"I like you, too," Susan said.

"You're... you're an extremely nice person and a good neighbor," she added weakly, overly aware of his hands on her shoulders.

"But not someone you'd want to go out with or be serious about," Jim said ruefully.

Susan held his gaze. "It's just as well, I'm sure. I know I'm not exactly your ideal woman. You don't agree with my sense of values any more than I agree with yours. I doubt you even like the way I look or dress. You have no use in general for interior decorators." Thinking became more difficult as his hands left her shoulders to stroke her back and draw her even closer.

"I've never wanted to kiss an interior decorator before—that's certain," he said softly, tilting her head back.

She dimly registered that he hadn't disagreed with any of the points she'd made, but the first warm, feather-light contact of his lips with hers sent the sharp, sweet ache of desire coursing through her. She heard the light thud of her handbag falling to the ground as she released her grip on it to put both hands around his neck....

Dear Reader,

Among the stellar authors in our January lineup is Lynda Trent, well-known for her weighty historical novels. What keeps her coming back to Silhouette **Special Edition**? Here's how she explains it:

"I write for Silhouette Special Edition to share a romantic fantasy with my readers, an emotional adventure in which a woman might be an heiress, a commoner or a Mata Hari . . . and still be loved by the perfect man. Within the broad scope of a Special Edition, she might dare to love a dangerous man; she might chance everything for a noble cause. I want to weave a tapestry of romance blossoming, of dreams fulfilled, and I want to share it with other dreamers."

Like the piratical hero of Lynda Trent's *Like Strangers*, the authors and editors of Silhouette **Special Edition** want to knock on the door to your heart . . . and open it to all the possibilities life and love have to offer.

Share your tastes and preferences with us. Each and every month we strive to offer you something new, something *special*. Let us know how we're doing!

Happy new year,

Leslie Kazanjian, Senior Editor
Silhouette Books
300 East 42nd Street
New York, N.Y. 10017

Books by Carole Halston

Silhouette Romance

Silhouette Special Edition

CAROLE HALSTON

is a Louisiana native, residing on the north shore of Lake Pontchartrain, near New Orleans. She enjoys traveling with her husband to research less familiar locations for settings but is always happy to return home to her own unique region, a rich source in itself for romantic stories about warm, wonderful people.

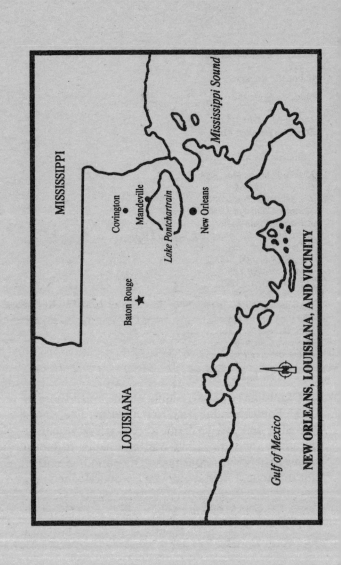

NEW ORLEANS, LOUISIANA, AND VICINITY

Chapter One

Susan freshened her lipstick, which was the same deep rose as her nail polish, powdered her nose and fluffed her blond hair. Then she slipped on a stylish oversized blazer before going outside and braving the July heat and humidity. The sidewalk was shaded by trees, but before she'd walked half a block her blouse stuck moistly to her skin. Her pastel hose felt like a damp casing on her legs, and her skirt drooped limply against her calves.

It took courage to dress smartly in south Louisiana during the summer, but in Susan's opinion, an interior decorator needed to show a sense of style. Especially one new in the business, who wanted to make a good impression and establish herself. Since there was no changing the climate, she didn't grumble or complain. Always the optimist, she made a habit of focusing on the positive side of everything.

Today she took in her surroundings with an interested, proprietary air. This was her new neighborhood. It was not where she would have chosen, under better circumstances, either to live or to operate her business. Nonetheless, she'd be doing both under the same roof, and she intended to make the most of the situation.

Moving to Old Mandeville, as people referred to the small town's historic lakefront district, had been an economy measure for her. She simply couldn't swing the rent on both business space in some fashionable location and the small house that had been home for herself and the two kids for the past year. Combining business and living quarters in a big, old-fashioned house on this street was a temporary solution. She had high hopes that it would turn out to be a wise move.

Like the several other streets zoned commercial in Old Mandeville, this one had a sleepy, residential look. Places of business were interspersed with homes, and shops were located in quaint old cottages and frame houses that dated back to the days when Mandeville was a summer retreat for New Orleanians. To a passerby, the main difference between a shop and a residence was that the former would have a discreetly painted sign out front, usually announcing that it sold antiques and collectibles, and the other might have a tricycle, temporarily abandoned by its small owner.

With no clearly defined shopping district, there was little casual drop-in trade. The only busy times for shopkeepers were sunny weekends and holidays when sightseers would park and browse. Understandably, most of the proprietors were lax about keeping regular business hours, as Susan had discovered when she began making the rounds to introduce herself. She hoped all that would change once she'd rallied support for her plan to breathe new commercial life into the area.

The potential was all there. Old Mandeville had architectural charm galore. The lakefront was always a scenic attraction, with frequent sailboat regattas and windsurfers often putting on a free show. Several good restaurants in the area enjoyed a thriving business, drawing visitors from New Orleans and nearby towns as well as the locals. The shop owners could easily share in that prosperity—even expand it. All they needed was some cooperative effort and promotion.

Susan's head was full of ideas for theme days and seasonal festivals, with the participating merchants and their employees wearing costumes and decorating their shops. Distinctive banners marking the occasion would hang outside each place of business, adding to the gala atmosphere. Tasteful advertising, which wouldn't be expensive when shared, would create an influx of well-heeled customers.

In a short time, a whole variety of other specialty shops would open up, and Old Mandeville's commercial district would evolve into a thriving colony of chic businesses. It would become a highly desirable location, perfect for an interior decorator, and she'd already be there, well on her way to success.

Susan sighed wistfully at her vision and came back to reality as she arrived at her destination. The house, painted a sober shade of green with white trim, was of the same vintage as the one she rented a couple of blocks away. Both had been built in the forties and had lapped wooden siding, fancy gingerbread trim and shutters that were operable, not simply decorative.

Her front porch, though, wasn't guarded by a huge mixed-breed dog that looked as though it could snap an ankle in two with one bite of its hefty jaws. Nor was her porch railing occupied by one of the least attractive cats Susan had ever seen, its shorthaired coat a mottled pattern of rust and black covering a lanky body that was all awkward angles. As though reading her uncomplimentary thoughts and resenting them, the poor creature emitted a piercing yowl.

Wondering if it was safe to enter, Susan studied a sign, hardly noticeable at first glance, that hung from the porch eaves. A length of varnished board had a single word *Furniture* routed into it. No wonder she'd had no inkling that Jim Mann was one of her new neighbors. He certainly wasn't advertising his whereabouts. When she'd asked about the sign, she'd learned that he lived here and had his woodworking shop in an outbuilding behind the house. According to her source, he used the two front rooms of the house to display the furniture that he built to sell.

It had been news to Susan that he made furniture. She'd only been aware of his custom cabinetwork. He was known as one of the reputable craftsmen on the north shore, none of whom she'd had occasion to employ for a client so far, since she hadn't been lucky enough yet to land a big decorating job where either new first-class construction or major renovation was involved. Any day, though, she'd get a break. Today she'd come, eager to meet Jim Mann personally and to make a valuable professional contact as well as to enlist his support for an active local merchants' group.

But she wasn't keen on sacrificing a good pair of hose, along with a chunk of her leg, to his dog. Double gates to the driveway stood open farther along the fence, suggesting that the animal didn't venture out to attack pedestrians, but he might still react viciously to someone intruding on his territory. A ruckus might bring his owner to investigate, she reasoned, and eased the gate open a few inches, prepared to jerk it closed again, as she called out cheerfully, "Do you bite, big fella?"

The dog yawned, showing enormous teeth, and thumped his tail once on the porch, as though mustering all the energy of which he was capable. When he watched without interest, barely keeping his eyes open, while she took a tentative step inside, Susan concluded that he was harmless and relaxed.

Pets were often said to resemble their owners, she reflected, smiling at the thought as she climbed the steps to the porch, encouraged by another lethargic tail thump from the big dog. If that theory held true in Jim Mann's case, she hated to think what the poor fellow looked like.

Apparently he hadn't considered the drawbacks of having animals, even more appealing ones, on the premises of a business. Not everyone liked cats and dogs. Some people had serious allergies and others deep-seated fears. At some point in the future, Susan might try to tactfully enlighten him on the subject if the increased customer traffic didn't cause the animals to seek a more peaceful place on their own, out of sight.

Out of hearing, too, she added ruefully to herself when the cat let out another plaintive yowl as she skirted the massive bulk of the dog to reach the door. A small index card was tacked to the door frame. She read the hand-printed message: FEEL FREE TO GO INSIDE AND LOOK, IF DOOR IS UNLOCKED. COME AROUND TO SHOP IN BACK FOR ASSISTANCE. J. Mann. A telephone number followed the name. Presumably those who didn't find the door open or anyone on the premises could call, if they cared to.

Shaking her head at what seemed both a very trusting attitude toward people and an indifferent approach to doing business, Susan tried the door. It was unlocked. "Is anyone here?" she inquired as she entered, feeling like a trespasser.

A welcoming blast of cool, dry air would have been too much to hope for. Older houses such as this one hadn't been built with central air conditioning, and Jim Mann could hardly be expected to keep a window unit running on the slight chance that a customer would show up. At least he kept the place well-ventilated, she noted approvingly. It wasn't musty or stiflingly hot inside, as she'd half-expected.

Even if it had been, though, she wouldn't have been able to take a quick glance around and then leave. She would have had to examine Jim Mann's furniture at close range. It was lovely, the designs starkly simple with a quaintly traditional look about them. Each piece had a fine-rubbed finish that felt like satin. There were trestle and drop-leaf tables of various sizes, ladder-back chairs, a narrow china cabinet with open shelves at the top, two secretaries, a chest, a bench, a settee with slender spindles forming the back, a music stand.

By the time she came to the last item, Susan had identified the severe yet graceful style as Shaker. Apparently it appealed strongly to her neighbor, who'd probably learned of it, as she had, from reading about the history of furniture. There was a stamp of authenticity in each piece that suggested to her that he had a book of designs and faithfully adhered to their dimensions.

It was, more than likely, a fortunate lack of originality on his part. The man was a fine craftsman, but from her impressions of him so far, she wouldn't put money on his aesthetic judgment. Based on the appearance of the outside of his house, his van parked in the driveway and his animals, she expected him to be a stolid, easygoing, unimaginative type.

He could definitely use her help in rearranging the two rooms to display his furniture to better advantage. She would like to suggest to him, too, that some accent items in brass and wicker would look fantastic. An antique coal scuttle, for example, and an old handmade basket filled with pinecones. Add a couple of hooked rugs to cover the bare wooden floor, some live plants, including a tall potted tree or two...

Susan could see the transformation vividly and sighed over the reality. Given an opening, she knew she'd probably find herself volunteering her services at a cut-rate fee or even for free, just because of the inner satisfaction her job gave her. She found it impossible to withhold her talents from someone who needed them. Creating a beautiful environment was a charitable instinct for her, as well as a source of deep personal pleasure. It was what she could do to make the world a better place.

As sole supporter of herself and two children, though, she needed to be paid and paid well. That awareness was ever present, giving her a sense of urgent purpose. Her expenses as a parent were going to escalate greatly during the next few years. Billy was thirteen and Joanie just two years younger. Up ahead were their high school years and then college. Susan was hoping somehow to come up with the money to provide more than just the bare necessities. She hated for her kids to be deprived because of what hadn't been their fault. It was bad enough for them not to have a normal family life because their parents were divorced.

She wanted to be able to dress them in the clothes they liked, give them a generous allowance and then buy a second family vehicle for their use while they were at home. When they went off to college, she hoped to be earning enough to pay full tuition and living expenses so that they wouldn't need to hold down jobs in addition to studying. She didn't want them to be drudges and miss all the fun.

Once they had their college degrees and were employed in their chosen fields, they would probably marry eventually. Susan had every intention of assuming the customary parental expenses in each instance. A typical mother, despite her own failed marriage, she knew she would be happy if

Joanie decided on a big church wedding, for which Susan would want to pay.

The fact that she couldn't spare the price of a ladder for an elopement at the present time didn't make her stop to wonder if she was asking too much of herself. There was nothing to be gained from self doubt, except a case of depression. If she kept a positive attitude and put forth a hundred percent effort, good things would happen. She would have all the work she could handle, make enough money to take care of her children's material needs, and someday have a few luxuries herself.

It was nice to know, too, that her well-earned success could benefit other hardworking individuals who had pride in their work, like Jim Mann. After seeing his furniture, Susan was doubly enthusiastic about meeting him, glad that she could be sincerely complimentary and could promise that she would be recommending him to future clients. She needed to inquire about his prices, though, she reminded herself, with a last glance around. Nothing was individually marked, and there was no posted list in sight. If he were asking too little, she would tell him and suggest that he could get more.

Out on the porch, the two animals hadn't moved from their places. Both seemed to be waiting for her to emerge. When the big dog whined hopefully, Susan paused to pat him on his broad head. He sighed so blissfully she had to smile. "You're just a big old softie," she told him. "And you're a pretty kitty," she lied to the cat on her way down the steps. The homely feline preened and began to wash herself, as though used to hearing the same fiction from a kindhearted owner.

As she rounded the corner of the house, Susan could hear the high-pitched whine of a power tool coming from the building at the rear, which she guessed to be Jim Mann's workshop. Large double doors stood open, but because of the glare she couldn't see into the interior as she headed toward it. Then her attention was sidetracked as she noticed for the first time that there was a shed attached to the side of the building. It had been blocked from view by the large, dark green van.

Parked beneath the shed was a sports car. Susan wasn't an expert, but she recognized it as an older Corvette, and noted the jaunty red and white color combination, the waxy sheen, the polished chrome with surprise. How old a man was her neighbor? she wondered. Was he married?

Her curiosity was impersonal, but she was glad nonetheless that when she reached the open doors of the workshop and got her first view of Jim Mann, his back was to her. Completely unaware of her presence, he was slowly feeding a length of board through a power planer, giving Susan more time than she needed to see that he was tall, with a lean, powerful build. The dark, faded T-shirt he wore tucked into his jeans was damp with perspiration and molded his broad shoulders and smoothly muscled back. His stance called her attention to his narrow hips and long legs.

With no choice but to wait until he noticed her, she focused on his head. His hair was dark brown and neatly trimmed, but sprinkled with sawdust. The strap at the back of his head presumably held on safety goggles to protect his eyes. The fact that he used them indicated that maybe she wasn't so far off in her estimate of his personality, if not his appearance. Even from the back, he was definitely... *virile*. The word didn't come easily because Susan wasn't used to noticing men that way.

At long last the board was finally through the planer. She became alert, preparing her face for a smile, as Jim Mann stripped off his goggles and reached for a switch. But in-

stead of deep silence, soft music filled the workshop, not
country and western or rock, but classical. Surprised at his
taste, Susan glanced and saw a portable radio on a work
counter. Then, just as she was opening her mouth to speak,
Jim Mann began to whistle an accompaniment to the com-
position that was playing. The sound ran along her spine
and aroused disturbing little ripples of sensation.

"Hello," she called out and was embarrassed at her own
voice, which seemed to convey a purely feminine greeting
she certainly didn't intend. "I didn't dare interrupt you,"
she went on brightly as he turned around. While he sur-
veyed her with keen dark eyes that were set in a face any
woman could find attractive, she kept on talking. "I'm Susan Casey. I just moved into the neighborhood and wanted
to meet you. We're both in the same line of work. I'm an
interior decorator," she added when his eyebrow quirked
skeptically and he gave her a quick male once-over.

"An interior decorator," he repeated in a pleasant voice
that held only polite interest. Susan felt an absurd little pang
of disappointment that she knew had nothing to do with the
purpose of her visit.

"I've only been over here on the north shore for a year. I
moved from Metairie," she volunteered cheerfully, watching him as he dusted himself off. His T-shirt was plain,
without a slogan or design, and it clung damply to a mus-
cular chest and flat stomach. His jeans weren't tight, but
they fit well enough to make a male statement. As he gave
his thighs a quick swipe, she got a clear view of his fingers
and could see that he wasn't wearing a ring of any kind.

"Jim Mann." He approached her with his right hand extended. "Nice to meet you, Susan. Welcome to the neighborhood."

His clasp was firm and brief, his tone fairly friendly, his
manner courteous. Susan couldn't have asked for the meet-

ing to go any better thus far, yet she felt another twinge of disappointment.

"I'm sure I'm going to like it here in Old Mandeville," she declared. "Everyone I've met so far has been friendly, and it's a unique location that's only going to get better with time."

Jim's expression was cautiously agreeable, but she could sense that she hadn't struck any sympathetic chord. "I think it's a pretty special place, myself," he said. "As for getting better, I can't think of any likely changes that would improve it for me." He made a casual sweeping gesture with one hand to indicate the machinery in his workshop. "It's nice to leave and come back expecting to find all my tools still here. My neighbors keep an eye on things for me when I'm gone, and I do the same for them. We help one another out occasionally, and yet generally mind our own business. It's a nice small-town atmosphere."

That doesn't suit everybody, he might as well have added. "I'm feeling twice as good about deciding to move here, after talking to you," Susan said lightly, hurt that he clearly didn't think she would fit in. "What I meant by 'better' is just more of the same spirit of cooperation you describe."

He raised his eyebrows, his quizzical expression inviting her to explain. She took the opening, with misgivings that she tried to drown in the enthusiastic sound of her own voice. "There's already an Old Mandeville merchants' group, I understand, which is a step in the right direction. It's just a matter of getting it active, calling meetings and discussing ways to improve everyone's business." He was frowning, looking doubtful, so she nervously rushed on to specifics, aware that she was talking too fast and too emphatically as she always did in high-pressure situations. "You, for example, have all that gorgeous furniture just sitting and collecting dust, because people don't know it's there. *I* didn't know it was there until very recently, and as an interior decorator I make it my business to know the work of skilled local craftsmen.''

In her sincerity, Susan clapped a hand to her chest. Flustered by his obvious effort to keep from smiling, she dropped her hand self-consciously to her side and continued with dignity, ''It's the same story with your neighbors and friends who have shops. They all have merchandise that would appeal to the right customers. Unfortunately only a few of those people ever find their way through the doors.''

''This isn't an area where you expect to do volume retailing,'' he said reasonably. ''Customers are more like guests and behave accordingly. Anybody who wants hordes trampling through should rent space in a mall.''

''Who said anything about hordes!'' Susan protested. ''I'm talking about well-to-do people with good manners who can afford the better things in life!'' She took a deep breath to control her exasperation. ''You do make your furniture for the purpose of selling it, don't you? You wouldn't be averse to more business of the right kind?''

The smile he'd been holding back out of politeness lit his face with humor and made him devastatingly good-looking. Susan had a warm, melting sensation that was unrelated to the temperature. It was impossible, for just a moment, to be offended that he wasn't taking her very seriously.

''But only of 'the right kind,' '' he replied. ''That's the whole issue. You see, I think more in terms of placing my furniture in a good home than of selling it. I might as well warn you before you start doing me favors and sending your clients to shop here that not just anybody who comes along can buy from me.''

Susan regarded him with wide-eyed amazement, realizing that despite his light tone, he was actually serious. ''You mean to say you actually turn down sales? You tell people, 'Sorry, but I won't sell to you, because I don't like you'?''

He smiled, amused, but shook his head and gave a straightforward answer. "Nothing that aboveboard. I give a ridiculously high price or say that a particular item isn't for sale."

"I noticed just now when I took a look at your furniture that you didn't have any prices on anything," Susan reflected, remembering her intention of telling him if he were asking too little. What a joke on her. On the basis of this brief conversation, she had wasted her time in coming here to meet him. Suddenly she felt discouraged and wilted by the heat. "Are you that independent in your attitude toward your custom cabinetwork?" she asked, just for the record.

"Not at all," he said kindly. "I stay pretty busy most of the time working for builders, but since neighbors get high priority, I'll be glad to give you a bid on a job anytime."

"I hope to take you up on that soon," Susan told him, not at all heartened by his promise. "Now I'll let you get back to your work." She offered him her hand briskly. "It was a pleasure meeting you, Jim."

"Thank you for coming by and saying hello, Susan."

His grip and his voice had a disconcerting gentleness. Walking away, Susan held her shoulders erect and took purposeful strides, in case he was watching her leave. She didn't want to trudge off, looking defeated, and further arouse his male sympathy.

There had been an unexpected truth in her final words. Meeting him *had* been a pleasure, but of an unwanted, purely feminine kind, rare for her, as well as pointless. There was no room in her life for a man. She didn't have the time or energy to spare for a male-female relationship and wouldn't have for years.

It shouldn't bother her that he hadn't exactly been bowled over by her. If he'd shown interest in her as a woman, she couldn't have encouraged him. He wasn't the type she would be interested in dating, even though he was undeniably attractive and surprisingly polished. When Susan did have the time for a social life, she wanted some glamour. Her ideal male companion would be a man who was comfortable in a suit and tie, who would want to dress up and go to nice places. He needed to be someone she could respect and admire, too, a man with drive and ambition.

Jim Mann's idea of dressing up was probably wearing his best jeans and a sports shirt. His notion of having a good time would be doing something casual, like getting together with friends for a crawfish boil on Saturday afternoons. Susan hated crawfish. With his good looks, the odds were overwhelming that he was a conceited male chauvinist, used to having women come on to him and cater to his ego. No doubt he liked his dates in tacky, sexy clothes, short skirts and low-cut blouses.

Susan built a convincing case that soothed her sense of feminine rejection and then she concentrated on the partial success of her visit. She had made a good professional contact in Jim Mann.

It was just too bad that he wasn't receptive to her idea of improving the neighborhood. Of the property owners and business proprietors that she'd met so far, he'd have been the best advocate to have on her side. He was the kind to speak his opinion with quiet authority and influence others.

For that same reason, she was glad he hadn't reacted more negatively. She would definitely rather Jim Mann be neutral than openly against her.

She was sure he could be a very tough opponent.

* * *

Now why had he gone and opened his big mouth? Jim asked himself with mild irritation as he got back to work. He made it his policy to work for builders, which saved him from having to deal directly with any interior decorators involved in the job.

Interior decorators were almost always a pain in the butt, concerned only with how things looked. It didn't seem to matter to them how much extra trouble and expense it might cost to get whatever effect they were after—which often as not was outlandish, in Jim's opinion. Mentally he shook his head, remembering his last job. He'd built a beautiful set of cypress cabinets, designed very simply to his own taste, without the raised panels and the fake country look that seemed to be the rage these days. Then the lady of the house had let her decorator talk her into painting the cabinets rather than finishing them naturally to highlight the wood. And she didn't want white or cream or some other reasonable color, but apricot.

Jim had point-blank refused to do the painting himself, saying that he was strictly a varnish man. Actually he was a purist and didn't even like the synthetic varnishes, such as polyurethane, but would consent to use them on the basis of their practical merits since they didn't hide the wood grain. Covering the grain of a fine wood destroyed its character and made as much artistic sense to Jim as gilding a marble sculpture. Still, he wouldn't put that past an interior decorator, either, not if the marble in its natural state didn't happen to suit the color scheme.

Still, he would have to keep his word if Susan Casey stuck around long enough to hold him to it. She was cute, with her big blue eyes that opened wide and mirrored her reactions. Jim smiled, remembering her amazement when he had told her that he didn't sell his furniture to everyone. Then she'd looked so downhearted, arriving at the conclusion that she'd wasted her time coming to see him, that his male sympathies had gotten the best of him.

By then he was finding her amazingly appealing, after his negative first impressions. At first glance he'd been put off by her carefully applied makeup, her blond hair, and the clothes that did nothing for her small-boned, slender figure. He disliked those pale-colored hose; they brought to mind some awful skin disease. And those jackets that were several sizes too big made a woman look like she was wearing some man's cast-off clothing.

Up closer, when he shook hands with her, he saw her long, lacquered fingernails, which didn't appeal to him, either. But her hand was small and soft and feminine, and she had an engaging earnestness that seemed completely genuine. He found himself thinking that it was especially a shame in her case that female fashion encouraged women to disguise their natural attributes and sacrifice comfort, in the bargain.

But then Jim himself had once invested a small fortune in ties, the most absurd article of male clothing, during those years he was out in the business world, single-mindedly climbing the ladder of success. On days as hot and humid as this one, he'd worn suits and sweltered while moving from his air-conditioned car into an air-conditioned building to call on clients.

He could hardly criticize Susan Casey for canvasing her new neighborhood, dressed with no regard for the climate, or even for trying to stir up changes that she would see as improvements for all concerned, not just for herself. He could admire her industry, even sympathize with her thinking, since there had been a time when he'd spent every waking moment furthering his own career and looking at the world around him in terms of potential business profit.

But this had been his neighborhood for the past six years, and he liked it fine the way it was. He would just as soon that Susan Casey found herself other territory to upgrade and left his turf alone. Jim wasn't really worried, though. He knew what she was up against, trying to get a cooperative effort going. The area tended to attract individuals, some of them real characters. Then there were old-time property owners who were better off financially than they might appear, their businesses more an excuse for being a collector than a serious moneymaking endeavor.

Susan Casey would get discouraged without any opposition from Jim. She would probably be among those tenants who came and went fairly quickly, and that would get him off the hook, since he had told her that neighbors get high priority.

It had been a pleasant interruption which he didn't immediately forget. Which of the several vacant rental properties in the neighborhood had she taken? he wondered, making the assumption that she was renting, not buying. Was her new address strictly her business location, or was she also living on the premises?

He should have gotten more information from her, even though he was only idly curious. If Susan Casey were unattached, he couldn't imagine the two of them becoming friendly. His last choice for female companionship would be an interior decorator.

Chapter Two

After five-thirty Jim called it quits. Flexing tired muscles, he decided to postpone straightening the shop until he had checked his mail, which had been delivered about mid-morning. Pulling down the tin flap of the box, he saw he had a couple of magazines, including the latest issue of *Fine Woodworking*. Pulling the journals out first, he tucked them under his arm and sorted quickly through the sheaf of envelopes: a statement from his broker, the telephone bill, the rest throwaway mail.

Glancing up to acknowledge a youngster who was wheeling his bicycle along the sidewalk, Jim noted the flat tire and the boy's disgusted expression.

"Looks like you've had some bad luck with your transportation," he remarked sympathetically.

"Yessir. Doggone tire went flat on me clear at the other end of the lakefront, at the turnaround."

Jim shook his head in commiseration, but he was vaguely surprised that the boy had walked to his house, well over a mile, just to get his tire pumped up. He wasn't one of the kids who lived in the neighborhood, but evidently he'd heard the news that Jim's shop was a free tire-pumping station. Jim never minded stopping what he was doing to render quick aid with his compressor. His memory wasn't so short that he didn't remember being a boy himself.

"Come on back to my shop," he instructed good-naturedly, gesturing with the mail in his hand toward the open entrance to the driveway.

"Sir?" the boy asked, looking uncertain.

Jim thought that maybe he was shy. "Your bicycle tire. I'll put some air in it for you. Then you might be able to make it home, if you're not going too far. From the looks of things, you need to get yourself some new tires."

His assessment was obviously bad news for the boy. He regarded the tires dejectedly as he replied, "I just have a couple more blocks to go. But if you wouldn't mind . . ."

"Not at all," Jim assured kindly, leading the way with long strides. "I don't remember seeing you in the neighborhood before. You must have moved in recently." He made conversation more for the boy's sake than from curiosity. His mind was on doing a quick cleanup and then going to the house for a shower and an ice-cold beer.

"Yessir. My mom and my sister and me."

The omission of any mention of a father gave Jim a likely explanation for the boy's dismay about needing new tires. His parents were probably divorced, and money was tight for the mother and kids, as was so often the case. Jim didn't understand how a man could shirk his responsibilities as a father, even after he no longer wanted to stay with the mother of his children.

"I'm Jim Mann, by the way." Jim spoke over his shoulder, thinking that this was the second time today he'd introduced himself to a newcomer in the neighborhood.

"I'm Billy Casey—wow, what a neat car! That's a 'vette. What year is it?"

They'd come in sight of the shed. "A '64," Jim replied absentmindedly realizing that his two visitors that day must be related, presumably mother and son.

"Do you mind if I look at it up close?" Billy asked in such a fervent tone that Jim couldn't refuse.

"No, go ahead," he invited indulgently and walked with Billy over to the shed. While the boy was totally absorbed in admiring the car, Jim looked at him more closely and couldn't see much resemblance between him and his mother. He was slender and fine-boned, like she was, and had sandy hair, but his eyes were hazel and his features different from hers. He must have inherited most of his looks from his father.

"How old are you, son?" he asked casually.

"Thirteen."

Jim would have guessed that he was younger, partly because of his size and partly because Susan Casey looked to be no older than late twenties. Unless she had given birth to Billy when she was a young teenager, she must be in her early thirties. It was hard to believe she had a son on the verge of entering high school. Could she possibly be the sister Billy had spoken of?

"You know, Billy, I think I met your mother today," he mused, as though the connection had just occurred to him. "She's an interior decorator, isn't she? Her name's Susan?"

"Yeah. I'll bet she's fast, huh?" It was clear that in the presence of a much more fascinating subject, Billy wasn't the least interested in discussing his mother.

Jim grinned. "You feel like you're going a lot faster than you are, when you're driving the speed limit. I actually don't take her out that often," he added hastily when Billy's expression grew wistful. "Now, let's see about that tire, shall we?"

"Yessir."

Jim was accustomed to boyish hints where his car was concerned, and always resisted the impulse to make even indefinite promises about taking a kid for a ride. He would be leaving himself open to pestering, and once he set a precedent, the news would travel, as it had with his compressor. He'd have every kid in town hanging around.

In this instance it would have been out of the question to weaken, knowing Billy's identity. Jim was more than half sorry he'd befriended the boy, even though he was a polite, well-behaved kid. Billy would surely go home and report to his mother about meeting Jim. She might make the wrong interpretation that Jim had acted out of an interest in her. He didn't have much confidence in the sound reasoning of any woman who'd chosen to be an interior decorator.

"When I saw you out front just now, I figured some of the kids in town had sent you here to have your tire pumped up," Jim remarked conversationally, just for the record.

"I don't know any of the kids in town," Billy replied in a discouraged voice.

"You'll make friends in no time," Jim assured him.

"I guess so. But we'll probably have to move again in another year anyway."

The boy's air of acceptance tugged at Jim more than complaining would have. Jim was searching for something cheerful to say that wouldn't be phony or inquisitive when his dog and cat appeared, in company as always, and provided a diversion.

"Gosh, that's a big dog. And an *ugly* cat—er, I didn't mean..." Billy's voice drifted off in apology.

"Uh-oh, she heard you," Jim said with mock gravity, as the cat made the yowling sound that was evidently her version of a meow. "Meet Beauty and the Beast." He fondled the big head of the dog, while he spoke soothingly to the cat, who kept her distance several yards away. "Billy was only joking. He thinks you're a lovely lady."

"Look at that! She acts like she understands you!" Billy exclaimed, laughing as the cat preened. "Are those really their names? Beauty and Beast? Doesn't *he* mind being called that?"

"He doesn't care what you call him as long as you put food into his bowl," Jim said affectionately. "Actually I don't know what their names are. They just showed up together a couple of years ago and seemed to like the accommodations."

"They were together? I didn't think dogs liked cats."

"These two act like they're friends from way back."

Billy turned his bicycle over to Jim and petted the big dog while Jim tended to the tire and answered Billy's questions. When Jim had finished, Billy thanked him earnestly, but didn't say goodbye. He parked the bike just outside the shop and came to linger in the open doorway and ask more questions about Jim's work and tools. The boy plainly hated to leave, and Jim didn't have the heart to dismiss him.

"I could help you clean up, if I wouldn't get in your way," Billy offered hopefully, watching Jim as he put the shop to rights. "To pay you back for pumping up my tire."

Jim pointed out the broom and assigned him an area of the concrete floor to sweep. "Now we're even," he declared a few minutes later when he was locking up. Billy stood nearby, making no move to get on his bicycle.

"I could come by tomorrow afternoon and help you clean up again," he suggested diffidently. "I wouldn't mind. I don't have anything else to do."

To hell with who his mother is, Jim decided. "It's always nice to have an extra hand, but leave yourself open," he advised. "You never know when something else might come up."

Billy nodded in mature agreement, but his face was alight, and Jim knew he'd be seeing the boy the next day and probably on a frequent basis until Billy adjusted to the neighborhood and developed other interests. The thought wasn't annoying. He didn't mind a boy dropping by. He always tried to treat any youngster fascinated with his workshop the same way Mr. Nicholas had treated him— hospitably, with patience and kindness, but most of all with respect. Adults tended to forget that kids wanted to be taken seriously, too.

Jim felt guilty sometimes that he didn't give the same attention to the children who came by his workshop that Mr. Nicholas had given him. When Jim was a small boy, the older man had shown him how to use hand-tools and had helped him with simple projects. Later, when Jim was old enough, Mr. Nicholas had tutored him in the use of power tools and let him use those, too.

The difference was that Mr. Nicholas had been retired and did woodworking as a hobby, while Jim, at thirty-six, was a long way from retirement age. Still, Jim could work a lot less harder. He had no financial pressures. He guessed it was just in his nature to be a workaholic, no matter what his occupation.

At least he wasn't in cutthroat competition with his fellow humans now, even though there was always an unavoidable element of rivalry in any field. Whenever he took a job, that naturally meant some other cabinetmaker wasn't offered it. But he'd never hustled work. It had just come to him, at first small jobs that no established woodworker would have considered taking. He'd done them for the chance to develop his skills and had charged according to his abilities at the time, not to undersell anyone.

Now his rate of pay was in line with the best cabinetmakers, who might still be better than Jim since they had more years of experience. One or two of them would always be better because they were exceptional, with that touch of genius that sets off a few in any field. Yet Jim was often first choice over the others because not only did he do high-quality work, but he was also more dependable and businesslike in his dealings.

He guessed he had just been born conscientious, because even when he was a kid with a paper route he'd had a sense of obligation toward his customers and had always delivered, rain or shine. Of course, the profit motive had been strong, from an early age, along with the drive to excel in everything he did. He'd had to schedule his life to fit everything in, studies, part-time jobs, family responsibilities, fun. There just hadn't been time for sports or for other interests. But he had never become so busy that he couldn't drop by Mr. Nicholas's shop for at least a few minutes and put in a little work on an ongoing project.

Bent on going to college and being a success in a career that would pay big money, Jim had had no inkling that those accumulated hours would turn out to be training for a future livelihood. Even when he'd taken a year off to get his head straight, moved over here to the north shore and set up a workshop, he'd had no thoughts of being a professional woodworker, but had kind of fallen into it. Now after just six years, a relatively short apprenticeship, he found himself with a solid reputation and twice as many work offers as he could handle.

On the one hand, he was proud of his accomplishment, but resentful of the decision that was being forced on him. "Why don't you expand your operation?" builders kept asking him lately. So far Jim had brushed aside the suggestion, making excuses about not wanting to put up with all the red tape and paperwork the government required of even small businesses.

The truth was that he was uneasy with how much the idea appealed to him. He'd given up a stressful high-powered career in favor of a peaceful existence. He found his work rewarding. He was happy, wasn't he? So why would he want to take on the headaches of supervision and complicate his life?

There was no question of ability. Jim had full confidence in his business acumen and management skills. He just didn't trust his own drive or know where it would lead him. He had paid the price of ambition once and found it far too dear.

Billy arrived on foot the next day, about mid-afternoon. Jim glanced up to see him trudging toward the shop, his hands in his jeans pockets.

"Guess I'm way too early," Billy said, uncertain of his welcome.

"Glad for the company," Jim told him cordially, stopping to mop his face with a bandana that was already soaked with perspiration. "Tire didn't hold the air, I take it."

"No, sir. Like you said, those tires are done for."

Jim waited, but that seemed to be the end of the subject. His curiosity got the best of him. "Tires on a bicycle wear out and have to be replaced, like tires on a car," he stated reasonably.

Billy nodded, his eyes moving around the shop interior. "My mom needs new tires, too. She's nervous about driv-

ing across the causeway, 'fraid she'll have a flat. What'd you
say is the name of that tall machine over there?"

"A drill press. I was just about to use it. You can see how
it works."

Jim got the picture and didn't probe any further. Evidently Billy would have to retire his bicycle from service
until his mother could afford to buy him new tires. The
boy's acceptance of the situation without whining and
complaining awoke admiration, but Jim couldn't help
wondering if it wasn't a case of poor management. Susan
Casey could apparently afford appointments at the beauty
parlor, cosmetics and fashionable clothes. A couple of bicycle tires weren't that expensive.

Billy became a frequent visitor, and Jim grew to like the
boy, who appeared bright and personable once he lost some
of his uncertainty. He was curious about Jim's personal life
and wanted his opinions on a wide range of subjects as well
as wanting to know all about Jim's work. It was evident that
he was starved for the company of an adult male, in the absence of a father.

Jim avoided directly asking sensitive questions, but in the
course of conversation, Billy told him enough so that Jim
could piece together the boy's family background. His
mother had left his father, moving Billy and his sister Joanie
with her into a rented apartment, when Billy was eight. Since
Joanie was two years younger than Billy, she would have
been six. Prior to the breakup, the four of them lived with
Billy's grandmother in her house in Metairie, the same New
Orleans suburb where Jim himself had grown up and where
his parents still lived.

A year ago Billy's mother had moved the two children
again, over here to the Mandeville area on the north shore
of Lake Pontchartrain. She'd rented a house in a subdivi-

sion, rather than an apartment. By the time Billy had made friends and adjusted to the change, they'd moved to the larger, but older house down the street from Jim, which served his mother for an office, too. She was branching out on her own after working as a decorating consultant for a paint franchise in one of the new strip shopping malls. Billy was trying not to let her see how much he minded the frequent moving because she would feel bad and worry about him.

Billy's father didn't emerge in an admirable light from just the bare facts that the boy divulged. His dad still lived with Grandma Casey. He'd held a wide variety of jobs, none of them the kind that would be high-paying. Jim gathered he wasn't college educated. Billy made no reference to child support payments or even gifts from his dad. It didn't appear that Susan Casey's ex-husband had been the greatest provider while she was married to him, and Jim doubted that she got much financial help from him now.

She evidently had a lot of determination, whatever else could be said about her. While working full-time as a sales-clerk for one of the big department stores in a Metairie shopping center, she'd taken night courses at the New Orleans branch of Louisiana State University, where Jim had gotten his business degree. He had to give her credit. It couldn't have been easy to be mother, employee and student.

Of all the fields she might have entered, though, he thought she could have made a better choice than interior decorating, something that was more worthwhile as well as easier to break into. With a good starting salary and steady advancement, she could have provided more stability for her kids, not moved them around so much, and could also have afforded minor expenses like bicycle tires.

It didn't once occur to Jim, even with his added knowledge of Susan Casey, that he might have made a mistake in discounting her as a serious threat to the neighborhood status quo. Then he was notified of a meeting of the local merchants' association, and when he inquired about the purpose for it, he learned that there was a movement afoot to revitalize the commercial area of Old Mandeville. The instigator was Susan, who'd apparently been very busy the past couple of weeks.

She had gone around introducing herself and had made a very favorable impression on the several people that Jim talked to. The consensus was that she had a lot on the ball and some good ideas. Her plan for a fall festival sounded like a winner. Didn't Jim agree? he was asked. Jim tried not to look annoyed as he admitted that he'd been out of touch and didn't know any of the details. Yes, he would definitely be at the meeting where Susan Casey would be in charge, he assured his questioner with a grim note in his voice.

His irritation grew as he recalled his meeting with Susan and saw it in a new light. She'd fed him some bait, making vague references to improving business in Old Mandeville, gotten his reaction and sized him up as an unlikely recruit for her cause, then cut short the selling pitch she'd used on the others. Was she hoping that he would remain ignorant of what was going on and bypass the meeting out of indifference? Or that if he did show up, he would sense that he was outnumbered and keep his mouth shut? She was in store for a surprise, in either case.

On the night of the meeting, Jim dressed in his best jeans and a white oxford cloth shirt that was a holdover from his executive days. Though casually dressed, mentally he was as alert and ready as if he'd been headed for a tough business conference wearing a suit and tie. He felt some of the same stimulation, and he had to admit he found the sensation pleasant.

He walked to the local restaurant whose owner had volunteered it as a meeting place on a night closed to business. There was good attendance, judging from the cars outside. Entering, he found the atmosphere was convivial, as he'd expected. Everyone was talking and laughing, and Susan Casey was circulating. Jim had several moments to observe her before he was noticed.

From what he could see of her outfit, it didn't do anything more for her figure than the garb she had been wearing the other time he'd seen her. She was too carefully groomed for Jim's taste, her makeup flawless and her hair looking perfectly arranged in the soft indirect lighting. Somehow, like before, he found her cute and appealing, though.

"Jim Mann! I haven't seen hide nor hair of you all summer!"

Jim and everybody else in the room heard Martha LeBlanc chirp out a delighted greeting. All heads turned in his direction, including Susan's. Her face was a picture of dismay, confirming for Jim that she'd been hoping he wouldn't show up.

"How are you, Mrs. LeBlanc? George...Miss Evans..." Smiling affably, he entered the group, shaking hands. By the time he got to Susan, she'd recovered her poise and managed a nervous smile. Her hand was as soft as he remembered, but also slightly clammy. "Susan, nice to see you again," he told her blandly, enjoying the scene more than he really should be, considering that he was angry.

With his height advantage, she had to tilt her head back to look up into his face. Jim met her blue gaze directly and could read only worry, intermixed with reluctant feminine recognition. There was no guilt or apology, no challenge.

"Hello, Jim. How are you?" she said, without any enthusiasm. Then when he had to turn his head to speak to someone demanding his attention, she slipped away.

Jim was disappointed at her quick retreat, but refused to go after her. He had been prepared for a wide range of behavior on her part, but not for this. His original doubts about her effectiveness as a catalyst for change returned to him as he waited impatiently for the meeting to begin.

Finally everyone took seats, after a great deal of milling around. Jim pulled out a chair and lounged comfortably, sitting in the middle of the room with his arms folded across his chest and one ankle resting on his knee. He wanted to be sure that when Susan stood up in front to address the group, there was no way that she could avoid seeing him.

"What does a stranger, a potential customer, see when he or she drives down this street for the first time?" she asked nervously, and then proceeded to answer the question, talking too fast and too emphatically.

Though not sympathetic to her purpose, Jim found himself willing her to slow down a little and not stress her words with such frequency. But then as she warmed to her subject and became less ill at ease, her rapid tempo and animated delivery no longer detracted from her delivery. The fast tumble of words, vivid play of expression, and exaggerated body language all conveyed enthusiasm and sincerity. He could feel the positive response she was generating in the room, see heads nodding and faces smiling, hear murmurs of agreement. Hell, Jim wanted to join the crowd, smile and nod and make approving sounds himself!

Her approach was visual and effective. Without being critical, she described the neighborhood as it was now, then contrasted that view with one of a thriving commercial district where more shops and businesses occupied the existing buildings and customers came and went with frequency. The transition could be brought about easily and inexpensively, she stated with cheerful certainty, causing no loss of charm or damage to historic values of the area. In fact, the prosperity she envisioned would ensure the upkeep of older structures by making properties more valuable.

"Any questions or comments so far before we get down to specifics?" Susan asked breathlessly, then paused to catch her breath. She beamed at the responses, some joking and meant to provoke guffaws and teasing remarks, but all favorable.

Jim listened with a pleasantly noncommittal expression, saying nothing and biding his time.

"How about you, Jim? You're being mighty quiet." Bud Dumas, the restaurant proprietor, addressed him in the lull as the remarks died down.

Jim sat more upright in his chair and put both feet on the floor, letting the group's attention focus on him. He saw Susan tense and watching him with dread written on her face. He had an urge to reassure her that was completely at cross-purposes with his views.

"I'm sitting here seeing a long line of customers outside your door, Bud, and asking myself truthfully whether I like the picture," he replied mildly. "On those times I was just driving by, I'd be glad for you that you were doing a land-office business, but the situation could be highly irritating when I wanted to come in myself and eat a meal, the way I do on the average of once or twice a week. You'd probably go up on your prices and cut down on the portions you serve, too." Jim waited, smiling, for the good-natured jeers of concurrence to quiet down before he continued in a more sober vein.

"To answer your question seriously, Bud, I'm happy with things as they are. I personally like the slow pace, the peace and quiet. It's nice knowing all my neighbors and not having a lot of traffic on the streets and strangers all over the place. I'd hate to have to get into that city mentality of locking and unlocking doors every time I take a step. I don't think anything now of leaving my shop wide open while I'm gone to the hardware store for a few minutes. That would have to change. I guess I'd have to carry around a bunch of keys, like a watchman, lock up every time I went to the house to get a cold drink or a cup of coffee and then be sure to lock the kitchen door behind me when I went back to the shop again." Jim had his listeners in the palm of his hand. He shifted in his chair, giving them a moment to relate his words to themselves before he went on. The attitude toward security was generally lax, he knew.

"Your business doesn't depend on a steady flow of customers, does it, Jim?" Susan spoke up hurriedly, a thin, desperate note in her voice. "You could be located in a more out-of-the-way place, and people would track you down, thanks to your reputation."

"I'd just as soon stay where I am, if I have a choice," Jim pointed out dryly.

"I certainly didn't mean to imply—of course, we all want you to stay..." Susan broke off, flustered.

Some element of her embarrassment intrigued Jim. He had to resist the temptation to carry on the exchange between just the two of them, excluding everyone else. It wouldn't do anything for her cause or his to make the issue personal.

"I know you didn't intend any offense, and there's none taken," he said equably. "I won't deny that my foremost concern is how the changes under discussion would affect me. As a property owner, I could only benefit financially if this area turned into a high-rent district, and I'm aware of that. I could sell out for a big profit or become a landlord and, either way, have more money in my pocket. But the question is whether it would be enough to pay me for what I was losing. What's a fair price for a place you like, when there's no guarantee you'll ever like any other one nearly so well?" Jim shrugged. "Now, if everybody's had a say on the general pros and cons, why don't we move on, Susan? How about telling us what you have in mind for boosting business in Old Mandeville?"

"I'd be glad to, Jim."

She looked and sounded torn, as though on the one hand, she was relieved to get past the hurdle of the open discussion and go to the next stage of selling her plan, but hated not responding to his remarks first. Jim sensed from her faintly troubled air that she didn't just want to override his reservations in front of the others, but to convince *him*.

Unless he was being completely taken in, his instincts told him Susan Casey wasn't a seasoned fighter or a selfish opportunist. For the sake of her own conscience, she wouldn't want to think that the change she was promoting would hurt anyone involved. In her mind, she'd evidently painted a rosy picture of prosperity for all and wanted everyone to buy it.

Jim could capitalize upon his insight and give her a hard time, but he didn't consider it necessary for the same reason he hadn't taken a more hostile stance in the discussion and discredited her motives. There was no reason to play hard ball. The neighborhood simply wasn't in any serious danger from her. She was a captivating cheerleader type, but it would take more than enthusiasm to organize the group she had assembled and carry through a promotional effort.

He could have bypassed the meeting and let this whole little tempest in a teapot blow itself out, but he wasn't sorry he'd come and he was in no hurry to leave. It was pleasant to be there, he reflected as he lounged comfortably in his chair, enjoyable to sit back, watch her and listen as she outlined her proposal for the fall festival he'd heard mentioned.

Her fall festival idea wasn't a half-bad notion, really. She had catchy, but simple suggestions for costumes and decoration. For such a venture to be a success, though, it would need to be well publicized and coordinated. The only person in the room he knew could do it, Jim himself, wasn't about to volunteer.

"We would need to settle on a date right away and get started with the publicity," Susan stated, almost on cue with his thoughts. "We can place ads in the newspapers, put out flyers, and hang posters around the parish where they're sure to be seen. I've worked up some figures on advertising expenses and done a sample ad and a sample flyer."

She stopped to distribute her handouts, moving briskly around the room. Jim got a whiff of her perfume, which wasn't light and flowery enough to suit her, in his opinion. To the sound of approving murmurs, he glanced through the several pages she'd handed him and came alert. The ad and the flyer were both damned good, the breakdown of costs was clear and detailed, with quotes of classified rates from the newspapers and estimates of charges from local printers. She'd gone to a great deal of trouble, with some efficiency.

"As you can see, the cost per individual business would be very reasonable, when it was divided," Susan remarked as she moved back to the front. She met Jim's gaze anxiously when he looked up with a slight frown. "Jim, do you have a comment or question? Have I overlooked something or made an error in my calculations?"

"No, it looks as though you've done your homework," he replied, trying not to sound ironic. *He* was the one who'd erred in typecasting her as a cheerleader. But he still couldn't manage to be worried. She'd need to be a combination quarterback and coach to carry this through. "How do you plan to deal with the fact that places of business are scattered? Miss Evans over here is going to feel badly if she pays her share and her shop is bypassed because she's on a side street."

"That's a definite concern," Susan declared, nodding and seeming appreciative that he had brought the matter up. "Of course, all the participating businesses will be listed by name in the advertising, but we need to do everything possible to make sure the customers find everyone. I thought we could have signs on street corners with arrows pointing toward the various shops and a banner hanging outside each place of business, something like this one."

Jim watched, with mingled annoyance and admiration, as she picked up a folded square of cloth and shook it out with a flourish for them all to see. Beaming with pleasure at the complimentary remarks from around the room, she went on to give the modest cost for having the banners made and then added, "After the festival, we can leave them hanging until the Christmas season, when we'd probably want to come up with a new holiday motif."

Jim would just bet that she already had some ideas about the design.

"I say let's take a poll and then settle on the dates, if we have enough support," someone suggested, and other voices chimed in agreement.

"Yes, let's do. I'm in favor of it. There's not much expense involved...."

"It certainly seems worth a shot."

"I think it sounds like fun!"

"Think of how the children will enjoy dressing up in costumes. I can just see my two little granddaughters in pilgrim outfits, playing hostess! They'll look *adorable*!"

Jim was the only member of the merchants' association in attendance who declined to participate. He held out good-naturedly against the invitations to join the ranks, but didn't oppose or challenge the cooperative venture. It would have been pointless. He would only have risked alienating his neighbors and strengthening the coalition in the bargain. The odds were all in favor of it breaking down on its own.

His best bet was to be a good sport and bring up a few sobering realities to give them something to think about as they went home.

"I'm glad Susan had the idea for the banners," he remarked cheerfully, "so that folks don't have any doubt in their minds where they're welcome. It wouldn't do to have them walking into people's houses. Or blocking driveways, for that matter. Parking is severely limited and is going to be a problem. You'll need the local police out in force, directing traffic.

"With Susan's ideas for publicizing the affair, there's no doubt that you'll get a big turnout, if the weather's good. The problem with a crowd, of course, is that there's always some little accidents. If I were taking part myself, I would be sure to double-check my liability coverage. Everybody's so lawsuit happy these days—a broken leg and it's off to court for a million dollars. And you people with the antique and gift shops will probably have some expensive items come up missing or broken. It's inevitable when there are a lot of customers jostling around. You just have to expect it and be adequately insured."

"Thank you, Jim," Susan spoke up, cutting him off before be could deepen the worry on most of the faces in the room. "I'm sure we all appreciate your bringing up these practical matters."

"Forewarned is forearmed, I always say," he put in mildly, smothering a smile. It was more temptation than he could resist to spar with her.

"Nothing ventured, nothing gained, is more my motto," she flashed back and then glanced at her watch. "I see that it's getting late. We've accomplished a great deal, deciding upon a common goal. Why don't we adjourn and meet again next week the same time, if Bud will be kind enough to volunteer his restaurant? At that time, we'll settle on a definite date and proceed with plans. In the meantime, I'll be talking with each of you." Her gaze collided with Jim's in a frank communication: Except for you. Then she glanced quickly away. "Good night and thank you for coming."

Jim stood and returned his chair to its place, in no hurry to rush off. He was surprised to find Susan almost immediately at his elbow.

"Could I bother you for a lift home, Jim?"

"It would be my pleasure," he replied, "but I'd have to carry you. I'm on foot, you see."

"Oh. Since we're going in the same direction, maybe you wouldn't mind walking with me."

"Mind? I'd enjoy the company." He smiled down at her. "Were you in a hurry or did you want to stay and talk a few minutes?"

"Actually I need to get straight home. I have two children that I don't like to leave alone at night—" She broke off and blushed when Jim couldn't keep from grinning. "You just can't be too careful," she said defensively.

"No, you can't," he agreed. "I'm ready whenever you are. Just lead the way and get me out of here before I can do any more damage."

She gave up the pretense and smiled back at him guiltily.

Chapter Three

I wish there was some way I could change your thinking,"
Susan said when they were outside. She was alive with
something other than satisfaction over his response to her
ploy to get him quickly away from the meeting, where his
presence had been a constant distraction for her. It didn't
help at all for him to be so big and manly.

"There isn't, though," Jim replied. "You might as well
save yourself the effort. Maybe we should walk on the
street," he suggested, glancing down at her high-heeled
shoes. "It's better lighted than the sidewalks and a little
more even. This time of night there's hardly any traffic."

"Good idea," Susan concurred, impatient with her silly
little twinge of disappointment at his practicality. They were
just two neighbors walking in the same direction, she reminded herself firmly, not a man and a woman on a date.
"Most of the streets in town badly need resurfacing, don't
they?" she remarked, setting a brisk pace beside him.

"Yes, the majority are in pretty bad shape. They've been patched and repatched. But I guess their condition helps to keep everybody within the speed limit."

"But it's not good on anybody's car, though, is it?" To simply agree with him was tempting, but Susan was bent on making her point. "I've been reading in the local paper about how the sewage system needs to be overhauled, too. And how more playgrounds and recreational facilities are badly needed. Just think of how much good could come of greater revenue from sales tax—"

Her last word came out in a dismayed yelp, as one foot sank down into a small pothole she hadn't seen because she was sneaking a quick glance at his face and noticing that he was smiling with amusement. Losing her balance, she would have fallen backward and sat down hard on the pavement if Jim hadn't been quick to grab her.

"Are you okay?" he asked, retaining a firm hold on her upper arm and keeping his other hand clamped at her waist to support her while she stood on trembling legs.

The concern in his voice combined with the strength she could feel in his fingers didn't do a thing to calm Susan's panicky heartbeat. "I'm fine, thanks," she assured him shakily and made a show of looking down and examining her shoe. "Thank heaven I didn't break the heel. This is one of my best pairs of shoes." She'd been lucky enough to find them on sale at half price. Otherwise she could never have afforded them.

"It was your ankle I was worried about," Jim said dryly, releasing her.

Actually she wasn't fine, she discovered when they started walking again. She'd apparently wrenched her knee and probably had sprained her ankle, too. Both twinged painfully with each step, but she set her jaw and managed not to limp.

"Are you sure you didn't hurt yourself?" Jim inquired, glancing over and taking in both her gait and her expression. "We could go back and get you a ride with one of the others."

The idea of a ride was definitely appealing, but Susan rejected the scene she could envision, with herself featured as a weak, injured female and Jim her rescuer. Besides, he'd said get "her" a ride, meaning he'd put her in someone else's care and still walk himself. This opportunity would be lost.

"No, I'm able to walk," she insisted and forced herself to step up her pace as proof. "It's not a long way to my house."

"Okay." Jim gave in, obviously not totally convinced.

"As I was saying, Old Mandeville is in need of a number of improvements that all cost money." Ignoring the shooting pain in her knee and ankle, she doggedly resumed the interrupted conversation. "Don't you agree that the town could use more sales tax revenue? Plus the extra income from other taxes levied on businesses?"

"Come on, Susan," Jim chided with a touch of impatience. "You haven't been marching around the neighborhood in ninety-degree-plus weather, pushing your ideas out of civic impulse. You have your own selfish reasons, just like I have mine for opposing you."

"Even so, you can't deny that the town would benefit from more business. But you don't even care about that. You're not thinking of anybody but yourself." Her accusation was more vehement than she had intended because speaking was an outlet for her physical pain as well as her frustration with him. Each step was becoming more and more difficult. "Do you mind if we walk slower?" she asked apologetically through clenched teeth. "My leg is bothering me a little."

Jim immediately came to a standstill. "I thought you might have hurt yourself back there," he said. "What is it, your ankle?"

Susan stood with her weight on her good leg, deeply grateful for the rest. She nodded and then volunteered reluctantly, "My knee, too."

He shook his head, looking faintly exasperated. Susan prepared to accept a well-deserved scolding, but he only asked concernedly, "How bad is the pain? Can you walk any farther?"

"I won't have any trouble making it the rest of the way," she assured him stoutly, not seeing that she had much alternative. No car headlights were visible in either direction. He certainly couldn't carry her in his arms the remaining blocks, although from the way he was sizing her up, she wondered if he wasn't estimating her weight. "I'm ready to walk again now," she said, disconcerted by her thoughts.

"Hang on to me and go slow," Jim instructed, offering her his arm. Susan took it and limped along beside him, feeling foolish.

"How're you doing?" he asked when they'd gone several steps in silence.

"Oh, fine. It doesn't hurt that much," Susan lied cheerfully.

"Then why aren't you talking? You haven't given up on me as a lost cause, have you?"

His humorous, indulgent note awoke a whole multitude of regrets in Susan. "I know you think I'm a real nuisance," she said with a sigh. "You wish I hadn't moved here and started stirring things up."

"I'd just as soon you'd targeted another area," Jim admitted.

His honesty hurt. Susan suddenly wanted to explain everything to him, to make him understand her enormous responsibilities that came first before all other considerations.

"Do you have anyone depending on you, besides yourself?" she asked earnestly. Since meeting him, she'd managed to ascertain that he wasn't presently married and hadn't been divorced, as far as anyone knew.

"If you mean, does anyone else look to me for financial support, the answer is no," he replied.

"Then you can't really understand my situation. I have two children to house and clothe and feed and educate. My ex-husband is supposed to pay a small amount of child support, but he doesn't. It's up to me to see that they have a good start in life, and I intend to do that." She spoke the last words between gritted teeth and couldn't keep from wincing. Walking had graduated from painful to agonizing.

"Let's take a breather and give your leg a rest," Jim suggested, bringing them to a gentle halt so that she wasn't jolted.

"Thank you, I could use one," Susan said with an indrawn breath of relief. "I hope I didn't sound like I was asking for sympathy just now, because I wasn't," she went on, self-conscious under his concerned scrutiny. He looked as if he was gauging her weight again. "I'm lucky to have two great kids. You've met my son, Billy. He's mentioned visiting you a few times. I hope he isn't being a bother."

"No, not at all," Jim replied. "I like Billy. He's a nice boy, and he's been a little at loose ends lately without a bicycle."

"He has a bicycle," she corrected. "It's several years old, and I'm hoping to get him a new one for Christmas, but his isn't out of commission, as far as I know."

Jim hesitated. "He didn't tell you then that he needed new tires."

"Why, no, he didn't," she responded, surprised and then dismayed. "He didn't say a word. Poor little guy, he knows that things are tight right now, and I've been so busy I haven't even noticed that he wasn't riding his bike." Susan squared her slumping shoulders and looked Jim proudly in the eye. "This is just a minor example of what I was trying to explain to you," she said resolutely. "I don't want my children to have to do without things. Now I need to get on home and check on them."

Dropping his arm, she mustered all her will and determination, wanting to proceed on her own strength, but before she could take the first step, Jim grasped her by the shoulders and anchored her firmly to the spot. "You shouldn't walk any more on that leg," he said, more to himself than to her. "You could have torn cartilage or even a broken bone and might do more damage. I'll just have to carry you."

"Don't be silly," Susan scoffed. "I'm not going to let you carry me down the street! Why, I'd feel ridiculous—" She broke off helplessly as, ignoring her protests, he bent and picked her up in his arms.

"Put your arms around my neck and hang on tight," he directed, setting out with even strides.

"This is so embarrassing," she murmured, but decided that following his orders wasn't the least bit repugnant. In fact, her whole response to being borne along in his arms had a disturbing element of pleasure she wouldn't dare reveal to him. "I know you're sorry you ever agreed to walk home with me."

"I'm just glad you're a lightweight," Jim replied good-naturedly. "Otherwise we'd be in trouble. I don't claim to be a superman."

"I weigh a hundred and ten. That's an awful lot to carry. If there's anything I need to do to make it easier for you, just tell me."

"You're going to have to take care of both sides of the conversation, for one thing, so that I can save my breath." Jim took his eyes from the street long enough to smile into her face.

The close-range view made Susan's heart do a wild flip-flop and send a spurt of warmth coursing through her body. "I'll just keep quiet and concentrate on being as light as possible," she promised, but could keep her word for no more than a minute or two. It was too intimate, feeling the hard pumping of his heart and the rise and fall of his chest, hearing his quickened breathing and his balanced footsteps on the pavement. Her own heart wanted to beat in time with his. She had to do something to fight the sense of becoming physically attuned to him, of being at one with his coordinated movements. In desperation, she chattered.

"I know I must feel like a sack of lead. You ought to put me down and let me walk some more. I think I could make it the rest of the way. Somebody we know may drive by any moment, and we could flag them down. It's incredible how deserted this street is tonight, when it isn't that late." And on and on.

He did put her down once to rest, easing her to the pavement carefully so that she could stand on her good leg while he caught his breath. Then he carried her the rest of the way, even up the front steps of her house, and deposited her at the door—again with consideration for her injuries.

"I know that was quite an ordeal for you." Susan leaned against the door frame, watching him flex his shoulders and arms and suck in a lungful of air. "I've never felt quite so foolish in my life, but I certainly appreciate the lift." She tried for a light note to ease her sense of awkwardness.

"I'll go home and get my van and drive you to an emergency room," Jim stated matter-of-factly. "You'll want to get that leg attended to tonight."

"That's awfully nice of you to offer, but it won't be necessary," Susan demurred. "I'll just take a couple of aspirin and soak my leg in hot water. It'll be fine in a matter of time."

Jim was breathing almost normally by now. "You should have X rays and a doctor's examination," he persisted. "If you're worried about leaving the kids here, they could ride along, too."

"I appreciate your concern, but I'll take my chances on nothing serious being wrong." Susan was pleasant, but firm. She didn't want to get into explanations that her medical insurance wasn't the best and she didn't need the extra expense.

Jim frowned at her, looking both worried and disapproving. "Okay, but you're not showing good judgment. Which shouldn't surprise me, I guess," he added.

Susan bristled at the criticism, but managed to hold her temper and not point out that it was her leg and her decision. He had been extremely kind and no doubt meant well.

"Is that a sexist remark?" she demanded lightly. "Any woman who doesn't take a man's advice is guilty of poor judgment?"

Jim shrugged. "Forget it."

"No, now you have my curiosity aroused. What exactly did you mean?"

"Just that I haven't met a woman in your field yet who showed any common sense," he answered bluntly. "Tonight, for example, you were more worried about ruining your shoe than whether you'd crippled yourself. Then, rather than admit that you weren't able to walk, you probably aggravated the extent of your injury. And now, you're being equally foolish, risking a sleepless night and complications.''

Susan's mouth was gaping open with her indignation. "Why, of all the insulting, know-it-all, narrow-minded, biased—" She broke off on a furious note. No synonym for men that she could think of seemed sufficiently unflattering and yet still accurate. "If I'd known the way you feel, I would have *crawled* home tonight on my hands and knees before I'd have taken help from you!"

To her utter outrage, he looked her up and down and then smiled with a kind of grudging amusement. "I have no doubt that you would have made it on your own, somehow," he said dryly. "You're not lacking in determination."

Before Susan could cope with his admiring note and answer, he had turned and was leaving, reaching the steps with two long strides and descending them with loose-jointed, masculine ease.

He stopped at the bottom to turn around and ask, "Do me a favor, will you? Don't let on to Billy that I told you about his bicycle's needing tires. It was none of my business, and I should have kept my mouth shut."

"I'm glad you did tell me," Susan said stiffly. "And I won't let on."

He nodded with satisfaction, evidently accepting that she would keep her word. "Good night," he called back over his shoulder, striding away.

"Good night. And...thanks," Susan managed to get out.

"Don't mention it."

Her anger deserted her and she sagged against the door frame, feeling the throb of pain in her leg and listening to the sound of his footsteps grow lighter. The thought that he had only a couple of blocks farther to walk to his place sent

a wave of depression through her. Why did he have to live
so close?

Then, on top of everything else, he had a low opinion of
interior decorators. It seemed one obstacle too many for
Susan to deal with, a low blow to the very foundations of the
optimism that had kept her going. Was she asking too much
of herself? she wondered, overcome with a sense of hope-
lessness. Could she carry through on all that she'd under-
taken?

The fall festival might be a dismal failure, an embarrassment to her, a disappointment to everyone. The neighborhood might never change for the better. Her interior
decorating business might never catch on. What if she tried
her hardest and still fell short, letting down all those who
were depending on her as well as herself?

The sound of an automobile roused her from the rare
bout of self doubt. Under the porch light, she would be visible to someone driving past. Jim might already have
reached home by now, she realized in a sudden panic and
hurried to unlock the door, even while she was discounting
the possibility that he would return in his van to forcibly
take her to get medical attention.

He wouldn't come back tonight if you called and begged
him, she told herself scoffingly, hobbling inside. But it
wasn't true, and she knew it. Jim Mann was the decent type
who would respond to a call for help from any one of his
neighbors, even her, whom he considered a troublemaker
and a dimwit.

Susan just hoped that she never *ever* gave him another
chance to play Good Samaritan to her again. About to close
the door behind her with a little bang, she changed her mind
and left it ajar enough to peer out and see the vehicle passing on the street.

It wasn't a dark-green van. Or a saucy red and white sports car. She shut the door quietly and locked it, thinking how different Jim Mann's two automobiles were. Did they express two sides of his personality? Actually neither exactly suited him, or at least the way that she perceived him.

He was something of a puzzle. Despite his reputation and the fact that she'd observed him in his workshop and witnessed his competence, he didn't seem like a man who had always worked with his hands. She didn't think of the average cabinetmaker as being so articulate and smooth mannered. Tonight at the meeting she'd gotten the impression that he was in his element. He could have opposed her more strongly, she'd sensed, and she had been glad that he hadn't.

Who was Jim Mann? What was his background? How did he happen to be living two blocks down the street from her?

She could have asked him those questions and had a more personal conversation, Susan reflected regretfully, as she took off her shoes and carried them, limping, through the old-fashioned central hallway. Instead she'd stuck to business.

It was just as well. They were hardly destined to be friendly, even if they hadn't been so totally at odds over Old Mandeville's future, not with his bias against her occupation, to which she was devoted.

"Hi, are you watching something good?"

She stopped in the door of the living room where her son and her daughter were engrossed in a TV program. The sight of them filled her with love and renewed her sense of purpose and commitment. As she limped on to the bathroom to fill the huge old claw-footed tub and soak her leg, she made mental lists of people to contact and things to do in connection with the fall festival.

Which was going to be a great success. She was *sure* of it.

* * *

Jim flipped on the TV when he got home and checked out all the channels, but nothing interested him. He left it playing, though, just for the background noise as he sorted through the latest issues of the half dozen magazines that he subscribed to.

He selected one, a business trade journal that dealt with all the latest trends in management. He had considered it required reading at one time and kept renewing his subscription now even though he had no particular reason to keep abreast. While he didn't pore over the articles, he at least scanned them each month.

But tonight he couldn't concentrate and tossed the journal aside, knowing that he was simply not in a mood to sit and read. He was too restless and stimulated. Having been primed to do battle at the meeting, he'd eased off and been left with that dissatisfied feeling he remembered experiencing in the past when he hadn't used up his aggression to meet a business challenge.

Adding to the problem was plain old biological need. It had been a while since he'd made love to a woman, and tonight had awakened the urge. Not that he had been aroused or had entertained lustful thoughts as he carried Susan Casey in his arms, but he'd gotten a male pleasure from the feeling of her arms tightly hugging his neck. With every breath, he'd drawn her feminine scent deep into his lungs until he felt drugged. Even her nervous chatter had been provocative, with her voice telling him that she was desperately resisting her female response to a feeling of helpless reliance on him.

He'd reacted like a normal man and had been reminded of his virility. He'd felt strong and in charge. Taking her to an emergency room had seemed the next logical step, an obligation he hadn't resented. When she'd refused, he'd been thoroughly annoyed by her independence, he had to admit, as well as concerned. Now that his irritation had faded, he was just left feeling frustrated.

What a stubborn, single-minded woman she was, all hundred and ten pounds of her. Jim shook his head, smiling, as pictures of Susan flashed vividly before his eyes. His problem in dealing with her was that she brought out the indulgent male in him. He found her refreshingly genuine despite her efforts to look sophisticated. She delighted him somehow, even while she was being an irritant, so that his inclination was to give her free rein to stir up a limited amount of trouble.

The best thing that could happen would be for her to get too busy with her interior decorating to spearhead the commerical boom she envisioned. She'd be far better off herself developing her own business and letting the others do the same. Even if her fall festival went over big, in the long run she was going to find out that people had to supply their own business incentive. Running a successful establishment depended on day-in and day-out concentration, not on an occasional party. Hadn't it occurred to her that there was good reason for the neighborhood status quo?

Not soothed, either mentally or physically, by his train of thought, Jim got up, deciding that he'd go down to a bar on the lakefront and have a beer. It was taking a roundabout way, but he drove by Susan's house and noted the lights burning. Was her leg hurting her like hell? he wondered, with an ache of sympathy. Did she wish she'd taken his advice and seen a doctor?

Half a dozen times Susan awoke during the night, because she had moved her leg in her sleep and been roused by the soreness and pain. Each time, in the seconds of groggy consciousness, she worried about whether she'd done serious injury to herself. Jim was a stern presence, looking on, but also a comforting one somehow. He accompanied her into her dreams as she dropped off again.

The next morning she felt almost embarrassed, as though he'd spent the night with her. To her relief, she could hobble around without any trouble, favoring her leg. In a couple of days, she was sure she'd be on the go again, and meanwhile there was plenty that she could do, using the telephone, plus paperwork.

Her biggest decorating job at present was a small condominium complex. She had been hired by the builder and had to operate within a restricted budget, but was making each unit slightly different by varying the wallpapers and colors. He wasn't paying her enough, but she was happy to have the work. It meant more experience and some money to help pay the bills.

Her few other clients were contacts she'd made as decorating consultant at the paint store where she'd worked a year before going on her own. The jobs were all small projects. She was almost donating her services to one older lady, a retired post office employee who was a widow living on a pension. Susan had helped her to work out a plan for redoing her living room in stages, as she saved the money. In a year's time, new carpet had been laid and draperies hung. Next would come furniture, one piece at a time. The project was the main interest of Mrs. Clara Jenkins's life, and Susan wouldn't think of abandoning her, even if she suddenly found herself busy with wealthier clients.

Mrs. Jenkins was proof of what Susan believed to be true of her occupation: interior decorating was an important service for everyone, not just the rich. It wasn't frivolous and useless, the way Jim Mann evidently saw it. Nor were good interior decorators impractical, though admittedly there were some bizarre types who aroused just criticism. But then every field has some who are not a credit to it.

As a cabinetmaker, Jim more than likely had had contact with a number of interior decorators. Susan could understand that one or two of them could have made a negative impression, but for him to harbor such a full-scale prejudice was definitely not reasonable. Jim had his good points, but he was obviously inclined to be narrow and judgmental.

Now that Susan knew that, she felt better about his opposition and his disapproval of her. He wasn't college educated, she assumed, and thus had missed the liberalizing experience of taking classes with all kinds of people with different opinions. Susan had been amazed at how college had opened up her own thinking as well as making available the career knowledge she was seeking.

At some future time maybe things would work out so that she could have a professional relationship with Jim and be able to show him he was wrong to be biased against all interior decorators. Hopefully he would come to see that her ideas for Old Mandeville were good, too. Despite his flaws, Susan didn't want to chase him out of the neighborhood.

Remembering what he'd said about Billy's needing bicycle tires, she questioned her son without mentioning Jim's name, as she'd promised, and determined that Billy had been walking everywhere. It also came out that he had been visiting Jim's workshop daily and had a well-developed case of hero-worship.

"Mr. Jim's teaching me to use some of his hand tools," Billy confided with a secretive air. "I'm making something, but I was going to wait and see how it turned out before I told you. Woodworking is fun, Mom. I want to take a shop class at school this year."

"We'll talk about that when school starts," Susan replied with a firm note. "Your first concern should be scheduling the courses that will prepare you for college. Now about those bicycle tires. I should be able to drive tomorrow. We'll take your bicycle and have some new tires put on so that you'll be able to get around." And not spend so much time with Jim Mann, who wasn't the influence she preferred for her son. "This afternoon how would you like to visit your friend Garrett and spend the night, or have him come here? I can't guarantee anything, but I'll check with his mother and try to arrange it."

Billy's face lighted. "Gee, Mom, that would be fun!" He thought for a second. "There would be lots to do here. Garrett and I could go down to the lakefront and watch the sailboats. I can take him by Mr. Jim's shop, too, and show him all of Mr. Jim's tools and his Corvette."

Susan had expected Billy to jump at the chance to go to Garrett's house, which was in the same subdivision from which they'd recently moved. She was pleased that he wanted to have his good friend visit him instead, in their new neighborhood, but she wasn't thrilled by the agenda.

"You're going to wear out your welcome with Jim, if you aren't careful," she warned. "As soon as we get your bicycle back in service again, you'll be able to ride around and meet some kids your own age. There must be some who live here in Old Mandeville."

"I'm going to need my bicycle," Billy reflected. "But I should be able to pay you back soon. I'm planning to get me some part-time work and earn some money."

"Part-time work," Susan echoed.

He nodded. "Mowing lawns and stuff. I could be a paperboy, like Mr. Jim was when he was my age, except that grown-ups deliver the papers in cars around here. Mr. Jim had all kinds of part-time jobs. He had enough money saved to buy himself a car when he was sixteen and got his driver's license. I've been thinking there's no reason I couldn't do the same thing." He shrugged his thin little shoulders as he confessed, with a note of shame, "If I can just get up the nerve to ask people. That's the hard part for me. They'll probably take one look and think I'm too puny."

Susan's heart melted with mother's love and fierce protective instincts. "You're not puny," she denied strongly. "But you don't need to spend your summer vacation doing odd jobs, anyway. Before you know it, school will be starting. Just enjoy your free time."

He didn't answer, and Susan could tell from his disheartened expression that she'd disappointed him with her response. Evidently he'd been wanting a vote of confidence that she hadn't given him. This was all Jim Mann's fault, she thought indignantly. Who did he think he was, anyway, setting himself up as a role model for her son?

"I'll call Garrett's mother," she announced, getting up abruptly. She didn't trust herself to continue the conversation at that moment.

"Thanks, Mom," Billy replied. "But if he can't come here, we'd better make it another time. You might need me to go to the grocery store or something. And Joanie wouldn't like me spending the night somewhere else. She gets nervous with all the spooky noises this old house makes. If anything happened after dark, she'd be too scared to even run for help."

Susan was deeply touched by his sense of responsibility and yet saddened to think that he wasn't carefree, at his young age. With a father in the house, he wouldn't have such concerns.

"Joanie and I both depend on you a lot," she said, not wanting to risk hurting his feelings.

A few days later she would think back and realize she'd been given fair warning of how he'd handle a nighttime emergency. It wouldn't have taken genius, either, to go a step further and guess the person he would ask to come to his mother's aid in a household crisis.

Chapter Four

Susan yawned and glanced at her watch, noting the time guiltily. She hadn't meant to spend the whole evening working in her office, but here it was a quarter to ten already.

After supper she had sat in the living room with Billy and Joanie, feeling that she should spend some time with them, but they'd been glued to the TV and had hardly seemed to notice when she'd slipped out. It was all but impossible for her to concentrate on some imaginary plot when there was so much to think about and do.

Her knee gave a slight twinge as she got up from her desk, but she walked normally as she left the room. In a week's time, she had largely recovered from the ill effects of stepping into the pothole and had put the whole incident out of her mind.

Billy and Joanie were still watching TV, but they'd clearly taken out time for their baths. Both looked well scrubbed and they were already dressed for bed. Susan regarded them fondly from the living room door, thinking how lucky she was. They were good kids and seldom complained. They even got along together remarkably well.

"Does anybody need to get into the bathroom before I take my bath?" she asked and got absentminded negative replies. A car chase was in progress on the TV screen with a great deal of tire screeching and stunt driving.

Smiling with a trace of envy for their tense absorption, Susan went on to the single bathroom in the house. It was considerably larger than the typical modern version and had old-fashioned fixtures both kids considered "weird." It had taken some adjusting for the three of them to have to share the one bathroom, when they'd been accustomed to two in their previous house. Susan missed the luxury of having her own private bathroom, however compact, adjoining her bedroom, but she didn't see the present situation as permanent. She had no intention of living at this location for years and years.

Tonight the sight of a towel on the floor near the stout pedestal sink drew a good-natured sigh. She bent to pick it up, registering the fact that it wasn't just damp, but sopping wet. Had Billy or Joanie spilled a glass of water and covered the puddle with the towel? she wondered as she wrung out the excess water into the tub and dropped the towel back on the linoleum. After she'd bathed, she would take it along with the other towels to the laundry room.

The problem with taking tub baths, as opposed to showers, she'd discovered, was that the former took longer because of the temptation to soak. The baths were wonderfully relaxing, though. All the tension was gone from her body, and she felt languid and supple as she pulled a knit nightshirt over her head. A one-size-fits-all shapeless garment with a cartoon picture on the front, it had been a present from the kids and was her favorite night wear, being both comfortable and modest enough to wear without a robe. There was no reason to look sexy.

Standing at the sink, she went through her nighttime routine methodically. Her hair pulled back from her face by a pink plastic headband she'd appropriated from Joanie, she removed her makeup, then used an astringent lotion followed by a moisture cream. Next she brushed her teeth vigorously and thoroughly, mindful that she hadn't been to the dentist now in a couple of years.

As she bent over to spit out the toothpaste, prior to rinsing her mouth, she felt for her plastic glass and knocked it off the broad porcelain edge. The sound it made hitting the floor seemed odd, somehow. Glancing down to locate the fallen glass, she immediately understand why and understood, too, why the towel had been lying there earlier. In the same spot was a puddle of water advancing from behind the sink pedestal.

With her mouth still in need of rinsing, Susan got her damp towel and swabbed the floor so that she could investigate without getting wet. Kneeling down, she peered behind the porcelain column and saw that two old, discolored pipes came through the floor and ran vertically along the wall. From a connecting joint in the one on the right, water oozed drop by drop and slid down.

The pipes must bring hot and cold water to the taps, she reasoned. The leaky pipe carried cold water, since it was on the right-hand side. Susan watched the trickle of water down the pipe onto the floor, debating about what she should do. Her landlord lived in New Orleans. She hated to call him at this hour when there wasn't actually an emergency, but on the other hand, she didn't want to be held liable for any damage to the bathroom floor. While the pipe wasn't gushing, the leak was steady and could possibly worsen. At the present rate, she could wake up tomorrow morning and find the whole bathroom floor flooded.

Probably that joint just needed tightening. Susan had a small pipe wrench in her kit of basic tools, along with several screwdrivers, a hammer and a pair of pliers. She could make an attempt at a repair. If she solved the problem, even temporarily, it would make her feel good as well as relieve her mind so she could sleep.

The kit was conveniently located on a shelf in the linen closet, there in the bathroom. Susan took a moment to hurriedly rinse her mouth before she got it and took out the wrench. Feeling resourceful but slightly nervous, she fitted the jaws of the wrench around the pipe joint, adjusted them for a snug fit and twisted delicately. There wasn't much room for manipulating the wrench, and her position was awkward up under the bowl of the sink.

The joint didn't seem to budge, and the trickle continued, unabated. Susan exerted a little more muscle, again with no noticeable result, then sat back wondering if perhaps she shouldn't tap the joint with the hammer. It would seem to serve the same purpose as banging a jar lid with a spoon to break the suction. Once she loosened the joint, she should be able to tighten it.

Taking care to be gentle, she tapped once, twice, and then three times. Confident by now of the sturdy qualities of the plumbing, despite its appearance of being old, she worked on the joint more vigorously with the wrench and administered harder and harder taps.

Billy's voice came through the bathroom door. "Mom, what are doing in there? What's that banging?"

"Mom, there was water on the floor in there tonight when I took my bath," Joanie chimed in, making her presence outside the door known as well. "I was going to tell you and I forgot."

Susan paused to catch her breath and cope with her frustration. She hated to admit defeat, after so much effort, especially since she was convinced she'd diagnosed the solution correctly and just lacked the strength needed to do the job.

"We have a water pipe leaking," she called out calmly. "I almost have it fixed."

Taking the handle of the wrench in both hands, she administered a series of vicious jerks, putting all of her hundred and ten pounds into the effort, and felt a surge of victory as the joint seemed to give. But the feeling was quickly doused, quite literally, with water. The pipe had come apart and the trickle had swollen into a full stream. Water was flowing down her arms and flooding the floor.

"Billy! Joanie!" she yelled, frantically joining the pipe back together and holding it with her hands, after getting thoroughly drenched. "The pipe broke! I'm having to hold it together, so you two are going to have to help. Billy, you go outside and see if you can figure out how to turn off the water coming into the house. Joanie, look in the yellow pages and try to get a plumber. Hurry and do as I say, both of you!" she urged, as they tried in vain to open the locked door.

The desperate note in her voice must have gotten through to them and sent them into action. There was a light flurry of footsteps as they ran barefooted in the direction of the kitchen. She could hear the panic in their tones but not what was being said as they held a terse conversation, with Billy doing most of the talking. The slam of the door meant he was going outside. A short time later Susan heard the murmur of Joanie's voice as she talked on the phone. Then, just seconds later, Susan heard a door slam again and then silence.

"Joanie!" Susan called out protestingly, knowing that there was no one to hear. Joanie had gone outside, too, hopefully to report to Billy that a plumber was on the way. She must have been persuasive or else made a very lucky pick because she'd had time to make only one phone call. Susan wished her daughter had thought to update her mother, who could definitely use a shot of encouragement.

Clutching the pipe was grueling. Her entire body ached with tension. Her awkward position put a strain on every muscle, but especially her shoulders and arms. She didn't know how long she could hang on, not stopping the flow, but at least lessening it.

An eternity seemed to pass. With all the windows and doors closed and air-conditioning units humming, outside noises didn't come clearly, but she thought she heard an automobile in the driveway. She *prayed* she hadn't imagined the noise and that the plumber had arrived.

You can hold on, Susan. Another minute or two, she coached herself grimly, feeling her muscles jump and tremble. Thank God, an outside door was opening. There was the sound of the kids' voices, mingled with a man's tone. The plumber was here! Susan sagged with the enormous relief.

"Mom, you can let go of the pipe. We turned the water off. Mom, open up!"

Billy banged on the door as he shouted.

"Just a minute," Susan called weakly. Unclamping her hands was almost an act of will. After backing out on her hands and knees, she stood up stiffly, noticing that she was soaking wet. Her nightshirt clung to the front of her, but she didn't have a robe in the bathroom, and modesty wasn't her primary concern after the ordeal she'd been through. Surely the plumber would overlook the fact that she wasn't presentable.

Unlocking the door and opening it wide, she addressed him gratefully, "I certainly appreciate your coming—" Pure astonishment as well as chagrin cut her words off abruptly, and she stared, dumbfounded, at the tall, dark-haired man standing there, with one of her children on either side of him. Jim Mann was regarding her with frank interest, taking in her appearance from pink headband to bare feet. "Where did you come from?" she blurted stupidly. "I was expecting a *plumber....*"

"I told Joanie to call Mr. Jim first and, if he was home, to ask him to come," Billy said eagerly. "I was sure he'd know how to turn the water off and what to do about the broken pipe, too. He drove right over in his van."

"You shouldn't have bothered Mr. Mann at this time of night," Susan scolded, trying to summon some vestige of dignity. She wanted to pluck at the wet front of her nightshirt and unplaster it from her breasts and stomach and thighs. Her nipples felt tight and hard and she knew, without glancing down, that they thrust against the knit fabric visibly.

"Billy did the right thing," Jim objected pleasantly. "It was quick thinking on his part. I'm glad that I was home."

He stepped forward and stood in the open door, glancing inside. Susan wanted to die from embarrassment as he took in the pipe wrench and hammer by the sink pedestal and the open tin box nearby containing the rest of her rudimentary tools. She braced himself for whatever he would say, knowing that the scene would have left her open to male condescension even if he'd been a total stranger and hadn't already branded her as a dimwit interior decorator.

"Your broken pipe runs water to the sink, I see," Jim said, not commenting on the evidence of her attempt at repair. "The plumbing in these older houses tends to be rather old-fashioned. Unfortunately, there usually aren't cutoff valves at strategic places.''

Susan met his gaze blankly, trying to visualize the plumbing behind the sink. "I didn't see anything that looked like a valve, but I might have overlooked it," she told him defensively, hoping fervently that there wasn't one. Otherwise, she was going to feel like an even bigger idiot.

He stepped carefully across the wet floor, and squatted down to peer behind the porcelain pedestal. "I don't see any, either," he reported and then maneuvered his big body into position so that he could reach the broken pipe and examine it.

Susan felt exposed and defensive all over again. "The leak was coming from that joint, where it broke off," she explained before he could ask any questions. "I figured that it just needed tightening. My mistake, I guess, was tapping it with the hammer to loosen it."

"You were hitting it *hard*, Mom," Billy corrected her earnestly from the doorway, where he and his sister were both standing, looking on with fascinated interest. "Joanie and me could hear you all the way in the living room."

Susan gave him a silencing glare and ordered in her no-nonsense mother's voice, "Go and get the mop, Billy. It's out in the laundry room, off the back porch."

"Couldn't Joanie get it?" he implored, not wanting to leave even for a minute. "Mr. Jim might need me to help him. Okay, I'll get it," he muttered, reading Susan's threatening expression.

Jim eased back and stood up, shaking his head. "About all I can do tonight, I'm afraid, is plug that pipe for you so that you can have water coming into the house for the toilet and the kitchen sink. I don't have much in the way of plumbing supplies on hand. Probably that whole pipe is going to need replacing. The threads were all corroded."

While she listened to his verdict, which tactfully did not mention the obvious fact that she'd worsened the problem, Susan was aware of a certain intimate novelty in having him standing there in her bathroom, tall and masculine and keenly observant. As he talked, he casually inspected her and then the toilet articles she'd just been using, as though connecting them to her scrubbed appearance. She wished she'd taken the opportunity, when he wasn't looking, to at least pull off the silly headband and fluff her hair.

"You've done enough already, coming over and turning off the water," she declared. "I'd never have let the children bother you if I'd known what they had in mind, but I do appreciate your trouble more than I can say. Now I'll call a plumber myself and let him take it from here. Maybe you could suggest somebody who lives within a reasonable distance."

Jim was frowning, looking much as he had the night of the meeting a week ago, when Susan had declined his offer to take her to an emergency room. "A plumber is only going to do the same thing and cap off the pipe," he pointed out. "He isn't about to start replacing old pipes at this time of night, when there's no emergency. You'll have to do without the sink until tomorrow anyway." His gaze switched discreetly over to Joanie, unself-conscious in her shortie pajamas. "From the looks of things, you've all had a turn in the bathroom and are ready for bed, anyway."

"We've already brushed our teeth," Joanie agreed, giving him a shy, flirtatious smile.

"Doing without the sink is no problem," Susan spoke up, flushed with warmth that was more than embarrassment. "I just didn't want to put you to any more trouble."

"I don't mind." Jim's eyes were back on her. "It won't take me more than fifteen or twenty minutes to go home and make a wooden plug, come back and tap it in. But it's up to you. I'll do whatever you decide.''

It was her broken pipe, just as it had been her injured leg a week ago, and he wasn't forcing a good deed on her again. Susan read his meaning with no trouble. He'd probably vowed not to make any more helpful overtures to her, just as she'd sworn not to let him act the Good Samaritan again. Yet here he was, leaving himself open to being refused once more.

"If you really don't mind, I'll take you up on it," she told him, the desire not to hurt his feelings stronger than her own pride. "Then tomorrow morning early I'll call the landlord and turn the problem over to him. He may have a plumber he uses. If any kind of similar problem happens in the future, though, I promise you that we won't be bothering you. The last thing I want to be is one of those pain-in-the-neck women who are always asking their neighbors for help."

Billy's arrival kept Jim from replying. "Here, Mom." Billy handed her the mop and then turned his attention eagerly to Jim. "Can I do something to help you, Mr. Jim?"

"The biggest job is getting this floor cleaned up. You could take care of that while I'm gone a few minutes," Jim suggested, man to man. "Your mom needs to put on some dry clothes, and, besides that, she looks a little done in." He smiled at Susan. "Plumbing is hard work, isn't it?"

"Exhausting," she agreed, smiling back at him sheepishly. It was impossible to resent such gentle, sympathetic teasing. "I don't think I've ever tackled anything quite that frustrating before. Maybe I just didn't have the right hammer."

His smile broadened with amusement as he looked down at the tool with her. "Probably you don't have the right vocabulary," he said. His glance took in Joanie and Billy, hanging on to every word. "Now I'd better get going and engineer my carpenter's solution to your problem so that you can all go to bed. Be back in a few minutes."

He cupped her shoulder lightly as he went past her. His touch was friendly and casual, like his voice, but Susan's heart beat faster and sent a warm surge of pleasure through her. "We'll be here," she called after him several seconds too late. "You can just leave the door unlocked and come on in, if you want."

"No, I'll lock it." His answer came back, male and decisive. "Better to be careful."

Both of her children as well as Susan seemed frozen, waiting for the sound of the door opening and closing, signaling Jim's departure. Joanie stirred to life first, stating in a wistful tone that came uncannily close to expressing her mother's mood, "I'll open the door and let Mr. Jim in when he comes back, Mom. I think he's nice, don't you?"

Billy jealously set his sister straight, before Susan could answer. "Mr. Jim is *my* friend, and I'll let him in."

"But you'll be busy mopping the floor," Joanie argued.

"I'll be finished by then."

"Not unless you get started," Susan intervened to point out. "What does it matter who opens the door, as long as somebody does?"

I'll open the door myself, she wanted to say and not just to settle the dispute. A part of her even wished that Billy and Joanie could be safely in their rooms and asleep when Jim came back. Disconcerted by her own foolish yearnings, she left her two offspring to settle their controversy and went to change into dry clothes.

In her room the sight of herself in the mirror brought her back to her senses. She stared at her reflection, appalled. She'd known she looked awful, but the reality was even worse than she had imagined. With her hair scraped back from her face in the juvenile hairstyle and no makeup, she was all eyes and looked totally bedraggled in the clinging, shapeless night shirt.

No wonder Jim had been so gentle and sympathetic, Susan thought dejectedly. He had felt too sorry for her to give her a bad time. Suddenly overcome with weariness, she peeled off the wet garment. Opening a bureau drawer, she took the top nightgown on the stack, another comfortable favorite, put it on and then a knee-length summer housecoat the children were used to seeing her wear. After slipping her feet into terry cloth slippers, she ran a comb through her hair and, without checking her appearance, went back to the bathroom with the situation firmly in mind. Jim Mann was just being a good neighbor, nothing more. He had no interest in her as a woman, which was entirely for the best.

Billy was mopping diligently while Joanie perched on the edge of the tub, out of his way and holding the hammer.

"I'll do that," Susan offered, holding out her hand for the mop, but Billy waved her off.

"No, Mom. Mr. Jim told me to. You can rest. Or just go to bed, if you want. I'll tell Mr. Jim you were tired. Me and him can take care of this."

"He and I," Susan corrected, hiding a smile at his masculine tone and reflecting that he could have a worse male model than Jim, after all. "Thanks, but I'll stay up." Despite her fatigue and level-headed perspective, she had no intention of making herself scarce.

Apparently afraid of losing any of the credit, Billy refused to let either Joanie or his mother finish drying up the floor with towels, after he'd accomplished what he could with the mop. But he did give the mop and the bundle of wet towels to Susan for her to take to the laundry room. Then he went outside to take up a watch, leaving Joanie posted at the back door, which he'd scrupulously locked, following Jim's example.

Jim arrived while Susan was in the laundry room, hanging up the mop and depositing the towels in the washing machine. She could overhear part of her son's report as he ushered his hero inside, including an account of her own refusal to go to bed, and then Jim's deep voice.

"Women have minds of their own, Billy. You might as well learn that." His tone changed, and she could guess that he was smiling at Joanie, who would be standing by, making a subtle bid for his attention. "I see that your pretty little sister stayed up to oversee the job, too."

"Everybody says that I look just like my mother," Joanie replied, giggling.

"You do, big blue eyes and all."

"In Mom's pictures when she was a little girl, she could be Joanie's twin," Billy volunteered importantly. "Now she says she has to get her hair color from a bottle."

Susan cringed, tempted to hide there in the laundry room and not put in an appearance. Then Joanie giggled again and confided, "You should see Mom when she puts the stuff she uses on her hair. Her hair turns this weird-looking color—"

"Joanie!" Susan reprimanded from the laundry room door. It was better to be revealed as an eavesdropper than to let the conversation continue. "You kids are telling all my secrets and boring Mr. Mann to death," she scolded, joining the group, her cheeks feeling like red flags of embarrassment.

Jim didn't look bored at all. His gaze touched on her hair with a kind of thoughtful interest and then he took charge, reminding the children of why he was there and leading the way to the bathroom. Susan followed along, half wishing that she'd worn a newer, prettier housecoat.

With Billy and Joanie both watching from as close as possible and vying with each other to ask questions, she had only an obstructed view from farther back. He didn't take long, as he'd promised, and left as soon as he'd finished, promising to turn the water on again once he was outside.

Susan was left with a sense of letdown. Lying in bed she had trouble falling asleep, despite being tired. Cupping her shoulder, she recaptured the feel of Jim's big hand and felt a warm shiver of pleasure accompanied by the ache of desire. In the darkness she tried in vain not to imagine his hand sliding down to touch her breasts as her nipples hardened and contracted the way they had tonight underneath her wet nightshirt.

Had he noticed? Yes, of course he had. His dark eyes had missed nothing, not the roundness and smallness of her breasts or their jutting peaks. Susan's certainty gave her an unfamiliar wanton thrill that didn't help in any way to make her drowsy or alleviate her sexual frustration.

The only antidote was a dose of common sense. Susan wasn't going to have an affair, she reminded herself, not with Jim Mann or anyone else. Her personal morals didn't condone casual sex, even if she weren't concerned about setting a good example for her children. Without such inhibiting factors, though, she and Jim still wouldn't have been lovers.

The subject hadn't come up tonight, but her plans for the fall festival were going well. She was optimistic that it would be a success and trigger the changes she considered an improvement to the neighborhood and which Jim strongly opposed. His male ego wouldn't let him admit that he was wrong and she was right. It was to be regretted, but he was bound to be bitter and resentful.

He was extremely attractive and masculine, evidently in his element when taking charge and giving a helping hand.

Susan could see how tempting it might be to play the weak, submissive female with him, but she was neither weak nor ineffectual, even though circumstances seemed to show her in that light. She was competent and forceful, with a mind of her own, with ambition and determination to carry through her goals. Was he secure enough to let a woman be herself?

Susan doubted it.

Then there was his point of view to consider. He might not be open to having an affair with her, even if she were willing. Susan wasn't truly confident that she appealed to him physically the way he appealed to her. For all she knew, he could be involved in a relationship with another woman, someone he approved of and liked, in and out of bed.

That last possibility was a thoroughly depressing thought, despite all her prior reasoning.

Jim drove the two blocks to his house, got a beer from the refrigerator and then went back outside to sit on the kitchen steps and drink it. A faint breeze brought the moist, brackish scent of the lake. The squeal of tires intruded on the night quietness from a distance and then the sound died away.

The beer tasted good. He was thirsty and drank in big swallows. When the can was empty, he crumpled it. Feeling the thin aluminum buckle under the strength of his fingers, he smiled, thinking about Susan wielding her hammer.

Tonight he hadn't gone to her house expecting to have his sympathies aroused or to enjoy himself. But he'd experienced both reactions.

Intellectually he knew, of course, that being a divorced woman with two children wasn't always easy, but seeing her in her flooded bathroom, with her sparse collection of tools, limp with relief that help had arrived, he'd comprehended in a very real way her role as head of her small household. She had to cope with any emergency that came up, deal with the day-to-day problems, without a husband to share the worry and irritation or to provide some mechanical knowledge and muscle.

The last two she definitely lacked, but she had enough gumption and determination to make up for them, enough to be dangerous, in fact. She'd beat the hell out of that corroded old pipe and broken it. Jim visualized the bright hammer marks and grinned, the way he'd wanted to do tonight and had somehow managed not to.

Then his next thought sobered him. That old house she was living in probably had electrical wiring that matched the plumbing. She wouldn't try her hand at playing electrician, would she? Plumbing disasters could do damage, but were relatively safe. She could kill herself fooling with electricity.

Jim would have a diplomatic talk with Billy and get across that the boy was to feel free, when an emergency like tonight arose or even when he was seriously uneasy, to call on Jim with or without his mother's permission. It was rather touchy, undermining her authority, but Jim just didn't trust her judgment. He'd hate to have some harm befall her when he was only a couple of blocks away.

She would have to be desperate before she'd ask him for help herself. Tonight when she'd opened the door and seen him, she had been mortified. Of all the men she would have chosen to see her in that predicament, he was her last choice, Jim had no doubt. Up to that moment, he was savoring his advantage, feeling in control but on his guard, ready to render assistance, but only to the extent that it was welcomed and would be appreciated. He knew from conversation with the two children that calling him hadn't been her idea.

The fact that the bathroom door was locked prepared him for her to be wearing some sort of nightclothes. It seemed reasonable to assume that she was in the bathroom preparing for bed when the plumbing gave way. Jim awaited the first sight of her with a normal masculine interest. Based on her daytime appearance, he didn't know what to expect, but definitely not what he saw. Never in a hundred years would he guess that she slept in what looked like a huge man's T-shirt, with a juvenile picture on the front of it, the kind of thing a coed might wear. Barefoot, not to mention soaking wet, she looked young and utterly defenseless and adorable.

Jim's stiff-necked attitude had deserted him. His main concern became making the situation less painful and embarrassing for her while he coped with his own instincts. His urge was strong to put his arm around her and give her a reassuring hug, but at the same time he was undressing her with his eyes. It was impossible not to notice that she didn't have anything on underneath the wet nightshirt and it was second nature to think about peeling it off tenderly. The memory stirred him even now.

Along with arousal, he felt a pang of conscience, not for reacting the way any man would have, but for deriving nothing but pleasure from what had been a very trying experience for her. He'd enjoyed the whole brief episode, including the presence of the two kids. Billy was a thoroughly nice boy, and Joanie, the little girl, was a doll, shy and sweet. She'd made a conquest of Jim on the telephone.

It had been a good feeling, he had to admit, to have the three of them, mother and son and daughter, relying on him. He supposed that sense of trust was one of the rewards of being a man with a family. The scene hadn't been true to life, of course. They'd all been on their best behavior, caught up in the novelty. The kids hadn't bickered or whined. Susan hadn't nagged and complained. Jim hadn't cussed and been harried, like a husband and a father.

And afterward, he hadn't stayed and taken her to bed. On that thought, Jim got up and went inside.

Chapter Five

The next morning Jim waited until a reasonable hour and called Susan's house. She wasn't home, but Billy was able to give a full report on the status of the broken pipe. His mother had contacted the landlord by telephone that morning, before Billy was even up. A plumber, whom Jim knew personally and would have recommended, was coming to the house before noon and should have the bathroom sink back in operation, at least by that evening.

With his mind put at rest Jim could go about his own business, which was a relief, as he told himself as he hung up. He had a busy day before him. Later in the day he would call and check again, though. And maybe catch Susan there. He was disappointed—and might as well admit it—that he hadn't gotten to talk to her.

That afternoon he was scheduled to meet Dave Myles, a general contractor, in one of the more exclusive subdivisions in the Mandeville-Covington area, where Dave was building a large expensive house and wanted Jim to do the cabinetwork. The owners were transferring to Louisiana from out of state, and the wife was to be on hand today—having flown in to confer with Dave. Jim had gone over the architect's plan, but needed some questions answered before he gave a price.

It was a big job, but not especially challenging. The house had a lot of extra built-in cabinetry, but the design was relatively simple. Working single-handedly, Jim would have to devote himself to it exclusively for a number of weeks, whereas if he had a bigger workshop and some help, he could oversee the basic, easy construction and attend to what required specialized techniques himself. Installation would go much faster, too, with more hands and muscle.

Hiring dependable, adequately skilled woodworkers was easier said than done, though. A few wrong cuts and mistakes meant wasted lumber and reduced profits. And even with good employees, he would have the upheaval of relocating his shop and then the inconvenience of not having it within walking distance of his house. There would be the expense of buying more tools and getting extra insurance coverage.

Why do it, when he made good money, more than he needed to support the life-style he'd chosen and liked? In addition, he had some solid investments, and was in a better financial position than the majority of young executives his age who commuted across the causeway in their foreign imports and conducted business on their car telephones.

Jim debated with himself until noon, while he assembled doors with raised panels for a set of cabinets he had nearly completed. Then he locked up and changed into clean clothes to go to Covington, where he had several errands to run. He planned also to stop for a bite to eat at one of his favorite lunch places where he was sure to run into people he knew. He felt the need for company, to get away from his thoughts. From Covington, he would keep his appointment with Dave Myles.

Driving past Susan's house, he noted the plumber's truck in the driveway but no sign of her own small economy car. Evidently she hadn't returned from wherever she'd gone this morning. Billy had said she needed new tires. Jim would take a look for himself, the first chance he got, and see just how bad they were. She might be riding around with no tread at all, risking her neck.

Out on Highway 190, he noted the commercial development with a critical eye. It seemed that every week another wooded section was being leveled by bulldozers. Then in record time a new strip shopping mall would spring up. More and more traffic lights were having to be installed. Six years ago when he'd moved to the north shore, the five miles from Mandeville to Covington had been a leisurely, continuous drive. Now it took twice as long, stopping and starting, and the view, in his opinion, was steadily being spoiled.

Of course, someone moving over here from the city more recently, like Susan, couldn't appreciate the changes. The north shore probably seemed rural to her, compared to New Orleans. She hadn't had the time, more than likely, to absorb the distinctive atmospheres of the small towns, all unique in their own way, each with a separate, interesting history. Thus she couldn't sympathize with Jim's reluctance to see them swallowed up in urban sprawl. It was some consolation to think that they would always retain some of their character, even at a future time when they were all a part of one vast city, as were sections of New Orleans such as the Vieux Carré, the Garden District and the Irish Channel.

In Covington, he turned onto Boston Street, which led downtown. There some of the original, old-fashioned retail businesses still prospered despite the competition of discount stores and shopping centers outside the town limits. On the fringes of the center of town, a number of specialty shops did well. They had taken over small cottages and frame houses on streets that were formerly residential, such as Lee Lane, which had become so well-known it drew shoppers from New Orleans and Baton Rouge.

Today Jim had to stop for a red light at the intersection of Lee Lane and Boston, giving him time to observe a tour bus discharging its passengers. If Susan had her way, his own street in Old Mandeville would be lined with shops such as these and attracting busloads, he reflected, shaking his head. He didn't think there was a real danger that she'd succeed, but he wished that she would abandon the whole idea, anyway.

She could operate a successful business at her location, exactly as it was, without turning the neighborhood into another Lee Lane. An interior decorator didn't depend on walk-in customers, but rather well-heeled clients who would refer her to friends, women like those who could afford Jim's custom cabinetry work.

If he got a chance to throw some work her way, he would, assuming that he was a good enough actor to make a positive reaction to the notion of hiring any interior decorator. Jim had time to doubt that ability as the light turned green and he was forced to wait another thirty seconds, while a group of chattering elderly matrons from the tour bus crossed the street, oblivious to the fact that they were holding up traffic.

Accelerating when the last gray-haired lady had stepped safely to the curb, he left Lee Lane behind him and drove to the Back Street Bar and Café, which catered to a wide range of types, from local attorneys and businessmen to blue-collar workers. His entrance was met with enthusiastic greetings and he exchanged a few words with friends and acquaintances at several different tables before he sat down at one with an unoccupied chair.

It was a small, informal kind of place, where the bartender and the waitresses freely engaged in conversation with the patrons and were spoken to by name. Jim was introduced to Lisa, a new waitress he hadn't seen before, who was waiting on his table. After she'd taken his order and left, the others filled him in on her. From Covington originally, she'd been around, having lived in more liberal places, such as California and New York. Now she was back and was renting an old house in Abita Springs, where there was an artists' community. She was a potter, supplementing her income by waiting tables.

Jim could understand the assumption that he would be interested in getting more information about Lisa's circumstances. She was cast in the mold of the women he'd dated the last six years here on the north shore, free-spirited and worldly and attractive in an earthy, natural style. Tall and willowy, but big-breasted, she wore a minimum of makeup and had long brown hair pulled back and held in a barrette at her neck. She carried herself with female confidence and had given Jim a frankly approving inspection.

He couldn't explain why she didn't appeal to him more, especially when he'd been feeling the need for a woman lately. When she brought his food, he flirted with her, and she reciprocated without any shyness. But some spark was still missing, and Jim left without making any overtures.

After stops at a hardware store and a lumberyard, he took a different route leaving town, avoiding Lee Lane, and drove to the subdivision, where he had to give the security guard at the entrance his name and destination. On the way to the house Dave Myles was building, he passed the clubhouse and tennis courts and had vistas of the green golf course.

Jim could easily have ended up living this life-style himself, commuting to a high-rise city office building from the suburbs and returning to an insular, perfectly landscaped environment, where his country club wife and indulged children awaited him. The prospect didn't raise envy. He preferred Old Mandeville and, unlike most of the laborers who were stopped in their vans and pickup trucks and quizzed by the guard, Jim knew the price written beneath the glossy picture. He'd paid a chunk of himself as an installment on success and money and power before he'd stopped to question the cost-to-value ratio.

Through choice, he used his hands now to earn a fraction of what he could be pulling down in salary and bonuses, but he slept well after a hard day's work and drank a beer because he enjoyed the taste, not to combat an excess of adrenaline with alcohol. His ulcers were gone, along with any desire for a cigarette, though he had once smoked up to three packs a day. Most important, he was able to appreciate a sunset, chat with a neighbor, drop everything and do a favor, relate to the people he dealt with as human beings, not as pawns in a game of manipulation.

He couldn't dull his ability to size up people and know how they thought, but he chose not to take advantage of it. His aggressive business instincts were too ingrained to disappear entirely, but he curbed them. As for meeting strangers with ease and making a favorable impression, that wasn't an asset he had developed, but one he had had for as long as he could remember. Without being conceited, Jim knew he had a natural charisma. Now he just didn't cash in on it.

Today he was pleasant, but direct in the meeting with Dave Myles and Joyce Crawford, a deeply tanned blond woman in her early forties. The three of them arrived about the same time, and got down to business after a minimum of small talk. Jim referred to the house plan, asked questions, and then made notations. His purpose in being there was to clarify exactly what would be expected of him as a cabinetmaker.

He felt no keen personal interest in either of his companions, and yet when, fifteen minutes into the consultation, Joyce Crawford brought up the subject of interior decorators and asked for names of those who were considered the best locally, Jim knew instantly how to go about getting Susan a shot at the job. He dispensed with his usual scruples over using his intuition and skill in maneuvering people, deciding that the job was too much of a plum for her to leave it lying on the table.

Deferring to Myles, he let him answer first, knowing that the general contractor would name a well-known decorating duo. Aside from their reputation, they were good friends of Myles's wife.

"Wouldn't you say, Jim, that Betsy Roper and Jo Ann Blanchard are considered the best?" Myles made the expected recommendation, enlisting Jim's support.

"It would be my guess that they've decorated more houses in this subdivision than any other decorators," Jim replied agreeably. "They must be doing something right. I'm not much on interior decorators in general," he confessed ruefully to Joyce Crawford. "But at least you're thinking of using somebody local, who might create a livable look, and not one of those far-out New Orleans decorators. They come up with some colors and ideas you expect to see in a magazine, but not in a house real people are going to live in." He shook his head and looked as if he were remembering past disasters, noting the blond woman's thoughtful expression with an inner satisfaction.

"I was thinking in terms of convenience, but New Orleans is close, isn't it?" she mused. "I could use a New Orleans decorator instead of someone local."

"Unfortunately, you don't even have to go to New Orleans to find one," Jim complained. "They're moving over here, too, along with the rest of the city."

Myles cleared his throat and spoke up. "If you'd like to see some examples of Betsy and Jo'Ann's work, it would be easy to arrange. As a matter of fact, I wouldn't be surprised if they turned out to be the decorators for at least one of your neighbors on either side of you."

Jim looked down at the house plan he was holding, hiding his glee with assumed indifference. It wasn't necessary for him to say more. Unknowingly, Myles had just finished killing off the front-runners among Susan's competitors for the job. How could the man not realize, at this point, that the woman wouldn't want to use the same decorator her neighbors had used?

"I'm sure they're very good, but my taste is rather cosmopolitan," Joyce Crawford said tactfully, and changed the subject. A few minutes later she got Jim aside and he let her pry Susan's name out of him.

Now the rest was up to Susan. If she got the decorating job and he took on building the cabinets, they would inevitably cross paths at the house. He found that he didn't mind the idea. Since there had to be a decorator involved, he'd just as soon the person be Susan.

Her car still wasn't in evidence when he passed her house an hour later with the intention of stopping in if she was there. Billy came by Jim's workshop, ruling out any excuse for calling that night and getting an update on the plumbing. The broken pipe had been replaced, a cutoff valve installed and the plumber's card left with Susan, who apparently had been in and out during the day.

"Mr. Sam told Mom to call him any time she had a problem with the plumbing," Billy finished up. "He said next time for her to give him first crack at the job. He told her the name of an electrician and said for her to be sure not to try to fix any wiring. Mom was embarrassed. She said for him not to worry, she'd learned her lesson and planned to stick to interior decorating."

It seemed that the talk Jim had planned to have with Billy, safeguarding Susan against herself, wasn't necessary. Jim was oddly disgruntled to have his concerns erased.

That evening he debated with himself, trying to decide whether he should warn Susan that she might be hearing from Joyce Crawford. If the woman from Atlanta didn't contact her, he would only be raising Susan's hopes for nothing. On the other hand, if Susan got a call out of the blue she might blow the opportunity, not knowing that her strong selling point was a shortage of references on the north shore. She should stress a New Orleans connection.

He ended up calling. Billy answered, as he had that morning, and sounded surprised and glad when Jim identified himself.

"Mom's not home," he replied in answer to Jim's request to speak to Susan. "She went to some kind of meeting. It has to do with a big festival the people who own businesses around here are going to have. She's the one in charge of everything."

"Give her a message for me, will you?" Jim tried not to sound as annoyed as he felt. "Tell her I gave her name to a lady looking for a decorator from the New Orleans area. The lady may be calling her."

If she wanted more information from Jim, she could try calling him. Tonight, though, she would be out of luck. As he hung up the phone, Jim decided irritably that he was going out. He might even head over in the direction of

Covington and possibly run into Lisa, the new waitress at
Back Street.

Susan was so elated that she felt as though she could float
home from her appointment with Joyce Crawford. Her first
big job had finally materialized!

All she had to do was meet the challenge, and she was on
her way to being one of the leading decorators on the north
shore. It was hard to believe that what she wanted so much
was now within reach!

Jim Mann had given her this incredible opportunity. She
was having problems taking that in, too. His role gave her a
strange, disturbing little thrill, even though she wished that
anyone else she knew, besides him, had been the one to give
her career this all-important boost. He was the last person
to whom she wanted to be beholden.

It seemed urgent to see him right away, thank him sincerely and yet be perfectly candid. He had to understand her
appreciation didn't cancel out her obligation to her other
neighbors to finish what she'd started, nor did it alter her
thinking about bringing Old Mandeville's commercially
zoned area to its potential.

Reaching her own house, she drove on past, torn between hoping that he was home and hoping that he wasn't.
As much as she wanted the confrontation to be over, the
coward in her longed to postpone it. For one thing, she was
still embarrassed about her plumbing fiasco. It was difficult to face him, remembering how awful she'd looked and
how ridiculous she'd appeared the last time he'd seen her.

His dark green van was parked in his driveway, in the
usual place, but pulling in behind it Susan noticed that the
large double doors to his workshop were closed. If he were
home, he must be inside the house, she concluded. Some-

how that possibility hadn't occurred to her and it made her more nervous.

Willing her heart to slow down to a normal pace, she revved the engine before killing it, the way she'd noticed men drivers usually did, and slammed the door unnecessarily hard after she'd gotten out. She wanted to alert Jim that he had a visitor, preferably even draw him outside to investigate.

On her way to the back entrance, it occurred to her that he might already be entertaining someone, perhaps a woman. The thought made her wish she'd stopped off at her house and called first. Then she remembered trying to call him the night before and again that morning, with no answer. Maybe he'd unplugged his phone, not wanting to be disturbed.

His dog and cat weren't in sight, she noted with regret. If they had been, she could have greeted them loudly and announced her presence. Billy had told her their names, Beauty and Beast, and their story. She guessed they were either inside or on the front porch, where they'd been the last time.

Climbing the steps, she could hear the hum of a nearby window air-conditioning unit over the pulsing of her own blood. The inner door visible through the wire mesh of the screen door had glass panes and must open into his kitchen. If he were in another room and very intent on whatever he was doing, her knock would probably go unheard. As she rapped her knuckles on the wooden door frame, Susan tried not to be more specific in imagining what room and what activity.

The door opened before she'd finished knocking, and Jim spoke through the screen, his deep voice surprised but welcoming. "Susan. Come on in." He shoved the screen door outward and stood holding it, providing an open passage for her. "I thought I heard a car engine."

"I hate to interrupt—I was expecting to find you out in your workshop. This air conditioning feels wonderful," Susan stammered as she stepped over the threshold, her shoulder almost grazing his chest. His friendly reception was disconcerting, especially after all Susan's qualms.

"Here. Have a seat," Jim invited, pulling out a chair for her at the kitchen table, where he'd obviously been working. A house plan was spread open on the tabletop, and there was a tablet covered with numbers and notations and a calculator next to it.

Susan sat, perching on the edge of the chair. She recognized the house plan—she had one just like it in her car.

"I'm not going to stay long," she promised. "I can see that you're busy."

"I was figuring out a bid on a job," Jim explained. "But I'm about finished. The longer you stay, the better. Then I won't have to go outside and work in this heat."

His light words accompanied by an engaging smile had a devastating effect on Susan's body temperature.

"I don't see how you stand it," she declared, wishing that he would sit down, too. The old-fashioned kitchen was roomy, with high ceilings, but she was conscious of his height, his build and his masculinity.

He shrugged. "You get used to it. As long as I don't get too acclimated to air conditioning, I'm fine. Is it cool enough for you in here, by the way?" His eyes rested on Susan's blazer. "I can turn the air conditioner to a higher setting. Or maybe you'd like to take off your jacket."

His tone was matter-of-fact, but Susan suddenly remembered what she'd been wearing the last time he'd seen her and held her shoulders more erect.

"It's very comfortable in here," she assured him firmly. "And I'll be going back outside in just a couple of minutes, anyway."

He turned and went over to take a glass from an upper cabinet, giving her a view of his broad shoulders and taut back. "How about something cold to drink?" he urged hospitably, opening up the refrigerator. "The selection is limited, I'm afraid. Would you like a soft drink or a beer?" He looked over at her inquiringly.

A refusal didn't seem to be among her alternatives, and Susan's throat was dry. "A soft drink sounds good, thank you," she said, relaxing her posture slightly. "But you don't have to bother with ice," she protested as he took out two identical cans and then got a tray from the freezer.

He ignored her, dislodging several cubes and dropping them into the glass. Then he popped the two cans, filled her glass and handed it to her. Susan took a quick sip, while he got the other can for himself. She was collecting her thoughts to proceed with the purpose of her visit when he pulled out a chair and sat down, closer than she would have liked with his big frame fully visible.

"Did the Crawford woman get in touch with you?" he asked as he lifted his can to his mouth.

"Why, yes, she did." Susan watched him swallow with his head tilted back, the strong column of his neck contracting. "That's why I'm here. I came by to thank you."

His keen dark gaze searched her face with a gentle concern she found puzzling. "Not for nothing, I hope," he said lightly. "Didn't you two hit it off? Have you talked in person, or just on the telephone?"

Susan realized that she'd been giving off the wrong signals. He thought she'd come to report a failed opportunity.

"Both, and we got along fine. She called this morning. I went over to her motel room. You won't believe the coincidence.'' Susan smiled, remembering. Her excitement was returning. ''We were both wearing the exact same colors. That broke the ice immediately. As you may have noticed, she has blond hair, too.'' She grimaced self-consciously, remembering her children's artless revelations to him, and added, ''Only she gets hers highlighted professionally, of course, so it looks much better.''

''I don't agree with that,'' Jim stated positively. ''But then I'm looking with a man's eye.''

Susan rushed on, too pleased and flustered to argue the point. ''Anyway, after we chatted, we discovered that we have amazingly similar tastes, the difference being that Joyce can afford to indulge hers.''

''She obviously likes expensive jewelry. Yesterday she must have been wearing fifty grand, between the rock she wore on a chain around her neck and the bigger one on her finger,'' Jim recalled dryly.

''Isn't that marquise diamond in her engagement ring just gorgeous?'' Susan demanded in a reverent tone and then sighed, looking at her own hand. ''Someday I hope to have one about half that size. I adore diamonds,'' she confessed. ''But then most women do, I suppose, along with fur coats and designer clothes.''

''Fur coats are a real necessity in this climate,'' Jim remarked with an indulgent smile. ''You can wear them during one or two months of cold weather and store them the rest of the year.''

Susan nodded sheepishly, agreeing with his practical reasoning. ''But there's just no substitute for the glamorous, luxurious feeling of having on a fur coat. I only know from trying them on in stores, since I've never owned one, but eventually, after I've gotten Billy and Joanie through college and set up for life, I intend to buy myself a full-length black mink.''

"Do you have in mind buying the diamond ring for yourself, too?" Jim asked.

Susan didn't get his meaning at first. "Why, yes. How else..." Her voice drifted off.

"You could have your diamonds and furs a lot sooner by marrying a man who could buy them for you," he pointed out. "That's how Joyce Crawford got hers, I'm assuming."

"Yes, but she was lucky. She married a college graduate, a guy with ambition. He's a high-ranking executive with a big corporation now. Those men aren't exactly growing on trees, looking for divorcées with a couple of kids. The kind of man I usually meet—" Susan broke off, suddenly realizing from Jim's expression that she was being very tactless. "It may take me longer to earn the things I want, but I'll appreciate them more," she declared. "Thanks to you, I'm on my way now, with my first big decorating job."

Her consideration for his male pride hadn't gone unnoticed. "You did get the job, then," he said in a rueful tone.

"Yes, I did, although I can still hardly believe it!" Her elation swelled under his pleased glance.

"I'm glad for you," he said heartily. "With a client like her in that subdivision, you should have your foot in the door."

"I can't tell you how grateful I am to you for making it possible," Susan told him fervently, not minding her indebtedness nearly so much at the moment.

"All I did was give her your name," Jim objected. "You had to sell yourself. Obviously you must have impressed her."

Aglow with the warm approval in his face and voice, Susan wanted to share the whole experience with him. "I took the hint from your message last night and played up the fact that I hadn't done much work over here on the north shore.'' She made a guilty face. "When Joyce jumped to the conclusion that I have lots of clients over in New Orleans, I didn't correct her error. Nor did I explain that the decorating firm I had worked for was really in Metairie, not New Orleans proper. Much to my relief, she didn't even write the name down. I was more of an assistant there and didn't have full responsibility for any major jobs. All in all, I wasn't entirely honest,'' Susan confessed.

"It doesn't sound as though you actually lied,'' Jim suggested in her defense.

"No, but I left out most of the truth. For example, when I gave Eloise Achord as a professional associate, explaining that she was head decorator for New Orleans's best-known furniture store, I didn't mention that Eloise was also one of my dearest friends. She ran the decorating staff at the department store where I worked as a clerk. She's the one who encouraged me to go back to school and become a decorator. I'll have to call her tonight and tell her my good news!''

"Could you call her early? I was thinking that I should take you out for a celebration.''

The casual invitation caught Susan completely off guard. She fought against her surge of delight as she stammered out a refusal, "That would be fun, I'm sure, but I have some other calls to make, too, and work to do—and the kids, I promised to take them out for pizza tonight—actually I don't have much time for a social life right now...."

"Don't you date?''

She shook her head, disappointed that he sounded merely interested, but not upset. "I went out a few times during the first couple of years after my divorce, but not since.''

His slow, attractive smile made her heart do a flip-flop. "I can tell that you're out of practice at letting a guy down easy.''

Susan sighed. "You'll want to take your invitation back anyway, once you hear what I have to say to you. As much as I appreciate the favor you've done for me, it doesn't change anything. I'm still going to be active in the Old Mandeville merchants' association and continue heading the committee planning the fall festival."

Impatience flashed across Jim's face, wiping out the friendliness and expression of interest. "Continue wasting your time and energy, you mean," he said in an exasperated tone. "Between your job and your children, don't you think you have enough to keep you busy? If you let the other merchants tend to their own business, you could even manage to have a normal social life."

He got up and went over to toss his empty soft drink can into the garbage pail. Susan stood up, too, feeling as though she were being dismissed. She couldn't even muster indignation as a self-defense against her regret for having to destroy her welcome.

"We're never going to see eye to eye, Jim," she said, having to look up at him as he stood several yards away and towered over her. "It's not your fault or mine that we have totally different philosophies. You're an awfully nice person, and I couldn't ask for a better neighbor. Every time I turn around I'm having to thank you, it seems. I wish I could do what you want, without letting down a lot of other people and compromising myself."

"I haven't asked you to do anything, except go out to dinner with me," Jim replied.

"But you would rather I didn't follow through with all my ideas I presented at the meeting you attended. Admit it. You think I'm going to ruin your neighborhood."

"I think you're going to make a futile, well-intentioned effort," he replied calmly, without any antagonism.

"You honestly don't expect me to succeed?" Susan asked uncertainly.

He shook his head. "Nope. Oh, your fall festival will probably get a good turnout, after you've single-handedly done most of the work organizing it. Afterward, your fellow merchants will go back to doing business as before."

"So that's why you haven't bothered to fight me?" she demanded, offended. "You don't give me credit for being a threat. And here I've been feeling terrible about making you unhappy with your own neighborhood."

He smiled at her tone. "Don't feel bad on my account. And I do definitely consider you a disruptive element. As for doing me a favor, there is something." Susan followed his glance over toward the open house plan. "Don't let your client paint my cabinets some repulsive shade, such as apricot."

She raised her eyebrows in response to his disgusted note. "I gather some decorator has done that in the past?"

He nodded.

"You sound very certain that you'll be doing the cabinetwork. I thought you said you were figuring up an estimate."

"The job is mine, if I want it," Jim replied. "The only question is whether I'll submit the estimate."

"If you do take the job, I would consult with you on the finish for your cabinets," Susan promised. "And do everything possible to make sure you're pleased with the final look." She blushed at her coaxing tone.

"That's an inducement," he said.

"Now I'll let you get back to your work." Susan walked over to put her glass by the sink. "Thanks for the soft drink."

He opened the door for her and then, over her objection, escorted her out to her car, which apparently interested him.

Susan replied to his routine questions about how she liked it and what kind of gas mileage it gave her, all the while finding his behavior rather odd.

"I'm due for a new set," she said when he bent and examined one of her tires with his hand.

"*Over*due," he corrected with a grave expression. "I wouldn't put off replacing them for another day."

"Are they really that bad?" Susan inquired, giving the closest tire a worried inspection. "Maybe I'd better not take the kids out for pizza tonight."

"They're that bad," Jim said firmly. "You stand the risk of having a blowout on the highway."

"I'll see about getting some new ones tomorrow," she said meekly. "I'm glad you happened to notice."

Jim opened the door on the driver's side for her. "I hate being the bad guy and spoiling your supper plans. Why don't I take you and the kids out for pizza?"

"They'd love that," Susan blurted, surprised. "But don't feel obligated... I mean, I know you're not in the habit... you might find it awkward... a woman and two kids..."

"Is that another roundabout no?" Jim asked with a smile.

Susan shook her head, smiling back at him. "No, it's a roundabout yes, if you're sure."

Chapter Six

The sound of Jim's van in the driveway made Susan conscious of the time. Jumping up from her desk with an exclamation, she hurried back to the bathroom to freshen up, knowing that her son and daughter would make Jim more than welcome in her absence. They were thrilled over the outing.

Emerging, she could hear voices in the kitchen and composed herself for her entrance, not wanting to appear as eager as her children sounded. He stood leaning against a counter and smiling down at Joanie, looking relaxed and exceptionally virile in jeans and a sports shirt. The sight of him intensified Susan's mixed emotions. She wished she were going out alone with him for the evening and yet knew it was best that she wasn't.

He heard Joanie out before he switched his attention to Susan and took note of her outfit. It was the same one she'd been wearing earlier—minus the blazer. "I came home and got busy working," she said lamely, picking up folds of her gathered skirt, which was a smart mid-calf length. Both it and her long-sleeved blouse were made of the same black and white print with splashes of aqua and yellow. She'd taken off her fashionable clunky jewelry, but kept on her Italian shoes. Made of black kid, they had narrow wedge heels and were wonderfully versatile. The complete ensemble was a source of pride and pleasure to Susan, since it had been put together with the resourceful, thrifty shopping necessary on her limited budget.

"We're in no hurry, if you'd like to change into something more comfortable," Jim said.

"Mom wears clothes like that," Billy explained.

"She dresses up every day and lots of time doesn't change until she gets ready for bed at night," Joanie added.

"Doesn't she wear jeans occasionally?" Jim asked, before Susan could cut in and protest at being discussed. She was mortified that her daughter's words might arouse his memory of her bedraggled appearance in the wet nightshirt. "Or a shorts outfit like you're wearing, Joanie? You look cute."

The latter question and the compliment brought giggles and jeers. In the commotion, Jim's eyes met Susan's in a teasing, provocative communication that said he'd like to see her, too, in a powder-blue tank top and short white shorts.

"I'm perfectly comfortable dressed like this, but I wouldn't want to embarrass anyone," Susan declared. "I thought you would all be starving and I didn't want to hold the party up."

"You look okay, Mom," Billy assured her kindly.

"I *am* starving!" Joanie announced dramatically, clutching her stomach. "Could we please go now, Mr. Jim?"

"Sure thing."

Susan watched him flip her daughter's blond bangs with a big gentle forefinger and was envious of the way both her children were standing close to him. She wished she had changed clothes, put on something casual that he would find sexy. A firm reminder that the kind of man she would be interested in would approve what she was wearing didn't ease her sense of regret for not having pleased this man.

As he ushered them all outside, he managed to make her feel like a special date, not an overdressed mother with two children tagging along. With his hand splayed lightly, but protectively against her back, he guided her to his van.

"Can I sit up in front with you, Mr. Jim?" Joanie wheedled, skipping ahead.

"Then I could sit in front on the way home," Billy negotiated.

Jim set them straight cheerfully. "Sorry, kids, but you're both going to sit in the back coming and going. Your mom is sitting in front with me."

He opened the door for her first, then lifted her effortlessly into the van. She tried to quash her feminine appreciation of his strength and solicitousness while he put Billy and Joanie into the back, and then came around to get in on the driver's side.

At the turn of the key, operatic voices came from the van's rear speakers, causing an outcry from the two youngest passengers and requests for the radio to be tuned to another station. Jim complied, finding a rock station, and then he turned the volume just loud enough, Susan noted, so that the two adults could talk in relative privacy.

"I gather the public radio station in New Orleans is your favorite," she remarked. "You were listening to it in your workshop, the day I came by to meet you." The recollection of watching him that day while he worked with his back to her and then hearing his soft whistle in the sudden quiet made her words sound far more intimate than she'd intended. "After the noise of your planer, the sound of classical music was quite a surprise," she added. "I'd been standing there for awhile, waiting for a chance to get your attention."

"It came as a surprise for me to turn around and see that I had a visitor. I had thought I was all alone in the world." Jim's sideways glance was clearly full of his own memories. Then, disappointingly, he became matter-of-fact. "The station is my favorite. I like the variety of music, from classical to jazz to bluegrass, and the in-depth news and interviews, too. Listening is a substitute for company, since I work for hours by myself "

"But don't you have to concentrate on what you're doing?" Susan asked. "Your work has to be so precise." She wished that he had stayed on the more personal conversational track. Her conjecture as to why he hadn't was disheartening; probably his first impression of her hadn't been any more flattering than his reaction to her appearance tonight.

"I have all the dimensions figured out before I start on a set of cabinets," Jim was answering. "It's like any other type of work. With a certain amount of repetition, it gets easy. That's why I like to break the routine with building furniture."

Susan visualized the two display rooms at the front of his house. Aside from dining room chairs, there hadn't been any duplications, she realized. Each piece had represented a new challenge for him.

"So making furniture is really just a pastime for you, not a business at all?"

"It's too labor-intensive to be a moneymaking proposition," Jim replied.

"Instead of just letting it sit and collect dust, though, wouldn't you rather sell it for a good price and make some profit, rather than none?" Susan tried not to sound impatient with his reasoning, which didn't make sense to her.

"I sell a piece occasionally."

She shook her head in baffled defeat. "You can afford to be casual about money, I suppose, since you aren't married and don't have a family."

"It's true I don't have a wife with a taste for diamonds and furs," he agreed, looking over at her with a smile.

"Or children to send to college." Susan refused to be coaxed into making light of his attitude. She found it disturbing that he was so obviously intelligent and yet apparently completely without ambition.

"Mom wants me to go to college." Tired of his sister's company, Billy had leaned forward to eavesdrop on his mother's last words and join in the adult conversation.

"I want you and your sister both to go to college," Susan corrected him, not altogether sorry for the intrusion, which kept her from speaking her thoughts too bluntly and hurting Jim's ego needlessly.

Jim turned down the radio volume. "I agree with your mother," he told Billy, drawing a grateful but surprised look from Susan, who hadn't expected any support from him. He met her glance and then added, "Personally I've never regretted getting a college degree."

"You went to college, Mr. Jim?" Billy was his mother's mouthpiece, saving her from blurting out the question with much stronger amazement and skepticism.

"I'm going to college to study to be an interior decorator, like you, Mom," Joanie piped up, before Jim had a chance to answer. She obviously wanted to be included, too, if her brother was.

"I might major in whatever Mr. Jim majored in and then be a cabinetmaker, too," Billy said, hero-worship in his voice.

"What *was* your major?" Susan asked Jim, letting the remark pass. It irritated her to suspect that he'd dropped the news of his college education mainly for her benefit and was reading her every reaction.

"Business administration," he replied.

"Are you serious? You have a degree in business?"

He looked over with a wry smile, taking in her wide-eyed incredulity. "*Cum laude* in my graduating class at Louisiana State University in New Orleans."

"You went to LSUNO?" Susan tried to place him on the familiar campus near the lakefront. "That's where I studied interior design—I don't actually have a degree," she added for accuracy before pursuing her train of thought. "Were you living on the north shore then? Did you commute across the causeway for four whole years to take classes?"

"No, I lived at home with my folks in Metairie. And I completed my course work in three years, not four. I was highly motivated to hurry up and get my degree."

"So you're from Metairie originally, like I am." Susan responded to the least fascinating bit of information. What had happened to that motivation? she was dying to know. How had he ended up a cabinetmaker on the north shore?

"Born and grew up there," Jim confirmed. "We may have more in common than you imagined," he suggested with another sideways smiling glance.

"Mom likes pepperoni on her pizza, Mr. Jim. Do you?" As Joanie tested out his hypothesis it occurred to Susan that he might already know more about her background from Billy than she knew about his. It was as pleasing as it was disturbing to think that he might have encouraged her son to reveal her personal history.

"Pepperoni pizza is probably my favorite," Jim told the little girl in a good-natured tone that held none of Susan's frustration over having her children as an audience.

"Mom likes mushrooms, too," Billy revealed with cautious disgust. "You don't, do you?"

"I have to confess I do," Jim admitted cheerfully.

"Billy *hates* mushrooms," Joanie blurted out.

"I eat them sometimes." Billy corrected her with a threatening note, reinforced—his mother could sense—by a silencing glare, which apparently had its effect since no contradiction was forthcoming from Joanie.

Susan suspected that her son's taste buds were about to undergo a forced conditioning. If his hero ate mushrooms, then so would he. She could sympathize with his admiration of Jim, who was consummately masculine. Fortunately Jim had many good qualities that she wouldn't mind Billy developing, but she couldn't approve of her attractive, personable neighbor as a male role model. That was even more true now that she had discovered he was college educated and yet lived as he did, earning his living by working with his hands.

Susan had nothing against honest manual labor. She held craftmanship in high regard, but she wanted her son to have much larger horizons than those of a skilled tradesman. His future was too important to her not to speak her feelings honestly. Her viewpoint would undoubtedly be an affront to Jim, another strike against any possibility of a friendly relationship between her and him.

It was no new conclusion that the two of them had no future, but she had to force herself to gaily join the discussion of pizza toppings that took up the remainder of the short drive to the restaurant. Jim's keenly perceptive glances in her direction indicated that she wasn't fooling him. There was a questioning undertone in his voice when he addressed her that asked gently what was wrong.

For him to be so sensitive to her mood made Susan feel worse. She was deeply appreciative of how good he was with her two children, too, not giving a hint that he minded their presence. If he felt awkward on their arrival at the Italian restaurant, escorting a woman and two kids inside, he gave no inkling of it. Spotting an empty booth, he guided them toward it past larger tables with extended families and tables for two occupied by couples.

As Susan fully expected, Billy and Joanie jockeyed for position, coveting the privilege of sitting next to him. He settled the issue as pleasantly and firmly as he'd assigned seating in the car, stating, "Your mom will sit next to me, and you two across from us."

"You have every parent in the place admiring your technique," Susan remarked to him in an undertone, as her son and daughter meekly obeyed. "Have you had practice or do you just have a natural aptitude for dealing with children?"

His smile and rueful expression betrayed that he was not as comfortable with the situation as he'd seemed. "I have nieces and nephews and get a lot of attention from them at family get-togethers."

Susan was oddly pleased at his answer, which seemed to indicate a lack of experience with occasions similar to this one.

"How many brothers and sisters do you have?" she asked, wondering if he took a date home with him for those gatherings and was used to having to claim a place next to him in the car or at the table.

"One of each. I'm the oldest and the only one unmarried. My mother hasn't given up on me yet, though."

"I have one brother and one sister, too, both married."
And her mother was hopeful that she'd remarry.

Susan restrained from mentioning that last fact in common. She slid into the booth, acutely aware of Jim's touch as he helped her courteously. Settling herself with him next to her, she had to suppress her selfish instincts at the sight of her two children, who sat eager and attentive, an obstacle to further private exchanges.

A waitress came with menus and took their order for drinks. She naturally deferred to Jim, who assumed the role of host, asking each of them what they would like. As soon as the girl had left, Susan disclosed what she'd decided upon in advance: She wanted to pay.

"You're our supper guest tonight and no arguments," she declared. "It's the least we can do to show our appreciation for your coming to our rescue the other night when our bathroom was flooded. Right, kids?" To her annoyance, Billy and Joanie were both silent, looking questioningly at Jim, whose expression showed that she was wasting her breath.

"I'll be happy to be your supper guest for a home-cooked meal. But this is on me tonight," he said. "Any time I take two pretty blondes out for pizza, I always pay." He winked at Joanie, who blushed at the compliment and giggled. "Plus, I owe Billy here something for coming by and giving me a hand in my workshop."

Billy beamed and avoided his mother's reproachful look for his lack of support.

"Could I visit you at your workshop sometimes, too, Mr. Jim?" Joanie requested prettily.

"Sure. Billy could bring you by with him. With your mom's permission, of course," Jim added with a glance at Susan, who'd stiffened.

Joanie didn't waste a second following up on the invitation. "Can Billy take me tomorrow, Mom?"

"We'll discuss it tomorrow," Susan replied, prepared to deal with arguments assertively. She would let Jim have the last word on paying the bill, but she was the boss of her small household and gave or withheld permission according to her best judgment. She refused to be railroaded into indirectly approving Billy's frequent visits.

"Tomorrow I won't be around much anyway," Jim spoke up, before Joanie could voice the plea forming in her face. "Or for the next few days. I'll be out installing cabinets."

Both of Susan's children looked so crestfallen at the news that he might have been announcing that he was moving out of state. She was left with the uncomfortable feeling that he'd read her clearly once again and had deliberately tried to ease the pressure on her.

"I wanted to see Beauty and Beast," Joanie lamented. "Billy told me about them."

"Those two aren't thinking of relocating, as far as I know," Jim consoled the little girl. "They'll be there whenever you do visit."

The waitress arrived with a tray and served their drinks. Conversation was suspended as she took their food order. They'd decided in the van to get two different combinations of toppings on each half of a large pizza. Jim pretended to become totally confused, matching up wrong choices, and had to be corrected by his two juvenile dinner guests who soon caught on that he was teasing them. Susan found herself smiling, too, and enjoying the fun.

By the time the waitress had good-naturedly verified the order to unanimous consent and gone away to place it, the atmosphere at the table was totally relaxed. Before the subject of visiting Jim at his shop could be resumed, he introduced another topic, asking, "So when does school start?"

Susan sat back, seeing no danger in his choice as Joanie made herself the center of attention first, filling Jim in on the grade she would be entering, and what her favorite subject was.

Then it was Billy's turn. "I'll be starting high school this fall, but you already know that," he said, sounding both boastful and sorry. Jim's prior knowledge was proof of conversations in private about which the boy was proud, but he was hampered from talking about himself by the fear of being repetitious, and boring his hero.

Susan took pity on her son and bragged, "Billy's a straight-A student. This past year he got first place on his project for the science fair at school."

"He's told me about it. It sounded really interesting," Jim said. "What science course will you be taking this year, Billy?"

"I don't know yet. I don't know any of my course—"

"Usually high school freshmen take biology, don't they?" Susan broke in, realizing suddenly that they were headed toward another sensitive issue. A discussion of Billy's schedule would put her on the spot again. "Whatever he takes, I'm sure he won't have any trouble."

"I wouldn't expect him to. He's a very intelligent boy," Jim said, giving her one of his keen, probing glances. "He's also good with his hands and catches on to using tools very quickly."

Susan's heart sank like lead as Billy's eyes lit up and went from Jim's face to hers and back to Jim's again.

"Billy told me that you were letting him use some of your hand tools," she said, smiling coaxingly at her son across the table. "He's being very secretive, though. He won't tell me what he's making. I figure it must be a present for his girlfriend."

"No, it isn't." Joanie giggled and clamped her hand over her mouth, but to Susan's despair, Billy didn't lose his expression of concentration as he cast his sister a scowling glance.

"I wish you'd tell Mom that she should let me take some woodworking classes in high school, Mr. Jim," he implored. "Maybe she'd believe you if you told her it wouldn't be a waste of time, the way she thinks."

"I didn't say taking woodworking classes was a waste of time," Susan corrected him, not meeting Jim's quick look, which felt razor sharp on her face. "It's just that you'll be busy taking college preparatory courses."

"But in high school you have electives," Billy argued. "Courses in things you're just interested in, like art and band and chorus. Isn't that right, Mr. Jim?"

"Some people are talented in those fields and go on to major in them in college," Susan put in as Jim shifted his weight, making her even more conscious of his big body next to her. It seemed that his broad shoulders were slightly farther from hers in his new position.

"Can girls take woodworking classes, too?" Joanie wanted to know.

"Of course not," Billy answered scoffingly. "Can they, Mr. Jim?" He ignored his mother, his usual source of authority, and looked to his hero for support once again.

"There have been lots of changes since Mr. Jim was in high school...." Susan trailed off lamely as Jim shot her an eloquent look that said he could speak for himself.

"My guess is that the industrial arts classes are all open to girls now," he stated, addressing both Billy and Joanie. "As your mother has pointed out, it has been a while since I was in high school. At that time shop classes, as they were called, were considered vocational and designed to teach practical skills for earning a living. Girls weren't supposed to become carpenters and welders and mechanics. Now, with the women's movement, there are women doing manual labor. Plus, there's the new idea that women should have the ability to be self-sufficient and not have to depend on men to do everything for them.''

He took a sip of his beer, while both of Susan's children watched and waited for him to continue. If she'd been giving the same answer, their attention would have wandered or they would be interrupting, she reflected as she sat mute, uncomfortably sure that he must be remembering her little tool box sitting open on her flooded bathroom floor.

''I would hope there's been an attitude change toward industrial arts classes in high school,'' he continued. ''They shouldn't be just for those students who aren't going to college. Everybody can benefit from basic mechanical knowledge, just to get along in the world, and some kids don't have any other opportunities to get safe hands-on experience with using tools.'' Susan knew he meant kids like Billy without a father at home to teach them. ''More important, though, classes like woodworking—and the other electives you mentioned, too, Billy, such as art and band— develop the creative part of us, the human being who has needs other than just earning money. I was too busy myself in high school to take any of them,'' he concluded, directing his last words to Susan.

''Did you learn woodworking from your father?'' she asked, going back to wishing that she was alone with him.

''No, from an old retired man in our neighborhood who had a workshop in his garage.''

''Mr. Nicholas, right?'' Billy supplied the name eagerly. ''He left you his tools in his will when he died, some of those same tools you have in your workshop.''

Jim smiled at Billy and nodded. ''You've been using several of them yourself.''

"Could I use them when I come to your shop?" Joanie pleaded. "You said yourself that girls need to learn to use tools, too."

"Mom hasn't said you could go to Mr. Jim's shop," Billy pointed out jealously. "Besides, you'd just hurt yourself and get in Mr. Jim's way." He turned to his mother and urgently changed the subject. "Mom, can I take woodworking in school? You heard what Mr. Jim said."

Susan groaned mentally. "Mr. Jim's views on a well-rounded education are certainly valid, but I'm not going to give an answer until I've talked to school officials and found out more about the recommended curriculum for college preparatory students. If you have an extra class period for an elective, then you can choose one. That's my final word, for the moment. And Joanie." Susan looked firmly into her daughter's round blue eyes, which were so like hers. "Mr. Jim is a busy man. He isn't running a child care center. Do you understand?"

"Yes, Mom," Joanie said meekly, but she darted a look of furtive hopefulness at Jim. Susan noted with exasperation that Billy was eyeing his hero, too, awaiting his reaction. One word of opposition from him and she obviously would have mutiny on her hands.

"Don't look at me for help, kids," Jim said lightly, fending them off with his hands. He smiled at Susan. "There's no way I'm taking on your mother. She's a tough lady."

His teasing camaraderie swept away all of Susan's prickly defensiveness. The warmth in his dark eyes set off a melting sensation. While she was resisting it, he glanced down at her mouth, introducing the breathtaking possibility of a kiss. Flustered, Susan looked away.

"Is that our waitress coming with our pizza?" she asked in an attempt to direct her children's attention elsewhere. It shocked and embarrassed her that she'd felt a longing for a man's lips on hers when she was sitting there in full sight of Billy and Joanie.

The ploy worked, with Jim's ready cooperation, and Susan regained her composure, but some intimate knowledge seemed to have passed between herself and him that couldn't be taken back. There was a vibrating awareness, a tension beneath the surface that added a disturbing element of pleasure for her because he was feeling it, too.

She was absurdly thrilled that he was attracted to her, inordinately pleased when he showed open interest in her habits and tastes and foibles as revealed by her children in the course of conversation, which skipped casually from one subject to another with no more sensitive issues arising.

"You like the night soaps?" he verified with a note of amused skepticism when the talk had shifted to TV programs, and Billy had volunteered her preferences. "All that sin and intrigue and fake glamour?"

"They're sheer melodramas, but I adore watching them," she admitted. "I like to see the fabulous clothes and jewels and the gorgeous houses, as much as anything."

"You don't like your men as villains?"

"What's a villain?" Joanie wanted to know. Billy leaped in with an apt definition and sought adult approval. The conversation moved on, with Jim's teasing question unanswered. It was a typical exchange in an enjoyable but frustrating evening.

Her children were having a marvelous time. The mother in her was delighted on their account and pleased that Jim seemed genuinely to like them. It was best, she knew, that they were present as chaperones and that she and Jim weren't alone, so there could be no good night kiss, no sexual overtures from him spoken in a low, husky voice.

Yes, it was definitely best....

Susan's heart pounded crazily at the thought of what she was wisely avoiding and then sank with the knowledge that she was safe from any temptation. There was no possibility of privacy. If Jim accepted an invitation to come in, the children would be there, vying for his attention. She couldn't send them off to their rooms with no television, telling them, "Mom wants Mr. Jim to herself."

Leaving them alone in the house at night, with no sitter, was out of the question, too. Susan wouldn't feel right even taking a walk down to the lake or going to a nearby lounge for a drink or to his place, should he ask her. Her reason told her she was fortunate to have a legitimate excuse to say no to those options for prolonging the evening together briefly, since there was simply no point in encouraging him. She had no intention whatever of becoming intimately involved with him.

With her refusal all worked out in her mind, Susan still felt a little thrill of uncertainty as Jim wheeled his van into her driveway and killed the engine. She had her mouth open to thank him and invite him to come inside, meaning to strike a polite, cordial note, when Joanie spoke up with unabashed eagerness.

"You could come in and watch TV with us, Mr. Jim. A real good movie is on tonight. Mom lets Billy and me stay up later during the summer when we don't have to get up for school."

Billy added his own recommendation of the movie, being more understated but every bit as hopeful as his sister that Jim would continue the evening with them.

"Mom would probably watch it with us, too, if you did," he said as an afterthought, as though Susan's presence in the living room might or might not be an influencing factor.

"It doesn't sound like your mother's kind of movie at all," Jim remarked, looking at Susan, who was sitting there feeling helpless and ambivalent. The situation seemed out of her control and whatever he decided wouldn't be satisfactory.

"We wouldn't have to watch TV," Billy suggested. "We could play cards or dominoes—"

"Or a game," Joanie put in to entice him.

"Another time, thanks." Jim was opening his door. He came around and opened Susan's and helped her climb down.

Billy and Joanie didn't argue or plead, but it was clear that they were disappointed. There was almost a tangible air of letdown as Jim walked the three of them to the back door. Susan tried to dispel it by giving her thank you speech in a gay tone.

"This was a nice treat. We had a delightful time—"

Jim smoothly cut her short. "My pleasure. Pizza doesn't usually taste that good. It had to be the company."

At the steps, he waited for Susan to get out her keys and locate the right one, then courteously unlocked the door for them and moved down out of the way. Billy and Joanie called their good-byes over their shoulders as they went inside. Instead of lingering, as Susan was expecting, they headed straight for the living room and the television set, and she could hear their voices fading away.

Standing on the top step, she found herself at eye level with Jim and separated by less than a yard, able suddenly to speak her parting words to him with no audience.

"Well, thanks again and good night," she said and cringed at how stilted she sounded. "Really, it was a nice evening. The kids couldn't have enjoyed themselves more. You were wonderful with them, very patient and kind. They don't usually take to someone the way they did to you."

"I'm flattered," Jim replied. "I like them, too. I also like their mother."

He reached out with both hands and, taking her by the shoulders, drew her down a step, so that she was in devastatingly close range. She only had to tilt her head back a little to look up into his face.

"I like you, too," Susan said, her heart beating wildly. "You're an extremely nice person and a good neighbor..." She bit her lip, hearing her words come out as a very lame compliment.

"But not someone you want to go out with or be serious about," he said, looking ruefully comprehending.

Susan held his gaze, acquiescing with deepest regret. "It's just as well, I'm sure. I know I'm not exactly your ideal woman. You don't agree with my sense of values any more than I agree with yours. I doubt you even like the way I look or dress. You have no use in general for...interior decorators." She completed her thought with difficulty because his hands were leaving her shoulders, stroking down her back and drawing her even closer.

"I've never wanted to kiss an interior decorator before. That's certain," he said softly, not disagreeing with any of the points she'd made. "Do you mind?"

Susan got bogged down with the question. Was he asking if she objected to his *wanting* to kiss her or was he seeking permission for a good night kiss? With his arms closing around her, pulling her against him, there was simply no possibility of rational thought.

"I guess not," she murmured, closing her eyes and tilting back her head as he lowered his lips to hers.

The first warm, feather-light contact sent weak pleasure coursing through her. She heard the light thud of her handbag falling to the step as she released her grip on it to put both hands around his neck. His embrace tightened slightly, but he didn't increase the pressure or intensity of his kiss. His mouth brushed against hers in a seeking motion as though he were exploring the lush, soft contours of her lips for pure pleasure.

Susan felt the sharp, sweet ache of desire and had to restrain herself from hugging him harder and pressing her body more intimately against his. But a little sound like a moan escaped from deep in her throat, betraying her. She pulled back, embarrassed as well as shaken by her own response.

"I'd better go in now," she said. "Any minute the kids will be coming to see what's happened to me."

Jim didn't relax the strong circle of his arms. "They'd see Mom kissing a man good night. Would that be so bad?" he asked huskily.

"It would be awkward to explain," Susan replied honestly. "I try to set a good example and wouldn't want them to think their mother makes a habit of kissing their male neighbors."

"Then there's the complicating factor that you would rather my workshop be off-limits for Billy. Am I right in picking up that signal? For him to see you in my arms, like this, puts you in a compromising position, doesn't it?"

Nodding her head required an enormous effort. "He's at an impressionable age, and I'm afraid of your influence," she admitted apologetically. "I don't mean to hurt your feelings, but I want Billy to set his sights higher."

Jim's arms dropped away from her, and Susan had no choice but to take hers from around his neck. She stood there with them dangling while he bent down to retrieve her handbag and then give it to her.

"Thank you," she said miserably. "I hate that I've insulted you, after you've done me one favor after another. You have such good qualities. You're thoughtful and kind and intelligent and—"

"Just generally one hell of a nice loser," Jim finished up on a pained note. "Your cool air is escaping, and you're letting all the mosquitoes in," he pointed out, glancing behind her at the open door. "I'm going to say good-night and take all my wasted good character traits along with my battered ego a couple of blocks down the street."

"I'm terribly sorry," Susan said sadly to his back as he turned and walked toward his van with long strides.

"Don't be," he called back. "It's been enlightening. Who knows? Maybe you've done me a big favor."

His words had a grim undertone. What had he meant? Susan wondered disconsolately as she went inside. She wasn't likely ever to know. After tonight, he wouldn't be asking her out again. She doubted that he would even take the Crawford job now, because of the possibility of running into her.

There wouldn't be any more personal conversations. Even the contact with him through Billy would be discontinued now, she presumed. The thought was depressing, considering that she'd done her son a service and safeguarded his future.

Chapter Seven

Jim drove home by way of the lakefront, taking a right-hand turn off of Monroe Street onto West Beach Parkway and then a left onto Lakeshore Drive. Normally it was a route he favored during less busy times of the day when he could enjoy the lake in its various moods, from glassy calm to violently choppy, with moss-draped branches of huge old live oak trees framing the view.

In the late afternoon when the heaviest influx of sightseers cruised up and down in cars, and joggers and bicyclists were out in force, he tended to avoid the lakefront. He usually drove farther along Monroe to his own street and turned off there, but that route took him past Susan's house. For the past three days, he'd been going and coming via the lakefront exclusively to avoid catching a glimpse of her or her children or, in turn, being seen.

Jim wanted to go back to the same state of mind he'd enjoyed before Susan Casey arrived on the scene. His male pride smarted every time he thought of her. He couldn't really believe that it hurt his ego as much as it did for her to have such a low opinion of him. As she'd said herself, she wasn't his ideal woman any more than he was her ideal man.

Out of sight, out of mind was the theory he was putting into practice, but it wasn't working. She kept coming to mind all hours of the day and night and didn't appeal to him any less, after insulting him.

The attraction she held for him was baffling. She wasn't really his type. Her shy response to his kiss had confirmed what his intuition told him—she wasn't used to having affairs with men. Perhaps she hadn't even slept with a man since her divorce, which could mean she had moral hang-ups about sex or romantic notions that lovemaking meant permanent commitment. Maybe she still felt emotionally tied to her ex-husband.

Whatever the reason for her almost innocent quality, Jim's common sense told him not to mess with her. Taking her to bed could hold some of the same risks as seducing a virgin. He didn't want to cause her or himself problems with guilt. Yet there had been that muffled little sound of passion she'd made that aroused him every time he recalled it and turned him all warm and possessive inside.

She might not admire him, but she was physically attracted to him. The spark of newness and mutual interest had been there between them from the beginning, along with the differences in outlook. Jim was confident that he could bring out the sensual woman in her, arouse her, satisfy her. He could be the lover of her fantasies, even if he didn't measure up to her standards otherwise.

But how could he make love to a woman who had told him straight out that she considered him a poor example of manhood for her son? That was a low blow. He thought she was wrong. He would never consciously be a limiting influ-

ence on Billy. But his present life was a lesson that stood on
its own, he supposed. As Susan had pointed out, Billy was
highly impressionable at his age. Maybe Jim might unin-
tentionally do the boy harm.

Would Jim want his own son following in his footsteps?
It was a question he hadn't ever considered before, and there
was no immediate and clear-cut answer. For that reason as
much as from stiff-necked pride, he intended to go along
with Susan's judgment and discourage Billy from spending
time with him. How he was going to do that without hurting the boy's feelings was a mystery. Jim couldn't stay away
from his workshop indefinitely.

If he expanded his business, the problem would be solved,
of course. Then he would be moving his workshop and
wouldn't be so accessible. He'd been thinking about the
matter almost constantly, along with thinking about Susan.

The only question was *when*, not *if* he decided to expand, he admitted to himself for the first time. Why not go
ahead and do it now? An immediate boost of spirits took
away any remaining doubt. He suddenly felt great. It was
time to move into a new phase, face up to a different challenge, not to prove anything to anyone, including Susan, but
because he was no longer satisfied. The truth was that he'd
become bored with the repetitiousness of his work. Susan's
coming along and ruffling the surface of his routine had
stung him to admit it.

Exhilarated, and with his mind clearer and sharper than
it had been in a long time, Jim turned up the volume of his
radio and whistled along with a rousing march as he drove
the last few blocks to his house. He wheeled into the driveway faster than usual and braked to a crunching halt, enjoying a sense of reckless power. His high spirits went flat on

him, though, as a movement caught his eye, and he glanced over in the direction of it.

He had a visitor. Billy apparently had stationed himself on Jim's kitchen steps to wait for his return. He was passing the time with Jim's animals, petting the dog and, no doubt, carrying on a conversation with the cat, following Jim's pattern. Now he was headed for the van, a spring in his step, his sensitive young face alight with boyish welcome.

Opening his door and stepping down, Jim came to another instant, firm decision that felt right immediately. No way in hell was he going to give this nice kid the brush-off. He liked him too much and cared too much about his well-being. Jim might not be the perfect male influence, but he was better than none, and he was what Billy had at the moment. His mother meant well, but she didn't understand a boy's needs.

He greeted the boy with a casual affection that was utterly sincere. "Hi, there, Billy. Nice to see you." It was good to see him. Jim had missed him the past three days. "What have you been up to?"

Billy was digging into his pocket and produced a small wad of paper money. "I've been doing some odd jobs like you did when you were a kid," he said, trying to be offhand. "I had to force myself to go up and knock on doors. I'm kind of backward, you know, like I told you. But it's getting easier, just the way you said."

"I'm proud of you," Jim declared, amazed at his own paternal feelings. Surely here was some proof that his influence wasn't all bad. Being able to approach people was certainly a valuable skill Billy would need in almost any career.

"I thought I'd open up a bank account," Billy went on eagerly. "I figure I can keep working odd jobs even after school starts, in the afternoons and on weekends."

Like Jim had done, too, but wouldn't want his own son to do.

"You could do that," Jim agreed, bending down to pet the dog's broad head. "Looking back, I wish I had devoted less time to part-time work and more to participating in extracurricular activities at school, though. I went overboard and missed a lot. But it's a great feeling to know you can earn money and be independent, isn't it?"

Billy grinned, nodding.

Jim got himself a beer and Billy a soft drink from the kitchen refrigerator. They sat companionably on the back steps talking. Billy related his labor experiences in eager detail and wanted to know what Jim had been doing. Jim filled him in on the cabinet installation he had finished up that day. The boy's comments and questions revealed all over again a quick intelligence. It was incredible to Jim how much he had picked up in just a few weeks, when he'd started by being totally ignorant of woodworking tools and techniques.

When they'd finished their drinks, Jim opened up his workshop and did a few odds and ends, mainly to give Billy a half hour or so to work on the small book stand he was making for his mother. Her name naturally came up. Billy reported that she had bought new tires for her car at one of the places Jim had recommended to her, and that she'd been pleased with the friendly service and the price.

"I'm glad to hear that," Jim said and meant it. It was good to know she had taken steps to make driving her car safer, also that the whole transaction had gone well for her. The thought of her having difficulties of any kind wouldn't bring him pleasure. She was wrong-headed about a number of things and was very stubborn, but she had the best intentions.

Locking up after Billy had left, Jim went inside, feeling generally good about life. The visit with the boy had left him both optimistic and confident. Things were going to work out well. Jim could trust his human instincts as well as his abilities. That evening he would take care of another work-related matter. He hadn't yet given Dave Myles an answer about doing the cabinetry for the Crawford house.

The past three days he'd been leaning heavily toward turning the job down, but he would take it instead. Once again there was no indecision remaining. Dave Myles was a well-respected contractor who built most of his houses in the wealthier subdivisions. He would be a source of future big contracts, more of which Jim would be able to handle with a larger workshop and several employees.

Encountering Susan on the premises was no longer a negative factor. Jim could handle a professional relationship with her, especially considering that the house wouldn't be near the decorating stage for some weeks. By then he'd probably have a totally new perspective and could look at her with different eyes. In the meantime, he did need to talk to her and put to rest her mother's fears about his adverse influence on Billy. She had no reason to worry, as Jim was sure he could convince her now that his pride wasn't an obstacle.

Myles was pleased that Jim was taking the job. The telephone conversation was cordial, but businesslike. Jim gave him projected dates when he should be installing cabinetry in the various parts of the house.

"That's what I like about you, Jim," Myles remarked. "You not only do good work, but you make my job easier. You've got a businessman's head on your shoulders."

Jim was briefly tempted to confide his plans, but didn't, preferring not to start rumors circulating until he was farther along. "I'll be at the house tomorrow some time to double-check the kitchen dimensions," he said in closing. "Maybe I'll see you there."

"Probably not," Myles replied. "I'll be in New Orleans all day. But you may run into Susan Casey, the interior decorator."

Jim caught Myles's pained note and was immediately curious. "What would she be doing there?" he asked.

"She's there every day, at least once," Myles explained. "I wish somebody would get the point across to her that she's a decorator, not a building inspector. Apparently she told Crawford's wife that she would keep an eye on things, and she's taking her promise seriously."

"She would," Jim said with dry amusement. He could see her so clearly, traipsing around the partially built house in one of her fashionable costumes, her heels tapping on the plywood floor. "I happen to know her personally since she lives in my neighborhood," he added. "What's the workmen's reaction?"

"Hell, they don't mind at all having a cute blonde coming around. I just thought I'd warn you that you might be quizzed on what you're doing, if she is there. I got the impression that you don't have much patience with interior decorators."

"I don't, so I'll be prepared." Jim tried to sound a grim note, but he hung up with a faint smile on his lips, not particularly appalled by the prospect Myles had raised.

The next morning he began a systematic survey of the Mandeville area by driving around and taking note of properties for sale or rent that might fit his purposes. He jotted down the names of realtors and their telephone numbers, secure in the knowledge that he could either buy or lease, depending on what he opted to do. If he couldn't find a building that was suitable, he could build one to his specifications. Obtaining a business loan would be no problem.

At noon he headed for the Crawford house, thinking about Myles's warning. Would he encounter Susan? he wondered. Deciding that he'd grab a quick lunch he pulled in at a hamburger joint, but the place was so crowded that he didn't park, but drove around to the take-out window instead. The crew would be knocking off for lunch, and he would have more peace and quiet at the house, he reasoned.

"Would you double that order, please," he added on impulse after he'd requested a burger, fries and a soft drink. He was awfully hungry, and food never went to waste around a construction site. His own rationalization made him grin. He was going prepared with an extra lunch and knew it.

The workmen were vacating the Crawford house, piling into battered pickups and vans, just as Jim arrived, and he had the place all to himself. With his house plan and clipboard tucked under one arm, he carried in his lunch bags with two of everything, more disappointed than he cared to admit that there was no sign of Susan's small compact car.

First he would do the job he had come to do and then he would eat, he decided. In the kitchen, he set the bags on a handy stack of lumber and then went back for a portable radio, encrusted with grime and sawdust, which he'd passed in another room. As necessary a part of the equipment for a building crew as were hammers and nails, it worked well despite its appearance and was tuned to a raucous pop station when he turned it on. The owner wouldn't mind his borrowing it, Jim knew.

After finding his favorite public radio station, which was playing big band music of the thirties and forties, he got down to work with his tape measure, whistling an accompaniment to a lively number that brought to mind a glamorous bygone era familiar from old movies. He could easily see Susan all decked out in the period fashions, dripping with rhinestones and exuding that beauty salon aura. She would still manage to look fresh and genuine, the little girl peeking out from beneath the polish and sophistication.

The sound of a car door slamming came to his ears faintly, but he didn't pay it much attention, unable to tell whether it was directly out front or in a neighbor's yard. Perhaps a minute later, though, he came fully alert when he heard footsteps in the house. A woman's footsteps, judging from the tapping of small heels, magnified by the cavernous emptiness of the rooms.

Jim paused, listening. Even without being forewarned by Myles, he thought he would have recognized that light, rapid feminine gait as Susan's. He smiled, remembering how she'd bustled along beside him the night of the meeting, making several steps to his one. Now she seemed to be making a beeline straight for the kitchen. There was barely time for him to finish the measurement he'd been taking and make a notation on his clipboard before she was there, speaking nervously from the open doorway to announce her presence.

"I don't want to startle you—"

"You didn't. I heard your footsteps," Jim assured in an amiable tone, retracting his tape measure as he stood up. Her expression showed clearly that she wasn't at all certain he would welcome this encounter. "There's not much danger of surprising someone in an empty house, like this," he added, taking in her outfit. She was wearing red today with jet black accessories. Her lipstick and nail polish matched the color of the outfit, he noted.

"That's true. In these shoes I sound like a whole herd of elephants walking around in a gymnasium." She was obviously relieved at his friendly manner, but flustered by his inspection. "I know. Elephants don't wear high heels," she went on quickly when he smiled, not finding her comparison at all apt. "They have sense enough to wear tennis shoes."

"No," he disagreed lightly, glancing down at her slim, smartly shod feet. "It's my understanding that they just have trouble finding shoes like yours in their size." He walked over closer to her, where he caught a whiff of her perfume and inhaled it. "You seem to be comfortable wearing shoes with heels. That must come from wearing them regularly and being light on your feet. My mother always takes hers off every opportunity, whenever she has to get dressed up."

"So does mine. It does take getting used to, and the trick is buying good shoes, which naturally are expensive. I can only afford them when they're marked way down, so I have just have a few pairs in basic colors. But aside from liking heels, I wear them because they make me taller," she confessed and then made a wry face. "Although they don't help much when I'm standing close to you. I'd have to be on stilts. But I didn't barge in here and interrupt you to talk about shoes. When I saw your van outside, I thought it must mean you had decided to do Joyce's cabinet work, and I wanted to tell you I was glad and also that I would keep my word and influence Joyce to choose a finish you'll like. And now—" She had to pause to take a breath. "I'll let you get back to what you were doing."

"I was about to stop and have some lunch," Jim said, gesturing toward the hamburger sacks. "Would you join me? I bought enough for an extra person, just in case someone came along."

"That was nice of you . . ." Susan looked at the sacks uncertainly. "I haven't eaten," she said and sniffed. "It does smell good."

"Surely you can't resist a hamburger from your favorite chain," he coaxed.

"How did you know—" She broke off, disconcerted by the answer to her question. Her children had divulged that information along with a lot more about her during the evening the four of them had spent together. "You don't seem to be at all . . . offended," she ventured hesitantly. "I wasn't sure you were even speaking to me."

Jim shrugged. "You dented my male ego pretty badly," he admitted candidly. "Then I accepted the fact that I might not be the answer to every woman's dream. So how about lunch anyway?"

"I'd love a hamburger."

"Right this way then." Jim escorted her gallantly over to the makeshift bench. "The atmosphere is a little rustic, but we do have classy background music."

"So I noticed," Susan said. "Don't bother," she protested as he pulled his bandana from a rear pocket of his jeans to dust off a spot for her. "This dress is washable. A little sawdust won't hurt it."

Jim went ahead anyway, using his handkerchief with a flourish, while she stood by watching him. Then she sat down daintily, both feet on the floor, waiting while he sat without bothering to clean his place.

"French fries, too," she remarked with interest as he served them both. "I had meant to come by earlier, but now I'm glad I didn't."

"So am I." Jim unwrapped his hamburger while she deftly ripped open a packet of ketchup. "Myles tells me you've been coming by often, checking on things." He took a bite under her startled scrutiny.

She took her time squeezing ketchup onto her fries. "He hasn't been particularly friendly. Does he have a bias against interior decorators, too?"

Her quick questioning glance was full of what she wasn't asking aloud. Had Jim bought the food with her in mind as a lunch companion?

"No, I don't think that's the problem," Jim replied, taking a sip of his drink. "It's just that Myles's wife is good friends with Betsy Roper and Jo Ann Blanchard. He may be taking some heat for not getting them your job. Also, since you're an unknown quantity for him, he may be a little paranoid that you are coming around too often, looking over his shoulder, so to speak."

Susan nodded. "I guess I could be giving the impression that I'm snooping around, and really I'm not. Mainly I'm just interested. And probably a little overeager. I'm still so excited about getting this job." She smiled sheepishly. "Also, to be perfectly honest, I've been taking advantage of having a legitimate excuse to come to this subdivision. The guard recognizes me now and waves me on past. I enjoy driving around and looking at all the beautiful houses and trying to imagine what it would be like to live in one of them."

Her wistful tone set off a peculiar twinge in Jim. He ate a french fry before he asked, "I take it you would like very much to live in a country club neighborhood like this yourself?"

"I would have loved having a nice big house while my kids were growing up, with or without the country club. But I missed the boat, I'm afraid." Susan went on, cheerfully pessimistic, "By the time I get them educated, they'll be off on their own, and I'll be at the condominium stage." She munched on a bite of hamburger.

"Doesn't remarrying figure into your plans at all?"

Susan blotted her mouth with a napkin, leaving a red imprint of lipstick. "No, not really. I'm not bitter, but marriage was a big disappointment the first time around. Besides, I just don't have the time or energy for the dating game, between being a mother and taking on a career. The odds just aren't that good, anyway, that I'd find a man I would want to marry who would be willing to take on a ready-made family." She crossed one knee over the other and swung her foot absently, relaxing and getting more comfortable. "What about you? Are you a confirmed bachelor? Don't you have any desire to get married and have a family?"

Her frank curiosity would have pleased Jim far more if it had been accompanied by a telltale self-consciousness. She felt free to question him since he wasn't in the category of men she'd want to marry.

"Sure, I'd like to get married," he replied carelessly. "The right woman just hasn't come along. And don't ask me to describe her." Susan was opening her mouth to interrupt and smiled guiltily at his prohibition. "Maybe without intending to, I've missed the boat, too, to use your expression. I'm thirty-six, which is past the marrying age."

"I seriously doubt you'd have any problem finding a nice woman to marry you," Susan scoffed. "You have to know you're an extremely attractive man. Plus you have so many good traits that would make you good husband material."

"For some other woman besides you, you mean. You as much as told me the other night that you would never consider marrying me," he reminded her.

She blushed at his playful reproach, but her reply was quick and spirited. "I would come as close to considering you as you would come to considering me. Go ahead and admit it. You don't like the way I look or my style of dress. A woman can tell those things. And you've made it quite clear that you have no respect for my occupation, which I happen to think is very important. You may think I'm a dumb, helpless blonde, but I'm not. I'm actually very levelheaded and independent and reasonably perceptive. I knew that first day I met you that I wasn't your type. What are you doing?''

Jim had leaned over toward her and picked her paper napkin out of her lap. Very deliberately and gently he dabbed lightly at the corner of her mouth. Her eyes widened and her mouth parted on an intake of breath, but she didn't draw back.

"Ketchup," he explained. "It's been driving me crazy."

"You should have said something," Susan murmured.

"Probably I should have," he agreed softly, smiling into her eyes. "I had trouble concentrating on what you were saying. I kept thinking of another way of cleaning it off, besides using your napkin. But since you don't appeal to me in the least, it didn't make sense to kiss you. And you wouldn't have enjoyed it either...."

He closed the small distance between his mouth and hers very slowly, giving her ample time to avoid kissing him, but she closed her eyes and tilted her head back for him instead. Then, while his lips were caressing hers, savoring her taste, he felt her hand coming to rest on his cheek. The warm light touch set off a wave of pleasure that rippled through his body. A telltale tightening in his groin warned him that he'd better stop, but the temptation to go for more depth was too strong. The way she opened for him brought fierce satisfaction, and her tongue was shy but not reluctant to couple with his.

Jim made a move to get closer, wanting to take her into his arms, and was brought back to reality by the sound of his soft drink toppling to the floor.

"That just goes to show you how much unpleasantness I saved us both by using your napkin, instead of my mouth or tongue," he said huskily, pulling back a few inches and touching his forefinger gently to the spot he'd wiped.

Susan sucked in a deep breath. "We would both have been totally repulsed, wouldn't we?" she quipped unsteadily in a weak voice.

Her dazed look brought a tender feeling to Jim's chest. To hide the emotion, he made a small production over his spilled soft drink.

"Look at the mess I've made," he declared, bending down to pick up his cup, which still contained some crushed ice, but no liquid. Susan insisted that he pour half of hers into it and they resumed eating, but without any real interest in the food. The meal was simply an excuse to sit there together longer and talk. She was afraid he was going to pick up the threads of the conversation again, and just as afraid he wouldn't, Jim sensed. He shared some of her ambivalence.

"A hamburger and french fries don't taste the same after a kiss, do they?" he commented lightly, to dispel the tension. "It's like sampling dessert during the main course."

"I suppose. I've never done that. Have you?"

"No. Actually I'm not much on dessert, although I can't turn down a slice of homemade apple pie or my mother's banana pudding."

Susan wrinkled up her nose. "I like fancy desserts, the kind that are so pretty it seems a crime to eat them."

"Do you like the looks or the taste?" Jim asked teasingly.

"Both," she admitted.

"How about the flaming desserts that the New Orleans restaurants are all so big on, like Bananas Foster? The ones the waiter fires up before he serves them."

Susan smiled and nodded. "I don't particularly like bananas, but I adore Bananas Foster. A good friend of mine, Eloise Achord, always takes me out to a fine New Orleans restaurant, like Commander's Palace or Antoine's, for my birthday. It's kind of a joking tradition that we order a dessert that comes in flames." She regarded Jim, briefly entertaining herself with a thought before sharing it. "If you ever met Eloise, you would think the way I dress is very understated by comparison. She's six feet tall and goes for really far-out fashions."

His meeting her good friend obviously wasn't very likely, in her mind. "You've mentioned Eloise to me before," he reminded her. "She was head decorator for the store you worked at as a salesclerk. So you two discovered that you both like fancy desserts and became friends?"

"Actually she felt sorry for me and took me under her wing. She's originally from New Jersey, you see, and moved to New Orleans because she fell in love with it on a visit. She just couldn't believe that I had lived in Metairie my whole life, just minutes from downtown New Orleans, and yet had never eaten in most of the famous New Orleans restaurants or had the benefit of what the city offers in culture and entertainment. Every chance she got, she would broaden my education. And still does," Susan added, "except that I don't see her as much now, of course."

Jim was a little jealous of Eloise's role, which he was fully qualified to take over himself and knew he would enjoy. He was as familiar with New Orleans nightlife as anyone, from entertaining former clients.

"We're not that far away from downtown New Orleans here," he remarked casually. "Just an extra half hour across the causeway. It's an easy matter to drive over and have dinner and take in some city nightlife—see a play, make the rounds of the clubs in the French Quarter, go dancing or whatever.''

"There's more than distance involved," Susan pointed out tactfully. "A night out like that costs a small fortune."

More than she thought he could afford. "So what if it does?" Jim demanded ruefully. "It's only money. I don't object to dropping a couple of hundred bucks for a good time whenever I want to. So how about Saturday night? I look quite presentable in a coat and tie. You wouldn't be embarrassed to be seen with me, I can promise you that."

"I didn't think that I would!" she protested, and then sighed. "I've gone and hurt your feelings again, haven't I? I didn't mean to. It's just that you work hard for your money, and I wasn't angling for a date."

"I was, and it's my money."

"That kind of date doesn't really seem like your idea of a good time," she said, voicing the thought hesitantly, clearly not wanting to trample harder on his male pride.

Jim took what consolation he could in her wistful note. At least she regretted not being able to cast him as her escort for a sophisticated night out.

"I have to admit that I was burned out on the wining and dining and nightclubbing routine when I moved over here to the north shore six years ago," he told her. "I had done so much of it in the line of business, entertaining clients."

Her eyes were huge blue pools of interest. "So you did use your degree? I wondered. You said you graduated *cum laude*, so I assumed you must have had offers."

"I did. I went with Huntington Manufacturing. It's part of a huge conglomerate. You're probably familiar with the Huntington name in office furniture."

"Why, yes, I am. Did you take that particular offer because of an interest in woodworking and furniture making?"

Jim smiled cynically. "I could have cared less what their product was. Huntington offered what I was looking for, which was money and advancement. I worked in sales, calling on corporate customers in the southeastern states. No nickel and dime stuff, but strictly big accounts that involved new office buildings or major revamping of old office quarters. It was highly competitive, but the sky was the limit."

"Didn't you like it?"

"I thrived on it. For nine years I lived and breathed work."

"Nine years!" Susan exclaimed. "Why, you must have been thirty years old, then, by the time you..." She faltered for the right word.

"Quit," Jim supplied. "The company didn't let me go. Actually I took a year's leave and then quit at the end of it."

"But why? Were you disappointed in the way the job had worked out? Didn't it pay as well as you expected or weren't you promoted the way you thought you deserved?"

Jim shook his head. "The money and the opportunity were both there. I was regional sales manager and had just gotten promoted the next step higher when I decided to back off and take a look at things."

"How does moving over here to Mandeville fit in?" Susan was too wrapped up in the story to hesitate asking questions.

"I just drove over to the north shore one day to look around, just to get out of the city, saw the house I'm living in now with a For Rent sign on it, and rented it that same afternoon. I moved over some woodworking tools that I had been keeping in storage. The old man I mentioned who taught me woodworking left them to me when he died—"

"Mr. Nicholas," Susan put in, remembering the information Billy had provided.

"Mr. Nicholas," Jim confirmed, speaking the name with affection. "He was retired and had a woodworking shop in his garage. I was fascinated with his tools, and he encouraged my interest and always made me welcome. He and his wife were childless, so I guess he enjoyed having someone to teach. Strange how things work out," he mused, shaking his head. "I owe Mr. Nicholas a lot."

Susan's expression was gravely doubtful. "He must have taught you a lot, for you to develop the reputation you have now in just six years."

"I've worked hard. One thing I've learned about myself is that I am a workaholic, no matter what I do for a living."

She bit her lip, holding back whatever it was she wanted to say, then prompted bleakly, "So you moved to Mandeville and became a professional cabinetmaker."

"I got drawn into doing woodworking commercially at first by taking on small projects for neighbors free of charge. They started recommending me, and one thing led to another. Here I am. This is not a tragic story," Jim chided gruffly. "You look like you're about to burst into tears."

"You don't regret your decision at all?" she asked earnestly. "You don't look back and think you made a terrible mistake?"

"I gather that you think I did."

Her slow head shake wasn't really a denial. "It's not for me to say, but I just can't understand how you could give up that kind of job to build cabinets for people's houses. Why, you could be living in a subdivision like this one yourself."

"It's not beyond the realm of possibility still," Jim suggested, "if I were to decide that I wanted to."

"You could go back to Huntington, you mean?"

"I don't think I'd have a problem going back with Huntington or with some other company. I'd have to start lower down the ladder again."

"But you don't intend to. I can tell." She sighed with bafflement at her conclusion. "You must have been making a huge salary."

"Plus a bonus that was based on the percentage of total sales in my territory. I was making very good money when I quit." Jim backed up his matter-of-fact claim with a figure that made her eyes widen with disbelief. "The problem was that I had all of the usual side effects of earning that kind of income. Aside from ulcers and a dependency on nicotine and alcohol, I was liking myself less all the time. Then a couple of things happened back to back that made me question whether any amount of money was enough to pay for health and friends and conscience. The answer I came up with was no." He shrugged. "I won't pretend that I haven't missed being in the fast lane every now and then, but there's a lot to be said for contentment and peace of mind."

"What were those couple of things that happened?" Susan asked after a hesitation. "Do you mind telling me?"

"No, I don't mind." Jim didn't realize until her gaze followed his hand that he'd reached to his shirt pocket for the pack of cigarettes he hadn't carried in five years now. "A guy that I grew up with, who was more like a brother than a friend, was killed in an automobile accident. I hadn't seen him in several years, even though he did his best to get together with me. A number of times he left messages on my answering machine, but I was in and out of town and always so damned busy, I just didn't have time to get back to him. 'Next time I'm home,' I would tell myself, and then suddenly there wasn't ever going to be a 'next time.'"

"How terrible," Susan said softly, reaching over to touch him on the arm. "I'm sorry."

Jim swallowed and went on dispassionately. "The next day after Chris's funeral, the man whose job I'd just been promoted to—he was on his way down the company ladder—committed suicide. He had a wife and three kids."

"But you weren't responsible!" Susan protested. "He must not have been doing a good job. Someone else would have taken his place, if you hadn't."

"I did nothing to prop him up. I wanted his job." Jim stated the facts, again with no emotion. "Ambition doesn't allow for any human considerations."

"But the very fact that you were so affected by both of these things that happened just goes to prove that you were too hard on yourself," Susan said staunchly and then lapsed into grave reflection. "It just seems such a shame. You were a victim of circumstance. If your friend hadn't gotten in that car accident and the man in your company had been a stronger person..."

"The chances are fairly certain that I wouldn't be sitting here, talking to you right now," Jim said lightly. He stood up and held his hand down to her. She looked at it and then up at him, surprised and puzzled by his behavior.

"That's a great tune to dance to," he said with a persuasive smile. "I'd like to give you a preview of what you'll be missing if you don't go out on the town with me Saturday night."

Susan glanced over at the dirt begrimed radio, her expression showing she hadn't been paying the music any attention. "You want me to dance with you *here*? Now?" she said incredulously.

"The dance floor isn't crowded," he coaxed, reaching down and taking both of her hands.

"But I'd feel so silly," she protested weakly, letting him pull her to her feet. "Besides, I haven't danced in ages."

"It's not something you forget," Jim assured her, putting his arm around her and drawing her close. "Just follow my lead. Hmm. That's nice," he murmured as she relaxed a little, some of the stiffness easing out of her body. "We dance very well together. Now, isn't this fun?"

He smiled down at her.

"I feel perfectly ridiculous," she said with laughter bubbling in her voice. "What if one of the workmen walks in on us? Won't you feel like an idiot?"

"He'd just better not try cutting in." Jim tightened his hold on her and put the hand he was clasping around his neck so that he could slide both arms around her. "If he wants to join the party, he'll have to get his own partner."

They finished out the number, dancing gradually slower until at the end they were standing and swaying in rhythm with their bodies pressed close together. Susan lifted her head from his chest and looked up at him with that same dazed expression she'd had after they'd kissed earlier, but there was anticipation in her eyes. She expected and wanted him to kiss her again.

"Thanks for the dance," Jim said huskily. "It was just an excuse to get you into my arms and do this—" he kissed her with tender passion "—but I enjoyed it."

"So did I," she said with a sigh. "Jim—"

The sound of car doors slamming and male voices and laughter came from outside. The workmen were returning. Jim kissed her again, and her lips clung sweetly to his, seeming to give him the answer in advance to the question he asked her as he reluctantly raised his head.

"Is Saturday night a date, then? You'll want to get a sitter for the kids. I know several older ladies in the neighborhood who would be very trustworthy." Her face had clouded over with what he assumed to be maternal concern.

"Jim, I know I've been giving off all the signals, and I apologize—I'm not a tease—but I won't go to bed with you," she informed him with a determined but desperate air that took all the sting out of the announcement for him. "I know it's a terribly outdated attitude, but I don't have affairs."

"Okay," he said pleasantly. "I can respect that. We could still go out and have a good time, couldn't we? If it will put your mind at ease, I give you my solemn promise that I won't ask you to go to bed with me." He smiled at her skeptical and faintly disappointed expression. "Just don't make me any offers and expect me to turn them down, though. I have to be honest and tell you that I would be very easy where you're concerned."

She blushed and glanced in frustration toward the open door. The workers' footsteps and voices signaled that they were entering the house now. But despite the risk of being seen at any moment, she let him steal a quick kiss before he turned her loose.

"Wear something glamorous Saturday night or you may feel underdressed," he warned her, as she walked over to pick up her purse. "I'm thinking black tie myself."

"Are you serious?" She was intrigued by the idea, as well as doubtful. "You don't need to go to the expense of renting a tux. That's not necessary."

"I don't have to rent a tux," Jim replied. "I have one hanging in my closet in a dry cleaner's bag. I may need some help with cuff links when I get to your house, though. It's been a while since I had French cuffs mastered."

She was looking at him strangely, and her voice was odd, too, as she said, "You own your own tuxedo."

"Along with a couple of dinner jackets and a variety of tucked and ruffled shirts. I'm all prepared to be a dashing escort. Is something wrong?" he asked as her expression seemed to get even more bleak. "You're not about to try to back out on me, are you? After you've raised my hopes."

She mustered a wan smile in response to his light, coaxing tone. "No, I won't back out. But if you'll excuse me, I really have to go now. Goodbye and thank you for lunch."

"You're welcome."

Jim was addressing her slim erect back. He stood there, puzzling over her sudden change of mood as he listened to the diminishing sound of her footsteps through the house. From the rapid clicking of her heels, she seemed to be leaving in an even greater rush than she had arrived, and her voice, returning the greetings of several workmen, was strained.

How could his owning a tuxedo possibly upset her? he wondered, and couldn't come up with any plausible answer.

Chapter Eight

Bolting from the Crawford house, Susan was a little frightened by her own emotion. It was a surprise turnabout, not a bitter twist of fate, that Jim had all the capabilities of being the urbane male escort of her imaginings. He had just chosen to be another kind of man. The fact that he had given up a successful career in higher-level management to become a skilled craftsman was difficult to understand, but not a tragic mystery. There was simply no reason to feel such an overwhelming sense of regret for what might have been. It was absurd.

Jim was seemingly very happy and well-adjusted in his present life. He had the quiet confidence of a man with a good measure of self-esteem. Who was Susan to say that he had made a mistake? It apparently didn't bother him at all to drive into this subdivision and glimpse the kind of lifestyle he'd given up. Why should Susan's eyes smart with a painful haze of tears as she passed one lovely house after another on her way to the guarded entrance?

The poignant ache in the region of her heart was for herself as well as for him, and that didn't make a bit of sense. Her future wouldn't have been linked with his, if he had stayed with Huntington Manufacturing and risen to the top. It wasn't likely that they would ever even have met. He wouldn't be living a couple of blocks down the street from her now. He wouldn't have carried her home from the meeting, come to her rescue when she'd flooded her bathroom, taken her and the kids out for a pizza supper, kissed her good night ...

Today wouldn't have happened. She wouldn't have felt so incredibly close to him, so vitally interested as she listened to him tell about his past. She wouldn't have stepped completely out of character and danced with him in a partially built house, given herself over to the close, strong haven of his arms for those wonderful few minutes.

If Jim were living in one of these big houses today, it stood to reason that he would have a wife, a very lucky woman who wouldn't be Susan. The thought caused a wrenching, jealous sensation, and yet his teasing accusation that she wouldn't consider marrying him was true. She couldn't afford to let herself even think of getting serious about him. They wanted different things out of life. They couldn't possibly be happy together.

Surely he felt the same way. He was just attracted to her and liked her, which was highly flattering. She could go out with him, have a delightful time, keep everything light and casual and under control. He would keep his word and not pressure her about going to bed with him. Soon he would lose interest, find someone sexually more willing, but would still continue to be neighborly and friendly, even with her working to bring on changes to his neighborhood that he opposed.

The realistic scenario, that should have soothed, brought on a fresh wave of anguish. Susan drove home, disturbed by her lack of enthusiasm for any of the tasks awaiting her. She couldn't even rely on her children's presence to restore her normal optimistic outlook.

Joanie was spending the day with a girlfriend in their old neighborhood, and Billy had been making himself extremely scarce lately, with only vague explanations. To his mother's surprise, he had turned down her suggestion that he might want to visit one of his friends today, too. She could have dropped both him and Joanie off at the same time.

"Are you sure?" Susan had pressed. "What are you going to do with yourself all day?"

"Oh, just fool around the neighborhood," he'd replied cheerfully. "I like it here now, Mom. Moving was a good idea after all."

Susan would have been delighted to hear that, if she'd had any evidence that he was making friends with boys his own age. She wondered how he was spending his time and suspected that he wandered around aimlessly, keeping an eye out for Jim. Joanie had asked her brother a couple of times the past few days, in Susan's hearing, if he had seen Mr. Jim and Billy had replied with a glum certainty, "No, he wasn't home today."

Thoughts of her son awakened guilt. Not once had he come to mind while she was with Jim, his hero, at the Crawford house. She'd temporarily forgotten her concern about Jim's influence on him, so wrapped up had she been in responding to Jim purely as a woman. The mother in her, finally awakened, made her see her date with Jim in a different context. How could she go out with him and expect to prevent Billy from spending time with him? How could she explain wanting to be with a man she couldn't encourage her son to admire?

Susan couldn't explain it to herself. Even realizing how selfish and pointless the desire was, she couldn't quite bring herself to the resolve she needed to make. She should break the date and tell Jim once and for all that she wouldn't go out with him. But she didn't want to.

Her own unwillingness to do what was obviously best was just another aspect of her emotional confusion. She didn't understand herself. How could she not heed her own best judgment? As though in blind search of the answer, she drove to the lakefront instead of going directly home. It was the most likely place for Billy to be killing time.

There was no sign of him. She looked closely when she spotted several teenaged boys throwing a Frisbee, but he wasn't one of them. Thinking that the harbor would be a natural attraction, where boats passed in and out of the channel, she passed up her street and went all the way to the end of Lakeshore Drive, but failed to catch sight of a slender fair-haired boy along the pier or sitting in the shade of the open-air building.

Of course, he could be at home, she reflected as she headed back and made the turn that would take her past Jim's house. Approaching it, she slowed down to a crawl, struck afresh with guilt. The purpose of taking this roundabout route had been the urge to drive past his place as much as it had been to look for Billy.

With the driveway clear, she could glimpse his red and white vintage Corvette under its lean-to shelter. The sporty little car brought up a practical matter that hadn't occurred to her before. On Saturday night Jim would have to drive them in the convertible or his van, neither of which was Susan's idea of an appropriate automobile for crossing the causeway, dressed to the hilt for an elegant evening in downtown New Orleans. She could imagine arriving in the convertible windblown and hoarse from shouted conversation. Or pulling up for valet parking in the van and alighting under the curious glances of couples getting out of their Mercedes and Lincolns. Taking her own small compact car was hardly a more glamorous alternative.

In any event, they wouldn't ride in style. Jim could don a tuxedo and look the part of the kind of man she would be interested in dating, but he wasn't really and didn't want to be. The transportation he offered was concrete proof of that. Susan should never have agreed to the date in the first place and should back out. *But she still didn't want to.*

Driving on, she glanced unseeingly at a boy pushing a wheelbarrow in a yard several houses along the street from Jim's. It took a second glance before the realization dawned that the boy was Billy. So absorbed had she become in her own personal dilemma once again that she'd forgotten about him temporarily. Braking, she pulled over to park in front of the house and then got out.

The wheelbarrow was piled high with dead tree branches and debris. Evidently he was doing yard work for the owner. When he didn't notice her, she called his name. At the sound of her voice, he started, slowly lowered the wheelbarrow and turned around, looking as though she'd caught him in the act of breaking a rule.

"Oh, hi, Mom," he called and trudged toward her, dragging the back of his hand across a sweaty forehead and then wiping the hand on his soiled jeans. His T-shirt was soaked with perspiration and his face flushed with the heat.

"I was just driving by and saw you," she said when he was several steps away from where she stood on the sidewalk.

"You don't usually drive home this way," he remarked.

"No, I don't," she agreed, feeling another wave of guilt because she couldn't say with complete honesty, *I was looking for you.* "What are you doing?"

"Cleaning up this lady's yard. Her name is Miss Ethel." He glanced back over his shoulder and lowered his voice discreetly. "She's kind of old and fat and can't stoop over."

"That's very nice of you to help her out."

He shrugged. "She's payin' me."

"I see. How did that happen? Were you walking by, and she stopped you?"

"No, I saw that her yard needed cleaning up, and I knocked on her door and asked if she wanted me to do it."

His admission was full of pride, as well as uncertainty as to how his mother would take it. A recent conversation came back to Susan. He'd mentioned wanting to do odd jobs to earn money, as Mr. Jim had done as a boy. Susan hadn't encouraged the idea, but evidently he'd gone ahead with it anyway.

"Have you been doing work for other people lately, besides Miss Ethel?" She kept her voice clear of any reproach.

He nodded and dug into his pocket. "See all the money I've made this week? Count it, why don't you?"

Susan took the folded bills from a grimy hand and complied with his eager offer. "This is a lot of money. You have been busy," she said. "Is Joanie in on what you've been doing?"

He shook his head. "She'd want to do it, too, and she's a girl. She'd pass out in this heat."

"So you've been keeping it a secret from everybody."

"Everybody except Mr. Jim. I told him. He was real interested and wanted to hear all about it. You aren't mad at me, are you, Mom?" he asked a little worriedly, trying to read her reaction. "I know you want me to have fun just being a kid, but I like making money. Like Mr. Jim says, it feels real good to know you can."

"I don't really like your not having told me, but I'm not mad," Susan reassured him. "As much as anything else, I like to know what you're doing because I love you and I'm interested." At least as much as Mr. Jim, she just managed not to add. "Was this Mr. Mann's idea that you should do odd jobs?" And keep it secret from your mother?

"No, it was all my idea. I didn't think that I had the nerve to ask people, though, and he told me I would get over feeling shy, after a few times. 'The worst that can happen is that you may get turned down,' he said. 'And then again, maybe you won't. Either way, you'll feel better about yourself for trying.' He was right. It was awful hard that first time, Mom. I'll have to tell you about it, but now..." He glanced over his shoulder at the laden wheelbarrow.

"Now you need to get back to work," Susan said lightly, despite a tightness in her throat. Her little boy was growing up, taking initiative, showing responsibility, with encouragement from Mr. Jim. "Later on when you get home, I definitely want to hear all about your jobs, though." She held out his money to him, wanting to hug him, sweaty T-shirt and all, but that would be an affront to his budding masculinity.

"Why don't you keep that for me?" he suggested. "That way I won't lose it. We're going to have to open me up a bank account, so I can start earning some interest."

"That's an excellent idea." Was it his own or had Mr. Jim suggested it? She would have liked to know, but didn't ask.

"So long, Mom." Billy started back toward his wheelbarrow, not trudging now but walking purposefully.

"Don't get overheated," Susan couldn't keep herself from saying.

"Don't worry, I won't," he called back over his shoulder. "I do need to get some of those colored handkerchiefs, though, to wipe the sweat."

He was referring to the bandanas that workmen used. Jim carried one, of course. He'd used his shortly over an hour ago to dust off a spot for Susan to sit on. In her son's eyes, if Mr. Jim preferred colored handkerchiefs, white wouldn't do.

Half amused and yet troubled, Susan got back into her car and drove on home. Perhaps she was being overly concerned about Jim's influence, which clearly was very powerful at the moment, but not necessarily lasting. Children went through phases. Billy was at loose ends this summer, moving to a new neighborhood where he knew no one. On a short-term basis, Jim might be the best thing that could have happened to him.

He seemed to be blooming under Jim's attention, developing confidence. As a mother, Susan had to be grateful, if a little jealous. Jim's approval was more important to her son than her own was right now. But once Billy got back in school and became busy and involved, his hero-worship would fade.

The strong attraction Jim held for Susan would go away, too, after he'd lost interest. Meanwhile it was okay for her to go out with him a few times. She was due a little fun. There was nothing wrong in her having a short-term platonic relationship with a man. The key word for both herself and Billy, where Jim was concerned, was *short-term*. Jim couldn't be permanent in their lives.

Susan's emotional turmoil quieted down once she'd put everything in calm perspective, but she felt strangely empty. The house seemed too quiet with neither of her children around. She put all her usual energy into her afternoon's work, but her normal enthusiasm was still lacking.

* * *

"Mom drove by Miss Ethel's today and saw me cleaning Miss Ethel's yard," Billy told Jim. "She never drives home that way, coming from the lakefront. When she said my name, I almost jumped out of my skin."

"What time was this?" Jim asked.

"Around noontime."

"Maybe she was looking for you." And maybe she had left Jim at the Crawford house and obeyed an impulse to drive past his place. That explanation was ridiculously pleasing to Jim. "So your secret is out now. How did your mother react?" he asked, aware that just keeping Susan in the conversation was the main reason for his inquisitiveness.

"She seemed a little upset, but she said she wasn't mad."

The answer wasn't what Jim had expected. It shed a different light on the boy's keeping his part-time work secret from his mother. Jim's impression heretofore had been that she wouldn't actually object, but simply hadn't given encouragement, and that Billy had wanted to surprise her.

"You didn't go against direct orders from your mother when you went out and took odd jobs, did you, Billy?" he inquired sternly, not liking the position that he was being placed in as a coconspirator.

"No, sir. Not *direct* orders," Billy denied earnestly. "Mom didn't come right out and tell me that I couldn't earn money. Honest."

"What exactly did she say? How did the conversation go?" Jim continued.

Billy frowned with concentration. "Let's see. She was asking me about my bicycle needing tires and said she would take me to get some new ones the next day when she could drive. She'd hurt her leg the night before, stepping in a pothole. Remember, I told you."

"I remember," Jim said. "Go on."

"I told her I would pay her back real soon because I wanted to start earning some money like you did when you were my age. I said I would like to buy myself a car by the time I could drive, the way you did. But the only trouble was me getting over being backward. She said I didn't have to worry about doing odd jobs. I should just enjoy my summer. That's exactly the way it went, Mr. Jim."

"I believe you, son, and I agree that you weren't disobeying your mother."

Jim got the picture clearly, and though it absolved Billy of blame, Susan's answer seemed like a negative reaction to Jim more than an honest and sensitive answer to her son. Aside from feeling like he'd had salt rubbed into a curing wound, Jim was frankly disappointed in her as a mother.

Almost against his will, he encouraged Billy to give a full rendering of the scene between his mother and him earlier in the day. It was all too easy for Jim to read between the lines. A major concern for Susan had been whether he himself was Billy's motivating force. After not having given the boy any moral support, she'd tried to put a guilt trip on him because he hadn't come to her and shared his sense of accomplishment. Instead he'd gone to Jim, which undoubtedly galled her. Still, there was no excuse for the fact that she hadn't patted Billy on the back and told him that she was proud of him.

It was difficult for Jim to hold up his end as the talk switched to other topics for the rest of Billy's visit. He apologized when Billy was leaving for being so absent-minded.

"That's okay," Billy said. "There was a favor I wanted to ask you. I wondered if you would mind lending me one of those colored handkerchiefs you use. The sweat runs all down in my eyes when I'm doing yards."

"You mean one of these?" Jim pulled his bandana out of his pocket and wiped his brow with an abrupt motion, remembering how he'd used it for another purpose earlier in the day.

"Just until I can buy some of my own. I told Mom today I needed to get some."

Jim took some grim amusement from imagining Susan's expression at that news. "No need to spend your money," he said. "I have a big supply, and I'll give you several to take home with you right now."

"Gee, that would be great!"

Billy didn't waste any time stuffing one of his free bandanas in a rear pocket of his jeans, the right-hand pocket, where Jim invariably stuck his. As the boy walked off, Jim saw that a red corner was dangling, like a signal flag, and was ashamed that his gift had been prompted by more than just generosity. Billy wasn't a battleground, and it wasn't right to use him to send messages or issue challenges.

Jim called Susan that night, spoiling for a confrontation. When she answered, he could hear adult voices in the background.

"Oh, hi," she said, lowering her tone, when he had identified himself. Her soft welcoming note, combined with his curiosity about who was there at her house, threw him off slightly, and he wasn't as forceful as he'd intended to be, coming directly to the point.

"Billy came by this afternoon, very relieved that he'd been found out earlier when you drove by and saw him. I wanted you to know that he has been acting on his own initiative, a fact of which he is rightly proud."

"You bolstered his confidence, though, judging from what he told me," she said in the same lowered voice. "I'm afraid I let him down when he gave me the chance to do the same. Mothers don't always say the right thing, unfortunately."

"Nobody's perfect," Jim said gruffly, his self-righteous aggression immediately dissipating. "I hope you're proud of him."

"Very proud. I told him so when he came home, pleased as punch with his bandanas that you gave him. I hate to cut this short, but there are some townspeople here at my house for a committee meeting . . ." Her voice drifted off, conveying more regret than apology.

"I thought I recognized Martha LeBlanc's voice. How's your fall festival thing shaping up?"

"So-so." It was a reluctant but honest admission.

"Are you getting more enthusiasm than true cooperation and having to do the work yourself?" he asked sympathetically.

"Pretty much. Before I let you hang up—" Her voice dropped even more and became muffled. Jim suspected she might have her free hand at her mouth, directing her words into the receiver for his hearing only. "What time should I be ready Saturday night?"

"Say about seven?"

She agreed on the time, then thanked him for calling and said goodbye in a more public tone. Cradling the phone, Jim felt about as tough and unrelenting as a marshmallow. He made half a dozen other calls, all to New Orleans, that a few minutes ago he had thought wouldn't be necessary. With dinner reservations at the big-name French Quarter restaurant he'd decided upon and tables booked at three night spots, Jim was all set for Saturday night except for leasing a car, which he would do the following day during regular business hours.

He would have been less than human if he hadn't regretted the lack of necessity for reserving a hotel room. There was no chance that they would spend the night together in town, even if the evening led to a mutual desire to do just that. Jim was resigned to driving home across the causeway during the wee hours and sleeping alone in his own bed.

Billy didn't mention his mother's date with Jim when he dropped by during the next couple of days. Jim wondered whether Susan was putting off telling her two kids until the last moment. He could tell at a glance, though, when Billy arrived on Friday that the boy knew. Sure enough, Billy brought the subject up immediately and dropped some totally unexpected, highly disruptive news.

"Joanie and me have to spend the night with Grandma and Grandpa Packard over in Metairie tomorrow night when you and Mom go out."

It was all that Jim could do to pull himself together and soothe Billy's disgruntled reaction to being excluded from the outing.

Chapter Nine

Susan hadn't felt any more fluttery and excited on prom night in high school. It was such fun dressing up and going all out to look her prettiest for a date. Opening the front door for Jim made her relive that anxiously self-conscious moment of undergoing inspection, followed by the flush of pleasure when he whistled and complimented her with his eyes.

There any sense of déjà vu ended. Her escort tonight was no gawky young man in unaccustomed evening finery. Susan stared in frank admiration at Jim, tall and suave and incredibly handsome in his tuxedo. She was bowled over by the transformation. He was good-looking enough in his work clothes.

"You look very beautiful," he said, smiling at her. "For the record, I like your dress. The color and the style are terrific on you."

Susan's peacock blue silk outfit was actually a skirt with tiered, irregular layers and a chemise top with flat narrow straps that left her shoulders bare. She didn't bother to correct Jim on the technical difference.

"Thank you. I ran across this today when I was shopping and couldn't resist it, since it was marked down." And was more alluring than anything she owned. "For the record, I think it's a crime against all women if you haven't worn a tuxedo in six years. Did you have any problem with the cuff links?" Susan blushed at her almost hopeful tone.

"No, I managed." He presented an immaculate white cuff studded with a gold link for her inspection and then, glancing at her little beaded evening purse that she held in her hand, asked, "Shall we go?"

"I guess Billy probably told you that he and his sister are spending the night with my parents," Susan remarked as she stepped across the threshold and got out her key. He hadn't mentioned the absence of any sign of her two children, and she didn't want to start out the evening feeling awkward about what interpretation he might be giving to the arrangements she'd made. After all, her purpose hadn't been to remove obstacles that would prevent the two of them from spending the night together.

"Yes, Billy did tell me that," Jim confirmed, closing the door and taking the key from her.

"My mother and father both complain that they don't see Billy and Joanie as much as they'd like, now that we're living over here. They were tickled pink at having the kids stay overnight with them," Susan explained while he was locking the door. "I was glad to save the price of a sitter and not have to leave the kids with a stranger."

Jim smiled at her as he gave her back the key. "It means we don't have any curfew, too. We can dance the night away, have coffee and beignets at the Café du Monde, and then watch the sun rise when we're driving home across the causeway. If that's what we want to do, and our stamina holds up.''

"That sounds like a fantastic evening," Susan said weakly, going all warm and tingly at his tone and the look in his dark eyes that said he was in favor of any and all options that included being with her.

He guided her down the steps with a light, protective touch that didn't do anything to make her feeling of being very special go away. Susan glanced almost with detachment at the driveway to see what he was driving, his van or his sports car. It really didn't seem to matter which one he'd chosen. The sight of a sleek, late-model sedan made her blink with surprise.

"You didn't go out and buy a car?" she asked uncertainly, thinking that perhaps he'd borrowed one from a friend.

"No, it's leased," Jim replied. "I was going to take it just for the weekend, but when I checked into the rates, I took it for a month instead."

"I feel bad, having you go to that expense," Susan protested.

"How bad?" He met her quick questioning glance with a grin. "Bad enough to help me get my money's worth and go out with me often?"

"It's a gorgeous car," she said, evading his light question.

"But not enough inducement? Is that what you're saying?"

"No, I just haven't ridden in it yet so I really can't tell," Susan parried and was treated to the sound of his appreciative laughter.

The car interior was luxurious, with cream leather upholstery, and Jim looked devastatingly handsome and masterful behind the wheel. When he turned the key to start the motor, soft music came from the speakers. It was like a scene from a romantic movie with every detail perfect.

They were soon speeding along on the southbound span of the bridge toward New Orleans, cocooned in air-conditioned comfort. On either side and ahead of them, Lake Pontchartrain spread out until it merged with the distant horizon, like a pearl-gray mirror in the mellow light of fading day. Conversation was light and relaxed, but not trivial, because it contained personal revelations that seemed to feed their mutual interest in each other.

"Did you drop off Billy and Joanie at your parents' house and then go shopping today?" Jim asked, glancing over at her. His dark eyes seemed to communicate the same unconditional approval that Susan felt every time she glanced at him.

"Yes, I treated myself to a whole afternoon of making the rounds of the shops and women's departments," she replied. "I hit Esplanade, Clearview and Lakeside shopping centers."

He whistled. "All in one afternoon? I'm surprised you're not exhausted. You say you 'treated' yourself. I take it you enjoy shopping."

"There are few things I would rather do," Susan admitted. "Aside from the practical necessity, I get a thrill from searching for bargains. Even though I do think longingly of being able to walk into a store someday and buy at full price, I doubt it will be any more satisfying. My guess is that you don't particularly like shopping."

"I don't, especially not for clothes. My approach is to go to the store that's most likely to have what I want, put myself in the hands of a good salesclerk, and get the whole business over as quickly as possible. I don't care to rummage through stacks myself and look through racks for the right sizes." He looked over and smiled at her expression. "You don't approve of that method, I can tell."

"It's definitely not the most economical," Susan pointed out. "A salesclerk's job is not to save you money."

He shrugged. "I don't mind paying the going price for a good quality of merchandise. I do object to paying extra for the logo of some designer who happens to be in vogue. My attitude toward spending money, in general, is that I just want a reasonable value in return."

"I'm looking forward to having that attitude one of these days," Susan remarked cheerfully. "Right now I'm operating on the elastic budget system. It's called 'stretch to make ends meet.' Fortunately, I've had a lot of practice and am something of an expert. Money was scarce when I was married, too," she said in a matter-of-fact voice when Jim looked at her inquiringly. "My ex-husband has never had to deal with your problem of being a workaholic, which, from what Billy tells me, you started to develop at a very young age. Did your parents instill a strong work ethic in you?"

Susan evidently wasn't avoiding the subject of her failed marriage, but was simply more interested in talking about him. He reflected a moment before he answered.

"You could say that, I guess. My parents are typical of the hardworking middle class who tend to emphasize money out of a sense of financial insecurity. When I was growing up, my father put in twelve-hour days, including Saturdays, at his job, driving a bread delivery truck." Susan recognized the large New Orleans bakery when Jim told her its name.

"My mother wasn't regularly employed outside our home," he went on, "but she sold cosmetics door-to-door in her spare time and had selling parties for various lines of plastic products and costume jewelry. She made fancy decorated cakes and took orders in the neighborhood. Every conversation in our house included some mention of money.

Expense was always a factor in the simplest decision. If my mother got a compliment on a dress she was wearing, she was sure to tell how much it cost. If my dad was asked how he liked our family car, he would answer in terms of what he'd paid for it and spent on maintenance. When I brought home a good report card, it was a cause for proud speculation that I would get a much higher-paying job than my father had and make a big income someday.''

Jim shrugged and concluded, ''So I picked up on the emphasis on making money and worked at odd jobs. Once I got a taste of having my own buying power and being able to get the things I wanted, almost anything that didn't pay seemed a waste of time.''

''That didn't include dating girls in high school, though, I'll bet,'' Susan remarked.

''No, it didn't,'' he admitted, smiling. ''I managed to squeeze in some social life, along with working and studying.''

''You were a good student in high school as well as college, I take it.''

''A solid B. What about you?''

''The same, but I didn't take hard courses like chemistry and physics since I didn't plan to go to college. My only ambition was to get married and have a family. What high school did you go to?''

The time melted away, and before they could possibly have driven twenty-four miles, they had reached the other end of the causeway and were soon on Interstate 10 heading to downtown New Orleans.

''We have dinner reservations at Brennan's,'' Jim told her. ''But there should be time for a drink at the Royal Orleans first. I thought I would park there.''

"I'm glad you picked Brennan's!" Susan exclaimed. "I read about the renovations and redecorating that the owners have done."

He looked pleased, and she wondered if he hadn't selected Brennan's knowing that she would have a professional interest in the face-lift the famous restaurant had been given.

It was an evening out of Susan's fantasies. At the Royal Orleans her senses were overwhelmed by the glitter of crystal chandeliers, the sheen of polished brass and the gleaming marble of the floors. She sipped a champagne cocktail that made her a little giddy, but Jim didn't seem to mind at all. They drew glances from other parties of well-dressed people, and Susan was fairly certain that their cocktail waitress underwent an interrogation at another table concerning their identity.

Then on to Brennan's, where in addition to a gourmet meal and excellent service, there was again the added pleasure of the whole ambience. She and Jim attracted their share of discreetly curious attention once more.

"I feel like a character in one of my night soaps," Susan confessed lightly, as she sipped her after-dinner coffee. "I'm having a marvelous time."

"Good. So am I," Jim said. "But I'm not so sure that I would fill the bill as a lead male character on one of those shows. Aren't the men rich, power-hungry, domineering types?"

"I have no complaints," Susan replied and smiled teasingly. "Besides, I'm not entirely sure you don't have one of those traits. You can be rather forceful."

"One out of three is better than nothing, I guess. Are you ready to try out a real dance floor?"

"After this big dinner, I doubt I'll be very light on my feet," she warned him and excused herself to go freshen up in the powder room while he took care of the check. Her eyes looking back at her in the mirror, dreamy with anticipation, gave her the real answer. She couldn't wait to dance with him, this time to live music with the lighting dimmed and no threat of any interruption.

The night spot located on the top floor of a big luxury hotel was filled almost to capacity. Eyes followed them when they were shown to the table Jim had reserved.

"Are you beginning to get a celebrity complex?" Susan asked him after they'd sat down.

"When a man takes out a pretty woman, especially a blonde, he has to expect some envious looks from other men," Jim said.

"I was under the impression that I was the one getting the envious looks from other women," Susan retorted lightly.

"We make a good-looking couple. Wait until they see us dance together."

"Don't say that!" Susan protested. "You'll make me so self-conscious I'll step all over your feet."

She didn't need to worry. Jim ordered a bottle of champagne and then led her to the dance floor, saying that the number playing was too good to waste. Seconds after he circled her with his arm and drew her close, she lost any sense of being conspicuous. Following his lead, she moved with him in slow rhythm, breathing in the faint, spicy scent of his after-shave. They seemed to occupy a totally private, sensual space.

"You're a wonderful dancer," she murmured, moving her fingertips against his shoulder for the pleasure of feeling the slight abrasion of his tuxedo jacket against her skin. Immediately his arm around her tightened, locking her into an even more heavenly embrace.

When the last note ended, she sighed with regret, raised her head from his chest and tilted it back to look up at him.

He smiled into her face with a tender expression and kissed her on the lips.

"You didn't step on my feet once," he said huskily.

"I tried to be careful," she quipped unsteadily. "These spiked heels I'm wearing could be lethal."

"That thought occurred to me, but I can stand up to a little pain to get you this close," he said.

The band had swung into a livelier tune. He led her back to their table with his arm around her waist, without asking her if she wanted to dance to it. They sat with their chairs close together and sipped champagne, oblivious to their surroundings. The next number was another slow one. After the first few chords, they got up without any discussion and went back to the dance floor to dance to it.

There was no sense of time passing or of minutes ticking away, as the hour grew later. Their champagne glasses were always magically refilled when they returned to the table and the band seemed to have an inexhaustible repertoire of wonderful love songs from different music eras. Susan was shocked when the band leader, announcing a break, mentioned that it was midnight, the witching hour.

"If you would like to go somewhere else, we can," Jim said as they sat down.

"Whatever you want to do is fine with me," she replied dreamily and then flushed with warmth when he smiled, making her words take on a more provocative meaning than she'd intended.

"Don't say that to me," he chided, toying with a silken strap of her blouse and sliding it back and forth no more than a half inch. "It's cruel. I have to keep my word, but I'm only human."

His fingertips brushing Susan's skin sent pleasure shocks through her. "What do you want to do?" she asked, her heart beating faster with panic, but also with a wild, sweet joy.

"I want to make love with you," he replied, his tone and his dark gaze blatantly intimate.

Susan tried to speak and had to swallow before she could get her one-word question out. "Where?"

He smiled and squeezed her bare shoulder with a warm, strong hand. "Preferably in a bed. But if you keep looking at me like that with your eyes as big as saucers, I'll feel like the big bad wolf taking advantage of Red Riding Hood."

"You've got the story wrong," Susan told him. "It was the wolf who had the big eyes. He was dressed up in Grandma's clothes, lying in her bed."

"That's right. He was a deceitful fellow trying to trick Red Riding Hood." Jim's voice was ruefully sincere. "I honestly didn't ask you out tonight with the purpose of seducing you. Until yesterday, when I learned that the kids were staying overnight with your parents, it wasn't even a possibility that the evening would end up with the two of us in bed. When and if we do make love, I want it to happen because you want to make love with me, too, not because you feel pressured."

"I'm not a sixteen-year-old girl!" Susan protested, feeling offended. "I can handle pressure from a man. Don't you think I knew this moment in the evening would arrive? I knew full well when I called my mother and arranged to have my children stay with her that I was leaving myself open to temptation."

"Is it a temptation for you to make love with me, Susan?" Jim asked softly.

"You know it is," she said reproachfully. "You know how attracted I am to you, how it makes me feel for you to touch me. Dancing with you is pure heaven, and when you kiss me, I turn to warm mush." Susan was turning to warm mush now, just from the way he was looking at her, his dark eyes possessive and pleased.

"But you haven't actually imagined me as your lover?"

She blushed, but held his gaze defiantly and countered with her own question, "Have you done that—with me?"

"The night you undertook to be a plumber stands out particularly in my mind. There was no way I could stop myself from mentally carrying you to your bedroom, undressing you and putting you to bed." He smiled. "Needless to say, I didn't just tuck you in and go away."

"I had trouble going to sleep that night," Susan confided, shamefaced. "Lying in bed, I imagined you touching me. Your hands felt simply wonderful."

"It will be good with us," Jim promised with a mixture of tenderness and male satisfaction. "I have no doubt."

"You do realize that I haven't had a lot of experience with men, don't you?" Susan asked uncertainly.

"I've made that assumption," Jim replied with a gentle lack of concern. "You married right out of high school and are hardly the type who would have fooled around on her husband. Since your divorce, you've dated very little, by your own admission, and could hardly have been sexually active."

"Just as long as you don't expect too much . . ."

"I expect to get a great deal of pleasure from touching you and holding you in private, from having you touch me, if you want to, from being aroused by you and satisfying you, if I can. It's you I want to make love with, not an actress in a X-rated film."

"Then give me a more specific answer to the question I asked you earlier. Where?"

"Here, at this hotel." He smiled, reading her expression, which must have reflected her suspicion as well as her concurrence. "And no, I don't have a room reserved, but there were vacancies when I checked earlier. If you would like to go to the powder room, I'll take care of it.''

Susan was besieged by nervous qualms as she sat on a velvet-upholstered sofa in the elegant outer room of the ladies' lounge, but she didn't want to retract what she'd agreed to do. There were butterflies in her stomach, but the flutters of emotion were made up of excitement and anticipation as well as doubt and apprehension.

The whole evening had had a fantasy element. Sharing a room with Jim in this luxury hotel didn't seem at all sordid, but was rather a deeper plunge into the world of sophistication and glamorous fun into which she'd stepped for one intoxicating night with him. Tomorrow she would return to reality, resume responsibility, act conscientiously.

Accompanying Jim to their room had a clandestine element that was stimulating as well as awkward. They shared the elevator with other couples going up to their rooms, too. Aware of discreet glances, Susan wondered if it was obvious that she and Jim weren't married. When he squeezed her hand, she looked up into his face to see him smiling at her and knew that he had read her thoughts.

''Don't ever walk into a bank intending to rob it,'' Jim advised her teasingly when they had gotten out on their floor and he was escorting her along the corridor, his arm around her shoulders.

''This is my first time at being a scarlet woman,'' Susan retorted, keeping her voice low. ''Did I look horribly guilty?''

''Not horribly. I doubt anyone got the impression that there was anything illicit going on.''

''You don't think we look like a married couple?'' she scoffed.

His smiling scrutiny made her heart race strangely. "I think we could very easily pass for newlyweds on their honeymoon."

Susan was saved from having to make any reply as he stopped her in front of a door and fitted the key into the lock. It was such a totally unexpected thing for him to say. She wanted to pursue it and discredit the idea and yet she didn't dare because of the feeling of being on dangerous, but thrilling territory.

The room was much larger than she had expected. It had a spacious sitting area with a couch and several chairs. There was a small bar and refrigerator. At the opposite end was a king-sized bed and a long low chest with mirrors. The colors were all muted greens and peach tones.

"This is lovely," Susan said, her shoes sinking into the thick, luxurious carpet as she took several steps inside and looked around with an appreciative but troubled eye. For the first time, she was considering how much spending the night together at the hotel was costing Jim. "A room like this must be very expensive. We could have driven back to Mandeville and saved you a lot of money."

Jim came over to take her loosely in his arms. "But I didn't want to drive back to Mandeville tonight and neither did you. It wouldn't be as private or as relaxed for either one of us. So don't worry about the expense. I'm a lot more flush than you realize anyway." He kissed her lightly and let her go. "Now why don't we both get more comfortable? I'll take off my jacket, and you can kick off those wicked shoes. While you check out the refrigerator and see what our choices are for something to drink, I'll turn on some music. Then we can put our feet up."

He was standing coatless at the television set by the time he'd finished talking. Susan drew in a little relieved breath, some of her tension fading, as she crossed the room to fulfill her assignment. He apparently was in no hurry to make use of the bedroom portion of the room.

"We have quite a variety. Beer, wine, soft drinks, club soda, tonic and little bottles of liquor," she reported from a crouching position in front of the open door of the little refrigerator.

"A soft drink sounds good to me right now. But you feel free to have wine or a mixed drink," he urged as he came to stand behind her. After switching radio stations several times, he'd tuned in soft listening music.

"I'd rather have a soft drink, too," Susan told him, glad of his choice. "I've drunk far more alcohol tonight than I'm used to. Do you want ice?" she asked, getting out two cans.

"No, but I'll fix the drinks. You go over and sit on the sofa."

"Why don't *you* go over and sit on the sofa?" she suggested, popping open a can. "I think I can manage here."

"No, darling, *I* will fix the drinks," he insisted. There was telltale laughter in his voice, but Susan's pulses had started stampeding in reaction to the endearment when she turned around to see him grinning at her.

"Take off your shoes. Sit on the sofa," she mocked, trying hard not to smile back. "I think you *are* the domineering type."

"Okay, okay." He raised his hands in pretend defeat. "You fix the drinks, then. I'll sit on the sofa, like a lamb, and let you wait on me. First, though, how about giving me a hand with these cuff links, since I'm asking nicely?"

Susan complied with pleasure.

"Now could I get you to undo this?" He turned around so that she could attend to the fastening of his cummerbund. "Thanks. You did that so easily." Jim took it from her, smiling, tossed it away and then pointed at his black bow tie, asking coaxingly, "One more favor? Getting dressed would have been so much easier if you'd just been there. I thought about that at the time."

Avoiding his eyes, Susan set to work on this third task, finding it no more difficult than the other two. "It's a good thing I kept on my shoes, or I'd have had to stand on tiptoe to do this," she remarked.

"Not necessarily. I could have bent over or given you a boost up, like this." He demonstrated, stooping to wrap his arms around her lower torso and then lifting her up and against him so that her face was level with his.

"This is too high," Susan pointed out breathlessly.

"So it is," he agreed. "But just right for kissing. How about a kiss before you finish up with my tie?"

Susan put her arms loosely around his neck and kissed him on the mouth, a little shy at granting his request, but also eager. His hold on her tightened as she pressed her lips to his, and her arms automatically followed suit, hugging him harder. The shyness melted away as she kissed him with less inhibition and then with passion. She felt a sense of feminine power mixed with melting desire as his breathing quickened and his response became urgent.

He broke off the kiss with a groan of male need. "I want you, Susan." The words, with no hint of his earlier playfulness, only called more attention to the hard evidence that she could feel for herself, with her hips welded to his body.

"I want you, too," she said, meeting his gaze.

A nakedly vulnerable look came across his face. His voice held a mix of tender gratitude and sexual intensity. "You have no idea how it affects me to hear you say that, sweetheart."

He put her down gently and caressed her bare shoulders, sliding the straps of her blouse down. "I've wanted to do this all night," he said huskily. "And this." He slid his fingertips down inside the bodice.

Susan shivered with the delicious sensations he was arousing. Her nipples were tightening into hard buds of aching impatience. She took both his wrists and brought his hands down to her breasts, on the outside of her blouse, and moaned softly with the pleasure when he cupped and squeezed the small mounds.

"That feels just too good," she told him weakly.

"It will feel even better with bare skin," Jim promised. "And I want to kiss your breasts, not just touch them with my hands. I want to see them, see all of you, without your clothes on."

"I hope you aren't disappointed. I'm not all that sexy."

Susan blushed at her own tone, which was totally lacking in either anxiety or reluctance. He picked her up immediately in his arms and carried her down toward the bed, saying, "Let me be the judge of that."

At the side of the huge bed, he set her on her feet and let her attend to her own undressing while he took off his clothes. It was incredibly intimate and sensual baring herself to him while he did the same for her, with neither of them hurrying or taking more time than necessary. Whatever shyness she felt was overshadowed by the desire to be provocative and by sheer feminine pleasure in his body.

Down to her strapless bra and bikini panties by the time he had taken off his shirt and slacks, Susan paused with her fingers at the front closure of the bra, suspending her own undressing as he stripped off his briefs. The sight of him naked and fully aroused made her go weak with desire, but awoke faint fear and uncertainty, too.

Her hands fell away as he came close, overpoweringly male and virile, but his voice was gentle as he asked, "Can I take over now?"

"Please," Susan said, the word sticking in her throat.

He caressed the tops of her breasts with his fingertips and then eased them beneath the lacy fabric to find her hardened nipples and rub them. Susan gasped with pleasure and felt as if her breasts were growing heavy for him as he unclipped the bra and took it off.

She moaned softly as he took possession of her sensitive flesh with his hands, cupping and kneading.

"I love that," she murmured, tilting back her head and looking up into his face, which was intense with his passion, but softened by pleased, protective emotion.

"No more than I do," he said. "I love being able to touch you like this." Holding her gaze, he caressed her nipples, using his forefingers and thumbs, and then pinched them, sending piercing shocks of pleasure through her. Susan gasped and closed her eyes. Before she could recover, he was bending over and taking one breast into his mouth, and she felt the suckling warmth of his mouth and the rough abrasion of his tongue. It was almost too delightful to withstand, but she grasped his head to guide him over to her other breast.

Meanwhile his hands were caressing her hips and buttocks and easing down her panties. His hands were wonderfully, incredibly knowledgeable, his right one especially, which stroked the insides of her thighs and coaxed her legs apart to claim the hub of her femininity. Now there was simply too much delicious sensation. She moaned his name aloud to tell him that when he cupped his palm and squeezed and then stroked inside her.

He kissed first one breast and then the other and then straightened so that his face was on a level with hers. Looking in her eyes, he stroked once again into her molten wetness, letting her see his own fierce, but tender satisfaction in her readiness for his lovemaking.

"Do you want me, Susan?" he asked, kneeling to take her panties the rest of the way down to her feet.

"No, not really," she joked unsteadily and then clutched his head as he kissed the sensitive juncture at her inner thigh, first on one side and then the other. "Please, Jim," she begged.

"Please what, sweetheart?" he asked her in a husky voice as he rose. "I'll do anything you want."

"Then make love to me . . . if you're ready, too."

He smiled and slid one of her hands down his body. "Maybe you could check for yourself and make certain, if you wouldn't mind."

Susan didn't mind. She wanted to touch him intimately, but he drew in a sharp breath at her caress and stopped her as she began fondling him.

"That's about all the research into the matter that I can stand, I'm afraid," he told her. "You'll have to take my word for it, sweetheart. I'm more than ready to make you mine."

But he was far too patient for Susan. Even after he'd picked her up and placed her in the bed after stripping off the bedspread and turning back the covers, he held back, kissing her and caressing her body.

"Please, Jim," she had to tell him again.

He raised his head and looked down at her. "Tell me exactly," he requested softly.

"I want you inside me."

"No more than I want it, my darling." He was poising himself for his entry, speaking in a low passionate voice. "I want to go so deep . . ."

The moment of union brought them both to an excruciating level of pleasure, and Susan wouldn't allow Jim a slow pace of lovemaking, though he asked her to help him not go so fast. She urged him on with her abandoned movements and whispered words to take her swiftly to a cataclysmic release. Reaching it, she cried out and then hugged him tight as he shuddered with his own surrender and went limp and helpless on top of her.

Chapter Ten

I'm embarrassed," Susan murmured as Jim rolled over, taking her with him, and held her cradled in his arms. "I had no idea that I was sex-starved. I acted like a wild woman."

"Don't be embarrassed," he said in an indulgent tone, hugging her. "I loved every minute of it. It did last a minute, didn't it?" he added, chuckling.

"You're just too good a lover," she accused. "I've never gotten that aroused before."

"I can take criticism like that all night," he replied. "I have to admit that I wasn't prepared for you to be quite so—passionate."

"I'm really not," Susan protested.

"No?" Jim eased his arm from underneath her and propped himself on his elbow beside her. Susan let him roll her gently over on her back, trying to hide her self-conscious reaction to his interested scrutiny of her nude form. "You enjoyed sex in the past, didn't you?'' he asked idly as he slid his palm in a circular motion over her abdomen and then moved his hand lower.

"I enjoyed sex to the normal extent," Susan said, feeling a pervasive weakness invade her lower torso. "My ex-husband was only nineteen when we married. He hadn't had a lot of experience, like you have, and married sex tends to get routine. It wasn't like this."

Jim bent over and nuzzled her nearest breast with his lips, murmuring, "I'd like a chance to give having sex with you become routine."

"You won't have that chance, though," Susan told him with an abstracted note, intensely conscious of his hand between her legs. "Tonight can't change anything."

"Then I guess I'd better take advantage of having gotten you in this compromising position," he said and bit her nipple, making her gasp and arch her back with mingled surprise and pleasure.

Susan was ready for him in minutes and tried her best to keep from urging him to the union that she wanted desperately, but again the pleasure that he gave her with his kisses and caresses was simply more than she could withstand. She begged and insisted that he end the torment and give them both satisfaction.

Her need was no less wild and urgent than it had been before, but he exerted more control this time and took her even higher, if that was possible, to a climax that was like a series of shattering eruptions. Afterward she felt the same embarrassment as before over her lack of inhibition.

"You're just incredibly good," she told Jim when she could talk.

He drew in an audible breath of exhausted satisfaction and tightened his lax hold on her. "Lovemaking like that isn't a matter of technique, darling. It's chemistry. I told you we would be good together. I could lie back and let you make love to me, and it wouldn't be less good.''

Susan was silent, hoping that he couldn't read her mind and know how titillating the idea he suggested was to her. ''Women are supposed to get more sexual as they get older, aren't they?'' she asked with a trace of worry.

''Does that mean you do want to test out my theory tonight and make love again?'' Jim inquired lazily. ''Just give me a few minutes of recovery time until I have the energy to roll over on my back.''

''No, it doesn't mean that,'' Susan denied laughingly, pulling away from him to clamber across the bed and get out on the other side.

''Please, sweetheart, you're not going out at this time of night to find yourself a younger man, are you?'' he asked with feigned anxiety. ''Pour me that soft drink you promised earlier. It will perk me up and then you can have your way with me.''

''I'm going to the bathroom,'' Susan called over her shoulder. ''Afterward, I intend to go to sleep.''

When she came out some minutes later, he was lounging comfortably in bed, sipping from a glass. The lights in the sitting room area had been turned out.

''I fixed a glass for you, too, just in case you're thirsty,'' he said, patting the place beside him.

Susan climbed over the expanse of mattress and settled next to him. He made no objection when she pulled up the sheet for modesty. She took the glass he handed her, self-consciously aware that he was taking notice of the results of her makeshift toiletry. She'd cleaned off her makeup, using a facial soap provided by the hotel and applied a little packet of cream.

"Since you've already seen the nighttime me, it shouldn't be so much of a shock anyway," she said flippantly, drinking from her glass.

"I think you look sweet and clean and pretty—and you smell nice, too," he replied in a warm, indulgent tone. When she looked at him, skeptical and uncertain, he smiled at her and kissed her on the tip of her nose. Then with a deep, contented sigh he draped his arm around her shoulders and pulled her closer, resting his cheek against her head. "Wait until you see the morning-time me, all bleary-eyed and scruffy, with a growth of beard."

It was incredibly intimate and cozy being there in the bed with him. Susan was yawning after a few sips of her drink.

"Sleepy, darling?" Jim asked. His voice was like warm velvet wrapping around her in a protective layer.

"All of a sudden I am terribly drowsy," she admitted, giving in to another yawn.

"Here. Give me your glass. I'll turn out the light."

Lying in his arms in the darkness, Susan shared her last waking thought. "I can't believe this feels so natural, going to bed with you—to sleep, I mean. You would think I'd feel awkward..." She sighed and drifted off to sleep.

Jim stayed awake, listening to her even breathing, just long enough to reflect that it was all for the best that she'd conked out on him. He might have shared his feelings about going to bed with her and knowing that she would be there with him the next morning. Aside from not wanting to rush things and put her all in a panic, Jim needed to get used to those feelings himself, get used to thinking in terms of *always*.

Susan was lying on her side, curled against Jim spoon fashion, when she awoke the next morning. He had one arm across her, so that she couldn't move without disturbing him. She stayed motionless, thinking of her children asleep at her parents' house across the city in Metairie. The sight of her clothes and Jim's draped across the chaise longue near the bed was proof of her irresponsible behavior.

How was she going to keep from looking different when she picked up the kids later today? Her sister and brother and their families would be there, too. How could she carry on a normal conversation and not seem furtive and secret?

"Good morning. Have you been awake long?"

Jim's arm tightened to gather her closer against him as he spoke the greeting from behind her. Susan could feel the vibration of his deep, sleepy voice in his chest.

"How did you know that I was awake?" she asked.

"Because you're all tense. Feeling some morning-after regrets?"

"Yes."

"Me, too."

"What kinds of regrets are you feeling?" she asked hesitantly, detecting no playfulness in his sleepy tone.

"I'm wishing we'd brought some casual clothes and had the whole day to spend fooling around in the Quarter, doing touristy things. We could ride in one of those mule-drawn carriages that are always lined up along Jackson Square, take a trip on the Mississippi River aboard a paddle wheel riverboat, maybe have our portraits painted by a sidewalk artist. Wouldn't that be fun? I've never done any of that."

"Neither have I," Susan said wistfully. A day like that with Jim *would* be fun. She had no doubt about it. "But we didn't bring casual clothes, and I have to be at my mother's for Sunday dinner at one-thirty."

"That lets out my next thought, then, that we could buy some clothes, since a hotel like this one is sure to have a clothing shop open seven days a week. There's plenty of time for a leisurely breakfast before we head back across the causeway, though. We can order room service. First, a shower sounds awfully good to me. How about you?"

"I'd like to take a shower, too, but you go ahead," Susan said, relieved and yet somewhat miffed that his itinerary apparently didn't include lovemaking. It was true that she wasn't in the mood, but she would have thought he might want to take advantage of his last opportunity.

He didn't even suggest that they could take their showers together. After kissing her on her shoulder, he got out of the bed and headed for the bathroom. Faintly disgruntled, Susan watched him go, stirred against her will by a feminine appreciation of his nudity. She wouldn't see him without his clothes on like this again, she reflected with a pang of dissatisfaction.

Left alone in the huge bed, she considered getting up and putting on her underwear rather than parading around nude when her turn for the bathroom came. But then she might appear to be trying to arouse his interest. Undecided, Susan lay there.

"I decided to shave first," Jim announced from the bathroom door. His face was lathered and he brandished a disposable razor that she had noticed the night before among the grooming aids provided by the hotel. "Why don't you make use of the shower, if you want. Or just keep me company? There's plenty of room in here."

His tone was welcoming, but Susan couldn't read any provocative message, and he went back inside the bathroom, leaving her to make her own decision. Flinging back the sheet, she got up and marched across the carpet, determined to match him for nonchalance. Barely glancing in his direction, she breezed by where he stood shaving and went to slide open the glass door of the large tiled shower compartment.

With a few deft motions, she turned on the spray and adjusted the water temperature. About to climb in, she remembered the disposable shower cap she'd seen last night and hesitated. She hated to get her hair wet, but also hated for Jim to see her wearing a shower cap.

"Need this?" he inquired and came over to offer her what she needed. There was nothing but friendly helpfulness in his expression.

"Thank you, I could use that," Susan said, irked by the whole situation. While he went back to his shaving, she donned the cap and got into the shower, closing the glass door firmly.

There was soap in the shower, but she'd forgotten a washcloth. Rather than step out of the shower and get one, she decided just to use her hands. But before she'd worked up a good lather, Jim was sliding open the glass door and handing in a plush washcloth.

"I don't know how you get along without me at home," he told her, smiling.

"I don't either, but somehow I do," she retorted and busied herself wetting the washcloth and rubbing the soap bar on it.

"If you need some help, I'm almost finished shaving," he remarked.

"No, thanks. I can manage," she replied, ignoring him.

He slid the door closed, apparently accepting her refusal, and went back to the sink. She could see him indistinctly through the glazed glass, while she washed herself vigorously, taking no pleasure in her shower. No sooner had she turned off the water than he came over again, no doubt to give her a towel, she reflected sourly.

"You're not through already?" he asked, standing squarely in Susan's way so that she couldn't step out of the compartment. "Your back and everything?"

"There isn't that much of me to clean," Susan pointed out. "Could you hand me a towel, please?"

"Aren't you going to offer to help me with my shower?" he inquired coaxingly.

"You didn't help me with mine."

"I offered, and you turned me down. It won't take long, since I'm only about twice your size. Come on. Be nice."

He was stepping into the shower compartment with her as he talked, and Susan had little choice but to give him room.

"I'll wash your back for you," she conceded.

"That's better than nothing. The perfect temperature," he approved when he'd turned on the water. "We could take showers together with no problem and save water."

Susan took the washcloth and soap bar from him. He turned and presented her with his back, sighing with pleasure when she applied herself to his shoulders first.

"That feels great," he said. "Take your time. My back is in need of a good scrubbing."

With a physique like his, he wouldn't have any trouble getting his back washed whenever he wanted. The thought made jealousy curl inside Susan.

"You have a good build, as I'm sure you've been told by lots of women," she said grudgingly.

"I'm glad you think so," he replied. "I like the way you're built, too. You have a very sexy figure."

Last night he'd made her feel that she was sexy, but not this morning, Susan wanted to tell him. "I'm finished with your back," she told him instead.

"Do it again," he requested softly. "This time with your hands. Please."

Susan's pulses quickened at his tone, which affected her whole body like a caress. Her sense of slight melted away, making way for languid anticipation as she lathered her hands. There was simply no way she could deny herself the pleasure of touching him at her leisure.

"My first view of you was from the back," she mused, stroking his broad, powerful shoulders. "The sight of you came as such a surprise that I was relieved you didn't know I was there right away."

"What were you expecting me to look like?"

"I didn't exactly have a picture of you in mind, but I wasn't expecting you to be tall, dark, and handsome." She slid her palm in circles over the taut muscles of his lower back and smiled to herself, recollecting, "I had just met your animals on your front porch and wondered if it was true, in your case, that pets resembled their owner."

Jim chuckled with amusement. "In other words, you were prepared to be sympathetic for the cross I'd had to bear my whole life, being so ugly. But you couldn't really tell that much, could you, with my back to you?"

"It was pretty obvious at a glance that you were...virile." Susan spoke the exact word that had come into her mind that same day, disturbing her with her own awareness. "Then when you turned around..." She paused to soap up her hands.

"You didn't change your mind, I hope," Jim said, turning to face her with the indisputable proof of his masculinity.

"No, I didn't," she told him, glancing down with frank satisfaction to see that he'd obviously enjoyed her attentions to his back as much as she had. "I saw that you were very good looking. Here you are." She held out the bar of soap to him. "Now you can take over."

He kept his arms down at his sides. "I would much rather have you continue. You did such a great job on my back." He smiled. "Except that I do usually wash below the waist, too."

"You didn't give me time. You turned around too soon," she told him, her whole body tingling under his warm teasing gaze that had dropped down possessively to her breasts.

"Shall I turn around again and let you finish?" he asked softly.

"No, that's all right."

With her heart beating faster, Susan proceeded to soap his chest with her hands and felt the quickened pumping of his heart, too. "Raise your arms," she instructed.

"Okay, but I'm ticklish," he warned and was able to stand only the most cursory washing of his underarms and sides. She couldn't resist tickling him deliberately and then she attended to the intimate hygiene that they had both been awaiting with sharp anticipation.

Jim groaned and closed his eyes at her warm, soapy touch, and Susan aroused herself with her own gentle thoroughness. Her breasts grew heavy and her lower body ached to receive the hardness she was sheathing with her hands. She urgently wanted to make love, without any further preliminaries.

"It's not easy to make love in a shower, is it?" she asked and met his gaze with a blushing boldness.

"Is that a way of saying that you want to dry off now and make love?" he asked, looking tender and indulgent. "Or that you don't want to wait that long?"

"I could wait, if you'd rather," Susan replied, her nerve failing her.

"But you want me right this very moment?"

"Yes."

"That's all I need to know," he said, touching her with his hands for the first time since he'd gotten in the shower with her. "I'm yours any time, anywhere, sweetheart. Whenever you want me, we'll figure out the mechanics."

It wasn't until afterward that Susan realized that she still had on the shower cap. "Why didn't you *say* something?" she asked him, stripping it off. "I completely forgot that I was wearing this!"

"That was quite a turn-on in itself," he replied, smiling at her mortified expression. "Besides, you look cute and sexy to me, no matter what you're wearing. Or not wearing," he added suggestively, bending down to kiss her breast. "Now why don't we dry each other off and order some breakfast?"

"Okay," Susan agreed distractedly, when he didn't straighten but began to awaken new delicious sensations with his mouth and tongue.

They made love again in bed, after he'd aroused her to a fever pitch with his foreplay, saying that he liked the preliminaries, even if she didn't.

"I like everything you do to me," Susan corrected him. "Too much."

"How are you and I going to live a couple of blocks apart and deprive ourselves of this pleasure?" he asked her afterward, when they lay in each other's arms, sated and lazy.

"We're just going to have to," she replied, sighing. "My conscience simply wouldn't allow me to sneak around and go to bed with a man. It makes things even worse that you live right there in the neighborhood, where we couldn't possibly hide what was going on between us. I couldn't look other people in the eye, not to mention Billy and Joanie, who are old enough to be suspicious."

When he didn't argue or offer any comment, she went on, "I know you're not going to be satisfied with a platonic relationship, not for more than a short time."

Jim hugged her, but made no denial. "What would you like for breakfast?" he asked, changing the subject. "I feel like I could eat half a pound of bacon and a dozen eggs."

Susan wasn't nearly so enthusiastic about food herself. She wanted to continue their conversation and get some reaction from him to indicate his thinking. Her only consolation, oddly, was that he might not be taking her seriously when she said she wasn't going to have an affair with him. Otherwise, he just must not be concerned about what the future held for the two of them.

Her pique soon faded. It was impossible not to share his good mood. Getting up, he went over first to turn on music and then, whistling along, brought the room service menu over to look at it with her.

"These omelets sound good, don't they?" he remarked. "But then so does everything else. Maybe I'll just order one of everything, and we'll have our own private breakfast buffet."

Susan was looking at the prices. A minimum breakfast for the two of them was going to cost him an exorbitant amount.

"We could just have coffee," she suggested. "And then stop and eat at a breakfast place or pick up something at a drive-in window. That would be a lot less expensive."

"But not nearly so enjoyable. Don't be so practical. Pick out whatever appeals to you. I'm feeling so extravagant that you could easily talk me into taking you to a jewelry store and buying you that marquise diamond ring you have your heart set on." He grinned at her.

"Lucky thing for you today's Sunday," Susan retorted, giving up the argument. "Or hadn't you thought of that?"

"That's right. The jewelry stores will be closed, won't they? By tomorrow I may have come to my senses."

"A lost opportunity," Susan lamented, looking at her hand. "I'll have the Monte Carlo omelet, then."

"Good girl."

Their hotel window overlooked the Mississippi River, they discovered, when Jim opened the heavy draperies to let the morning light flood in. They breakfasted, looking out at the view, which included the dock where the old-fashioned riverboats embarked daily. One of the charming little ships had a calliope atop it, Susan recalled as she thought wistfully of the day in the French Quarter that Jim had outlined earlier.

"I suppose I could telephone my mother from here and tell her I wasn't going to be able to make Sunday dinner," she said. "I could give some excuse, saying I needed to stay in Mandeville, and arrange to pick up the kids tonight." Or even tomorrow. Susan avoided Jim's eyes, afraid that he would read her thought, which filled her with as much excitement as guilt.

"We can come back and spend another day in the Quarter any time we want," Jim pointed out. "August is hardly the best weather anyway. I'd like to bring the kids sometime, too. They should get a kick out of a riverboat ride, and unless I miss my guess Joanie would like having her portrait sketched by an artist."

"She would be thrilled," Susan concurred, trying not to sound as disgruntled as she felt. "It's just not as easy as it sounds to get a free day."

"I would love to have you all to myself today," he told her, "but you're not going to feel good about being dishonest with your mother. You looked conscience-stricken, just talking about it."

It was on the tip of Susan's tongue to inform him that lying to her mother hadn't been behind her guilty air, but before she could, he changed the subject, asking if her brother and sister were also expected by her parents for dinner that day. She answered that they were and then replied to his inquiries about them and their families, with not nearly the amount of interest that he seemed to be taking in the conversation. His cheerful acceptance of her plans for the afternoon, which would leave him on his own back in Mandeville, wasn't in the least pleasing. Apparently he didn't anticipate being at loose ends for something to do.

In fact, she began to wonder if he hadn't already formulated his own plans, which didn't include her. When they'd finished eating, he didn't rush her, but he didn't show any inclination to linger in the hotel room, either. He called and arranged to have their car brought to the entrance and then paced around the room, while they waited, and told her not to be embarrassed about departing in last evening's clothes.

"For all anyone knows, we could he headed to a big fancy wedding," he pointed out.

"I don't feel awkward," Susan told him, sitting stiffly on the sofa. "Don't worry. I'm not going to walk out of here with shame written all over me." Shame might come later, but at the moment what she was feeling was hurt and resentment.

"I'm more worried that you might give off the impression that last night was a big disappointment for you," he countered with a coaxing smile. "Could you act a little friendly toward me when we're leaving, just for the sake of my male image?"

As he came to sit beside her on the sofa, she got up abruptly and walked over to the window. "This may be old hat for you, but it isn't for me," she said, looking out through a glaze of tears. "I'm afraid I can't be quite so casual, even if what happened with us has no meaning."

He had followed her and his arms closed hard around her tense form, letting her feel his strength. "You're wrong, darling. I'm not at all casual—damn," he muttered as the phone came to life and trilled insistently.

"They're calling from downstairs about the car. You'd better answer it." Susan was as alarmed as she was soothed and thrilled by what she heard in his voice. She composed herself and walked quickly over to the door after he released her with a frustrated sigh.

"How's this for a wedding guest expression?" she asked lightly as he hung up the phone after a few terse words and turned to look at her.

He didn't answer as he walked over to her. It took all Susan's courage to hold his dark intent gaze. Her heart pounded with a crazy mixture of hope and fear as he reached her and she tilted back her head to look up into his face.

"Don't encourage a man to tell you he cares about you, Susan, if you don't want to hear it," he said quietly. "That's not fair play. Ready?"

"Yes," she managed to get out through a tight throat, too confused to risk saying anything else. She wanted to apologize for her behavior and confess that she didn't understand it herself. But as much as she yearned to ask him if he did care she just didn't dare.

"Don't look so tragic," Jim chided gruffly as he accompanied her along the corridor to the elevator, not touching her. "We're all dressed up for a wedding, remember, not a funeral."

Susan did her best to assume a cheerful expression during the few seconds that they waited for the elevator, but then relaxed the effort when the doors slid open to reveal no other passengers. Feeling his gaze, she glanced up to see that he was watching her with a grudging smile tugging at his lips.

"I know. I'm a terrible actress," she said contritely. The prospect of getting back into his good graces was immensely heartening.

He ushered her in with his palm at her back and pressed the button for the hotel lobby. "Your face and body language do tend to give away your state of mind," he said and stopped fighting the urge to smile.

Susan gave some startled consideration to the statement. Just how much had she given away just now, in the hotel room? "You do mean *general* state of mind, like happy or sad?"

He shrugged in qualified agreement. "Favorable or unfavorable, too. Given the subject and the situation, I can zero in fairly closely on your reaction."

"I'll certainly have to be careful, then, what I'm thinking around you, from now on."

"Only if you want to keep what you're thinking secret."

"You have me at a disadvantage," Susan complained lightly, happy that he hadn't corrected her assumption that there would be a "from now on" for them. "You aren't at all transparent to me."

"Then you'll just have to ask me any time you want to know what I'm thinking." And had the courage to listen to the answer, he added with his inflection and smile.

"Are you always good at reading people?" she asked breathlessly.

"Yes, but I don't always bother, especially when what I see is as painful as it is intriguing," he replied and offered her his arm as the elevator came to a smooth stop. "Here we are at the lobby. How about a big happy smile?"

Susan took his arm and managed to fill his request without any trouble as the elevator doors opened, and he led her out into the spacious, elegant lobby.

Chapter Eleven

There's something I'm curious about," Susan remarked when they were driving on the northbound bridge of the causeway. The trip from downtown hadn't taken long, with the light Sunday traffic. "I wanted to ask last night, but was a little embarrassed."

"What is it?"

"You're such a responsible type of person, I was just surprised that you didn't bring up birth control or offer to take precautions." She flushed with warmth, meeting his glance. "Don't tell me that I rushed you and didn't give you the chance."

"There was a hurried element," he agreed with a teasing smile, but then went on soberly. "I assumed, since you didn't bring the matter up, that it was either a safe time for you or that there was nothing to worry about. Was I wrong?"

"What do you mean, nothing to worry about?" Susan asked, registering his lack of concern.

"Just that two seems to be the recommended number of children these days. Some women take steps not to have any more when they feel that they've completed their family. My sister had a tubal ligation after her second child."

"You thought I might have done that, too." Susan was silent, coping with the knowledge that he had given calm consideration to the possibility that she might be sterile.

"But you didn't?"

"No."

"Is this a safe time for you?" he inquired uncertainly, but still without any grave concern.

"Yes. But I'm amazed that you didn't make sure. What if I had just gotten carried away, and my judgment was dulled by champagne and because I was having a wonderful time? What if I had gotten pregnant?"

"Then I would be a father," he said reasonably. "That wouldn't be the end of the world for me. But I realize you might feel differently."

Susan met his glance, not knowing how to answer. The thought of becoming pregnant with his child around a host of conflicting and disturbing feelings, but none of them unpleasant. He wouldn't abandon her with the problem or hear of her having an abortion, which she wouldn't want to do. He would marry her.

"It would be quite an adjustment for me, at this stage of my life, to go through diapers and formulas and colic again." She lacked the nerve to address any issue other than the disruptive presence of a baby.

"I can certainly understand that," Jim said in the same reasonable tone. "You probably wouldn't want to go through being pregnant again, either, which can't be too much fun. With your small build, childbirth must not have been easy. My sister had a very hard time with both of her children."

"I loved being pregnant, and I didn't have a hard time," Susan corrected him. "The difficult part isn't having babies or even getting them through the early stages when they need constant care. Being a parent is just such an enormous responsibility as children grow up. That's what people don't always realize."

"But it must be rewarding and rather fascinating to relate to your own children as individuals," he suggested.

"It is," she admitted.

"Yours are both such attractive, bright, likable kids. You must feel a great sense of pride and accomplishment when you stop to realize that you brought them into the world and have helped to make them the way they are."

"I do feel proud and very fortunate, but obligated, too, to be the best mother I can possibly be for them. If I were to remarry, it would have to be with the understanding that they could never take a back seat in my life."

He nodded. "That's as it should be, even if a half brother or sister came along. Or wouldn't you consider having more children?"

Susan swallowed, searching for the least offensive way to say something he was sure to find devastating to his pride. "Not unless I had a very strong sense of financial security," she said, trying without much success to be matter-of-fact, not apologetic. "Otherwise, not only would I be letting down the two children I already have, but I would be letting myself down, too. I don't mind working hard and economizing for another eleven or twelve years, until Billy and Joanie are through college, but no longer than that. Then I want an easier life for myself, with a few luxuries. I suppose you think I'm a very selfish, materialistic person to feel this way," she ended miserably.

"No, I don't think that," Jim denied, his rueful tone and pained expression giving away the fact that he was feeling insulted.

Susan knew that to apologize would only make things worse. "You would want a child of your own, if you married?" she asked, sighing.

"Only if the desire were mutual," he replied, not sounding especially confident.

It would be, Susan ached to assure him. She couldn't imagine that a woman could be married to him and not want to bear his child. The picture that came to mind of him looking pleased at the news that he was going to be a father cut right through her. She could see his awed expression at the first view of his own tiny infant, too. He would be awkwardly gentle, but he would want to hold and examine it, and share in the miracle.

"You would be a good father," she told him wistfully.

"Do you think so?" He seemed pleased at the idea.

"Yes, I do. You really shouldn't miss out on having your own children." Susan blushed at her reluctance to give him that advice.

"Then I guess I'd better find myself a wife who doesn't mind being barefoot and pregnant."

For several minutes they rode along in a silence that surprisingly wasn't strained and uncomfortable. Still, Susan found herself feeling not very pleased that he didn't seem to find the conversation as upsetting as she did or as inconclusive.

"What are you going to do this afternoon?" she asked him.

"I don't know. I was just wondering that myself," he said. "I'm having doubts about what I had in mind doing."

So he had had plans. "What was that?"

He smiled at her faintly accusing tone. "I had thought that if your mother was like mine, she would have more than enough food and wouldn't object to an extra guest for dinner. I was going to try to wangle an invitation and drive back to Metairie with you to pick up the kids."

"She always cooks twice as much food as we can eat." Susan was pleased and surprised, but also a little daunted at the idea of showing up at her parents' house with Jim. "You would be very welcome, if you still want to."

"My other option is a crawfish boil some friends are having over in Madisonville. There might be an unattached female or two with standards not as high as yours. Don't you think I'd do better to go to it?"

"Do you like crawfish?"

"Not especially."

"My mother is a good cook, and Billy and Joanie would be tickled pink." She met his gaze, which told her frankly she hadn't said the right thing to persuade him. "I'd love the company driving back. I can drive, and you can just sit and relax and talk to me. Shall I call my mother when I get home and tell her to set another plate?"

"Why don't you do that? It's too hot for a crawfish boil, anyway." He smiled at her.

"When you asked me all those questions about my family at breakfast, were you trying to decide if you wanted to take a chance on inviting yourself to dinner?" Susan inquired, much happier now about the whole breakfast scene in the hotel room and his matter-of-fact acceptance of her plans.

"You don't take a hint easily, do you?" he said, grinning. "I gave you every opportunity to say, 'Why don't you come along and meet everybody for yourself?'"

"I just didn't dream that you would want to. I hope you won't be bored."

"I won't be. Don't worry about me."

The last seemed a general reassurance that made Susan feel terrible all over again about the sensitive conversation they had just had. Then he reached out and laid his hand on her abdomen, remarking, "I'll bet you would look cute pregnant, but no danger, you say?"

"Almost none," she said, feeling oddly bereft. "Your bachelor days aren't numbered."

"Oh, but they are," he contradicted cheerfully, drawing his hand away after a gentle little pat. "I've decided that it's time for me to marry and have a family. Once a man reaches that psychological state, I understand, it's all over. In six months to a year, I'll have myself a wife."

"You don't want to rush into anything, though, do you?" Susan said, jealousy twisting inside her. "You want to find someone who will make you a good wife. If you get in a big hurry, you could be sorry."

"If I were in a big hurry, I'd go to that crawfish boil this afternoon, wouldn't I?" he asked soothingly.

Instead he was wasting his time with her, at Susan's own urging. "I guess you would," she agreed grudgingly, but still couldn't drop the subject. "I know you said once that you didn't have a 'right woman' in mind, but you must have some preconceived ideas. Do you want a wife who's strictly a homemaker type or would you consider marrying a career woman who wouldn't give up her own occupation?"

"Some combination of those two sounds good," Jim replied. "But I think it's best to keep an open mind, don't you? If I had preconceived ideas, I would only end up changing them. The 'right woman' for me is someone I want to spend the rest of my life with. If she feels the same way, we can work everything else out. There has to be give and take, a certain amount of compromise on minor differences."

"But you would both have to want the same kind of life, have the same basic sense of values."

"Yes, of course. Otherwise, we'd be in for serious problems. But don't you think we've had enough heavy conversation for one day? Tell me how your fall festival is going. What's the date on that, anyway?"

Susan answered him reluctantly, not wanting to drop the subject, even if it gave her no pleasure. He didn't seem to notice her lack of enthusiasm and asked questions that led her into a detailed explanation of how she'd organized the local merchants into various committees that weren't making as much progress as she would have liked in carrying out her plans. His comments were insightful and sympathetic, and he even made several very astute and helpful suggestions.

"It's too bad I don't have you behind me," she couldn't help remarking. "I could certainly have used your business knowledge and experience in dealing with people."

"We would only have butted heads. I would probably have tried to take over," he said, smiling, but good-naturedly serious.

"Because you don't like a woman being in charge?"

"Because it comes natural to me to be in charge."

"I don't think I would have minded turning the whole thing over to you," Susan mused. "Not once I realized that you were more capable than I was."

"This way you'll get all the credit, plus some good publicity for your interior decorating business," he pointed out. "You shouldn't be shy about having your name mentioned and your picture included in the newspaper coverage."

"What worries me is that I'll also get all the blame for whatever goes wrong," she confided. "When I stop to think about the hundred and one possible foul-ups, I get the jitters and wonder if I wasn't crazy to take a project of this size on."

"A few things will undoubtedly go wrong, but it sounds like you have all the bases covered," Jim remarked reassuringly. "There's nothing you can do about the major factor, which is the weather. If you need me to give you a hand at the last minute, when everything has to come together, I will."

The casual offer took Susan completely by surprise. "Why would you do that, when you don't want the fall festival to succeed?" she asked. "You haven't changed your thinking about bringing in more businesses into the neighborhood, have you?"

"I'm not any more in favor of the idea, but I'm not as opposed to it now," he replied.

Susan was filled with a sudden foreboding by his answer and his unconcerned air. "Why aren't you?"

"Because I've decided to relocate my workshop and, in view of my sudden urge to get married, I've become more flexible in my attitude toward living where I am. The woman I marry might prefer to live in a different kind of house in a different area." He smiled at her. "You came along and knocked me right out of my rut. It's all going to work out for the best, and I'll end up being much happier, so don't look so upset."

"But I *am* upset. I feel terrible. Even if the fall festival is a gigantic success, our neighborhood isn't going to go commercial overnight. Don't you think you're being hasty, moving your workshop? Why don't you wait and see?" Susan urged, but he was shaking his head in a gentle refusal of her logic.

"I need more space, and it isn't feasible to enlarge my present building. I'm going to hire some helpers."

"Billy is going to be heartbroken when you move your workshop," she protested.

"By then Billy will be in school and involved in his studies and extracurricular affairs. You don't approve of his spending so much time in my workshop, anyway," Jim reminded her, with no accusing note in his voice. "I would expect you to be pleased that he won't be able to drop by any time he wants."

Susan *should* have been pleased about all of Jim's plans for his future. He was alleviating her worries about the danger of his becoming too entrenched in Billy's life or hers. With his workshop in a different location, Billy would lose contact with him. She would hold to her principles and not make love with him again, thus forcing him to look elsewhere for a woman who was also a marital prospect.

She guessed that the fair thing to do, since she couldn't encourage Jim's interest in her, would be to not see him again. She probably should tell him to go to his crawfish boil this afternoon, and not come with her to her parents' house. If he asked her out after today, she should say no.

But it wasn't as though she was misleading him. She had been upfront and open to the point of cruelly damaging his pride. He had to know that his relationship with her couldn't lead to anything permanent. If he wanted to be with her anyway, Susan couldn't deny herself the pleasure of his company.

"Cheer up. Everything is going to be fine." Jim's confident prediction interrupted Susan's troubled train of thought. "When we get to Mandeville, I'll get out at my place, and you can take the car on to your house. That should attract the least amount of attention. Then you can pick me up and drive, if you want to."

"I'd love the chance to drive this car," Susan told him, perking up.

"Drive it as much as you like. In fact, you can park it in your driveway and use it. Nobody has to know that it isn't yours."

"But don't you intend to use it?"

"No, I'll be driving my van. It's a shame for the car to sit and collect dust when you could enjoy it. The gas mileage isn't bad, and the car is insured."

"That certainly is a generous offer," Susan said, sorely tempted. "This is the kind of vehicle I would have, if I could afford it."

"Then treat yourself. I insist."

Susan didn't argue. Accepting meant he wouldn't be using the sedan to take out any other woman besides her. She felt as though she were buying herself a month's time when she would have some claim to him.

There was a sense of letdown as she drove the car home, after leaving Jim at his house. For the sake of discretion, she supposed, he hadn't so much as given her a quick goodbye hug or kiss. Nor had he suggested that she might want to come back as soon as she'd changed and steal a private half hour or so with him. They had a whole hour before they needed to leave again, twice as much time as Susan needed to get ready.

"You'll pick me up a few minutes before one?" he'd asked and then suggested, after she had agreed, that she could pull into the driveway and blow the horn. He would be listening for her and would come out immediately.

It wasn't until Susan had parked and gone into her house that it occurred to her that she hadn't even bothered to notice whether the coast was clear in the immediate vicinity. At least she must not have given a furtive impression, if one of her neighbors had been in evidence. So far a guilty conscience wasn't proving to be a major problem, she reflected somewhat worriedly.

As she took off her silk outfit in her bedroom, she thought about Jim a couple of blocks away, shedding his own clothes, and she felt a sensual awareness of her body as she stripped down and put on clean underwear. Guided by the desire to please him, she picked out a pale blue cotton dress that was simple and feminine. Remembering their discussion of shoes some days ago, she slipped her feet into frivolous little sandals with tiny heels. She took her time as she made her face up lightly, applied a pink glossy lipstick and fluffed her hair. Then she was ready with thirty minutes to spare.

Surely Jim was ready by now, too, she reasoned. Men never took as long to dress as women did. It was silly for her to twiddle her thumbs and pace the floor. If nothing else, they could drive on over a little early and perhaps take a tour of his old Metairie neighborhood. And since she was picking him up ahead of time, she would go inside rather than blow the horn, which was conspicuous anyway and seemed inconsiderate of others on a quiet Sunday afternoon.

Susan launched into all her explanations as soon as he opened the kitchen door for her, wearing dress slacks and no shirt. She could hear his TV playing in another room as she entered, explaining her early arrival. He'd apparently been watching a sports program.

"I just have to put on a shirt," Jim said after he'd taken in her appearance. "You look very pretty, by the way. I like that dress, too. Why don't you come into the living room and sit down a minute while I finish dressing?" He gestured toward an open door.

"There's no hurry," Susan said as she preceded him to the next room, which was furnished in plain masculine taste with a large sofa and chairs. "I suppose this was originally intended as the dining room," she remarked, glancing around.

"I'm sure it was," Jim agreed. "The two front rooms of the house were probably parlors. There's just one bathroom, the same as in your house, and three bedrooms. Feel free to walk around," he offered as he started over toward an interior doorway through which she could glimpse a hall. "I won't be long. Should I wear a tie?" he asked without slowing down.

Susan drifted after him, watching him disappear into a room across the hallway. "No, that won't be necessary," she said. "None of the other men will have on ties, just slacks and nice shirts."

"That's about what I figured."

His voice came from inside the room, which she assumed to be his bedroom. In the hallway, she hesitated, glancing inside the open doorway and edging closer to the threshold, working up her nerve. He'd given her leeway to look around, and she'd slept with him the night before, for heaven's sake. It was certainly no big deal to show some curiosity about his bedroom.

"Can I come in?" she asked.

"Sure. I don't have any secrets from you after last night." He had slipped on a shirt and was buttoning it. As she entered, he looked up to smile at her. "How's this shirt and slacks combination?"

"Very nice. Judging from them, you don't put yourself in the hands of clerks at lower priced stores." She walked over closer to him and pretended to be interested in the contents of his closet.

"I can't buy just any shirt or slacks off a rack because of my height," he pointed out.

"Oh, that's true. You need a longer length on the sleeves and the pants legs." It was difficult to sound casual with her stomach tightening and her breathing growing faster as he reached down to unfasten his slacks. She tried not to be blatant about watching as he proceeded to tuck in his shirt. "I noticed when I was shopping for a Father's Day present last year that some of the major chain department stores have sizes for tall men now." She mentioned two stores that were household names and standbys for family shopping in the medium-priced range.

"Those stores are fine for buying jeans and work shirts," Jim replied. "But the quality just isn't there for other clothes. I probably wouldn't know the difference if I hadn't gotten used to wearing much better. I'm ready." He turned toward her with a smile and the air of presenting himself for inspection.

"You look very handsome. My mother and my sister are going to fall head over heels for you, I have the feeling." Susan moved closer to him, her pulse rate quickening, and reached up to fuss with his collar, which was perfect as it was. He stood patiently, not touching her. "This shirt does have a nice fit," she remarked, smoothing her palms along his shoulders.

"It's one of my favorites," he replied. "Now we'd better go, don't you think? I don't want to be late and start off on the wrong foot with your mother."

"We have plenty enough time for you to at least kiss me," Susan said petulantly, putting her arms up around his neck. "If the idea appeals to you at all, that is."

"I'll mess up your lipstick," he warned, but his arms were closing around her.

"I don't care. Hold me close," she murmured, tilting back her head and closing her eyes with pleasure as he complied with her order. His lips on hers, warm and firm and possessive, felt so incredibly good that she moaned softly in her throat and tightened her hold around his neck to encourage him to kiss her with passion and depth.

But he didn't kiss her harder or accept her invitation as she parted her lips for him. Instead he eased the pressure and lifted his head. Then, after hugging her painfully tight, he released her and took her hands down from behind his neck and held them.

"We don't have time for more than that," he said huskily. "Otherwise we'll end up making love and missing dinner or else arrive at your parents' house in a state of frustration."

Susan was already in a state of frustration and a state of annoyance, as well. "It's good that one of us keeps a clear head and has self-control," she said peevishly.

"Aside from not wanting to be rude and inconsiderate, I'm only abiding by your rules," Jim told her. "Just this morning you were very definite about not wanting to have an affair. You gave me your reasons, which are all valid. Since then, you haven't changed your mind, have you?"

"No," Susan admitted.

"Well, then, be fair. I can't kiss you, especially in my bedroom, and not get turned on. Just now, I didn't want to tuck my shirt in and zip up my pants. I wanted to take my clothes off and take yours off, too."

Susan drew in a breath, going weak at his words. "I wouldn't have stopped you," she confessed. "You're right. I'm saying one thing and acting another way."

"It's not going to be easy for me to be around you and not think about how much I'd like to have you in my bed. Not just for a quick bout of lovemaking, but all night, every night."

"That's totally out of the question," Susan said quickly, to suppress the sharp longing that welled up inside her. "I guess I'm still under the spell of last night. My conscience will wake up again and I'll get everything back in perspective as soon as I bring the kids home and get busy with work. After all, I'm used to getting along without a man.''

Jim squeezed her hands. "You aren't feeling any guilty pangs yet?"

"None," she confided sheepishly. "I went to my house just now without the first worry that somebody might see me coming home at noon all dressed up in last night's clothes. I was too upset with you because you didn't kiss me goodbye or suggest that I hurry and change and come back. When you opened the door without your shirt on and acted like a perfect gentleman, I was disappointed, and then I followed you in here, as bold as brass. I'm shocked at the way I'm acting and a little embarrassed, but it's like I'm somebody I don't quite recognize. Right now—"

"I think this is enough of this discussion," Jim cut in hastily. "Or at least let's continue it in the car."

Susan let him usher her toward the door. "I'm surprised you don't have a king-sized bed," she remarked, glancing toward his bed, which was neatly made up.

"That's a queen-sized, which has the extra length, just not the width," he replied. "A king-sized one is more than I need." He smiled down at her. "Sleeping in that one by myself tonight is going to be lonely enough."

Susan thought of her own bed, which was a standard double. She suspected that it was going to seem much larger tonight, with a lot of empty space.

On the drive Jim sat back, relaxed, in the passenger's seat and steered them clear of intimate conversation. He made no effort to stimulate any physical awareness between them, but Susan was attuned to his slightest movement and intensely conscious of little sensual details, like how his slacks were snug on his thighs and accommodated his masculine form. His voice and his presence gave her pleasure in addition to her enjoyment of him as an intelligent and interesting companion.

On arrival at her parents' house, she assumed a casual, breezy manner and introduced Jim as a neighbor who had been very nice and helpful. Billy and Joanie, who had already filled everyone in on Jim, were more enthusiastic than she would have liked in greeting him, but his behavior was impeccably right. He was polite and cordial and at ease, but didn't touch her or look at her with anything more than warm interest.

Leaving him to fend for himself with the men and children, Susan joined Becky, her sister, and Mary Ann, her brother's wife, in helping her mother with last-minute dinner preparations. She tried her best to be blasé as she agreed with the female consensus that he was an extremely good-looking man. On trips into the dining room, where the table extended almost wall to wall with the extra leaves inserted, she could hear enough of the conversation going on in the living room to determine that he was making a favorable impression on the males in her family, too. She could tell from her father's voice that he had taken an immediate liking to Jim.

When the food was on the table and her mother had summoned everyone to come and eat, Susan was careful of her expression, giving Jim a pleasant friendly smile as he came to stand near her. Then Joanie took it upon herself to be helpful in assigning places to sit, informing her grandmother, "Mr. Jim likes to sit next to Mom."

Susan felt her cheeks grow warm at the amused glances, but before she could say something light, Billy was speaking up with a jealous note, "I've already told Grandma that."

"I appreciate you kids looking out for my interest, but I think your grandmother is capable of figuring out seating arrangements for herself," Jim said ruefully, smiling at Susan's mother.

"They don't give me any credit, Jim," she said indulgently. "Grandma's just an old fogey to them."

The embarrassing moment was smoothed over, thanks to him. He sat next to Susan and gave every indication of being perfectly comfortable and of enjoying his meal immensely. He even took second helpings, endearing himself further to her mother, while Susan ate without any real appetite, feeling the strain of trying to appear as if she weren't paying any special attention to him.

Evidently she wasn't successful. Later when she was helping clear the table, she came in for some feminine teasing from Becky and Mary Ann.

"You give yourself away every time you look at Jim, Sis," Becky said, grinning delightedly.

"What do you mean, 'give myself away'?" Susan demanded defensively.

"She means you give the impression that you could eat him for dessert," Mary Ann chimed in, smothering a laugh. "Not that I blame you. He's some hunk and nice, too."

"He is very nice," Susan assured them. "But he's just a friend and neighbor." She picked up a stack of plates and carried them to the kitchen, flustered but also strangely resentful that Jim's manner of looking at her had escaped any mention. Her own reaction baffled her. She should have been relieved and grateful that Becky and Mary Ann hadn't detected any telltale intimacy in his glances, but somehow his discretion wasn't any more pleasing to Susan than his self-control had been earlier.

The whole afternoon seemed endless for her, and it was another source of annoyance that she never once caught Jim glancing at his watch or got any inkling that time might be dragging for him. He managed to talk to every single member of her family, including her nephew and two nieces, and charmed one and all. Susan was amazed at his memory. He had apparently retained every bit of background information she had given him.

The only person he didn't seek out and draw into conversation was Susan herself, who made a point of not sticking by his side. But he drew her eyes like a magnet, and her ears strained to pick up his comments. His laughter raised a jealous tide of pleasure inside her. It was difficult for her to concentrate on her own conversations, a fact that her mother innocently commented upon.

"Susan, you seem to be a hundred miles away today, honey. Do you have something on your mind?"

"I noticed the same thing," Becky remarked from across the room, exchanging a knowing smile with Mary Ann.

Susan could feel herself blushing and hear the defensive note in her voice as she insisted that nothing was bothering her. Try as she might, she couldn't help stealing a glance at Jim, but he was engrossed in a discussion of golf with her brother, Mark, a golf enthusiast, and seemed oblivious to anything else.

If he had looked up and caught her eye, Susan knew that the moment would have been even a greater test of her composure, yet it irked her that she could be totally distracted by him, while he was apparently not at all bothered by her presence. From all appearances he was enjoying himself thoroughly, not wasting any regrets on spending the afternoon like this, among people who were strangers to him, rather than being alone with her.

When it was finally late enough to leave, he was no help at all in hurrying their departure and was the last one in the car, this time taking the driver's seat.

"You certainly were a hit with the whole family," she remarked before they'd gone half a block.

"I didn't sense that I was quite that popular," he replied, looking over at her questioningly.

"Grandma said you were welcome to come any time, Mr. Jim." Joanie spoke up from the back seat before Susan could think of a way to answer.

"She meant that I was free to accept any time your mother might want to invite me again," Jim told the little girl.

"I could invite you," Billy pointed out.

"And me, too," Joanie said. "Will you come with us next time to Grandma Packard's, Mr. Jim? It was more fun with you there. Didn't you think so, Mom?"

"Everyone enjoyed meeting Mr. Jim and talking to him," Susan evaded, thinking to herself, everyone who got the chance to talk to him.

There was no opportunity for any private exchange on the drive home, which seemed interminable compared to her three more recent rides with Jim. She tried to uphold her end of the four-way conversation and not feel frustrated by her children's presence, but it was impossible not to think ahead and wish there was some way she could have at least a brief time alone with him when they reached Mandeville.

Apparently he wasn't of the same mind, though. He drove straight to her house, raising her hopes, but before she could even invite him inside herself, Billy and Joanie were both urging him to come in and watch TV. When she didn't second the invitation immediately, Jim declined.

"But how about a movie tomorrow night?" he asked.

Susan had to wait until the enthusiastic reactions died down before she could answer. "I have a committee meeting."

He nodded. "Is it all right if I take the kids, then?"

"Yes, of course," she said, but words stuck in her throat. He could have suggested another night when she wasn't tied up or at least looked disappointed.

"Don't bother about supper for them. We'll have something to eat before the movie."

"They'll enjoy that." She hesitated before taking the car keys that he was holding out to her. "Now you'll have to walk home."

"It will be good to stretch my legs after sitting down so much today. Good night." He slipped his hands into his pockets and backed away a step. "Good night, kids."

"Good night, Mr. Jim," Billy and Joanie chorused in unison after him as he strode away.

Susan's farewell, spoken with a tight throat, was drowned by her children's youthful voices.

Chapter Twelve

Susan glanced at her watch anxiously. The meeting was over finally, but no one was making a move to leave. Jim and the kids could return at any moment, and he might not come in if he saw the cars parked outside. It was bad enough that she hadn't seen him and said hello earlier.

Billy and Joanie had kept watch for him and gone dashing out, yelling their goodbyes to her, as soon as he had pulled up, driving his van. By the time Susan got to a front window, they were climbing in. She had watched the dark green vehicle pull away from the curb, feeling like a martyr.

The meeting hadn't been very productive. Susan took her share of the blame. It had been difficult for her to keep her mind on the proceedings. She had kept wishing that she had rescheduled it for another night and had gone to the movies with Jim. Just the thought of sitting with him in a darkened theater and sharing glances and smiles, even if they didn't hold hands, had raised a longing inside her.

She sighed, glancing at her watch again, and then tensed at the sound of car doors slamming out on the street. "Excuse me, that must be my children coming home," she said, moving quickly across the room toward the front hallway. Any concern about her dignity was lost in the urgency to stop Jim before he drove off and tell him that the meeting was over and everyone would soon be gone.

But she was too late. Jerking open the door, she saw the taillights of his van disappearing down the street. He had done just what she had feared he would do.

It wasn't easy for her to be civil to the departing committee members who had followed in her wake, belatedly taking the hint that they should go home. She had to stifle her impatience as they lingered on the porch and straggled along the front walk, still chatting as if they had all night and nothing to do.

Just managing not to close the door with a bang of frustration as she went inside, she headed straight for the nearest telephone and called Jim's number. He would have been home less than ten minutes and could come back or at least she could talk with him for a little while.

Except that he wasn't home....

Susan let the phone ring a dozen times before she hung up, sick with disappointment, and went to interrogate her children. They were glad to tell her where they had eaten and what movie they'd seen.

"How did Mr. Jim like the movie?" she asked.

"He liked it," Joanie assured her.

"Yeah, he laughed a lot," Billy added in agreement. "So did Miss Lisa, this lady that watched the movie with us. She's a friend of Mr. Jim's."

"When Mr. Jim introduced us, Miss Lisa said to just call her Lisa, Mom, but I told her you liked us to call grown people Mr. or Mrs. or Miss," Joanie reported virtuously.

"She said she was glad there are still some parents teaching their children manners."

Susan somehow managed to keep her lip from curling and to not make a sarcastic remark, but she couldn't keep her voice entirely free of outrage and incredulity as she inquired, "This Miss Lisa met the three of you at the movie?"

"She didn't meet us," Billy explained. "She just came by herself. We were standing in line buying popcorn, and she came over and said hello to Mr. Jim. He acted real surprised to see her. She asked why he hadn't been in to eat in the restaurant where she works, and he said he'd been busy."

"Miss Lisa's a waitress," Joanie put in.

Susan felt better that the encounter was accidental, but she still wondered, knowing there were six movies playing in the theater where they'd gone, several of which were more to adult taste.

"So since Miss Lisa was there to see the same movie, you all sat together," she conjectured with a grim note.

"No, she came to see another one," Billy corrected. "But when we told her what we were going to see, she said she'd heard it was funny and would just as soon see it, too. She asked if we minded her sitting with us, and Mr. Jim said we wouldn't."

The only thing he could have said in politeness, whether he welcomed an addition to his party or not. Still, he wasn't home right now.

"Then after the movie, he brought you straight home and didn't want to come in. I know you must have invited him."

"He said it looked like your meeting was running late, so he would pass for tonight. Maybe next time you could go with us, Mom," Billy said consolingly, responding to his mother's downcast expression.

"Don't worry. I will," Susan said, tormented by the question her children couldn't answer. Where was Jim now?

COMPROMISING POSITIONS 215

Had he gone somewhere to meet Lisa? Even if he hadn't and was just out for a drink at a local place, he could encounter other interested, available women who couldn't fail to appreciate not just his looks and masculinity, but his personality and charm as well.

"Mr. Jim gets mail from them."

Billy's comment intruded upon her jealous, troubled thoughts. He and Joanie had switched their attention to the television screen, where a broker's commercial that they both found entertaining was playing.

"I know because I get his mail out of the box for him lots of times," he went on for Joanie's benefit and then, seeing his mother's gaze fixed on him, added, "He always thanks me for bringing it to him and saving him the trip."

"I'm sure he trusts you not to be careless and drop anything," Susan said, just as glad that her surprise and curiosity had been misinterpreted. What kind of correspondence would Jim be receiving from a brokerage firm? "When you say Mr. Jim gets mail from that company, you mean that you've noticed more than one envelope?" she asked, wondering if such companies solicited clients. If so, she'd never been on a mailing list.

"I don't remember exactly, but at least three or four," Billy replied.

"Mr. Jim probably gets a lot of junk mail, like we do, and just throws it away without reading it," Susan speculated, fishing for more information.

"I'd like to get Mr. Jim's mail for him sometime, too, Mom, but I've never even gotten to see his shop," Joanie complained. "It's not fair!"

"You might lose some important bill or something," Billy pointed out with brotherly superiority.

"No, I wouldn't!"

Susan left them to settle their own conflict and went to take a bath. It had been such a long day and a longer evening, ending in frustration and disappointment. She hadn't gotten to see Jim or speak a word with him, and now she would go to bed and lie there and wonder whether he would be sleeping alone tonight, too, and wishing she were there with him.

She was almost certain that he would be doing both. For all her jealousy and insecurity over hearing about tonight's episode with Lisa, she didn't think he would be open to advances from another woman right now. *He wanted Susan.* The knowledge filled her with joy and made her feel very special, but also put her values and judgment to the test all over again.

Immersed in a tubful of warm water, she reveled in the thought that he was hers, even temporarily, and then despaired at thinking that her conscience ruled out having an affair with any man. Yet how could she deprive herself of intimacy with Jim when she went weak with longing at the mere thought of his lovemaking? How could she not be *close* to him, with no physical barriers, for at least a while?

Sitting with the children in the living room after she'd bathed and gotten ready for bed didn't bring her any closer to resolving her dilemma. Their presence didn't make the moral issue stronger or lessen her temptation to compromise her principles. Not sleepy, but not interested in the television program they were watching, she finally got up and went to bed.

She was lying in the darkness, debating about whether to try calling Jim again, when the phone on her bedside table rang. The sound of his voice made her heart leap with gladness and cleared away all her indecision.

"I just drove by your house and saw that the cars were gone. I figured it was safe to call."

"This must be telepathy. I was lying here in bed, thinking about trying your house again."

"Any time I crossed your mind today or tonight, it was telepathy," Jim replied. "You called here earlier?"

"A few minutes after you dropped the kids off. The meeting was over, but they all hung around. When I heard your van, I went to the door as quickly as I could, but you were already gone."

"I was pretty disgruntled and stepped on the gas," he admitted. "I went down to the tavern on the lakefront for a beer and ran into a couple of guys I knew."

"The kids had a great time."

"I had a nice time with them, but it would have been a whole lot nicer if their mom had been along."

"Their mom's evening couldn't have been a bigger loss," Susan confided, warmed to the core by his tone as well as his words. "I was feeling too much like a martyr to concentrate on that darned committee meeting. Then you didn't come in, and when I talked to the kids, after getting no answer at your house, they told me about your waitress friend at the movie, and I turned green with jealousy."

"There's no cause for you to be jealous of Lisa. I know her only slightly, and I'm not interested in her." Jim sounded indifferently matter-of-fact, but his voice changed as he added, "Having her sit with us made me miss you that much more."

Susan melted at the revelation, but she still felt a certain feminine curiosity. "Because she reminds you of me or because she's different?"

"She's entirely different in almost every respect. Tall and brunette." He hesitated. "A more liberated type."

"Attractive?"

"Yes, she's fairly attractive in her own style. Right now I'm just finding myself partial to slim little blondes with big blue eyes."

"Lisa isn't slim?"

"She isn't overweight, but she's, well, full-bodied. If it will put your mind at rest, I didn't even sit next to her at the movie." There was a note of amusement in his voice. "Joanie sat on one side of me and Billy on the other. Since you weren't there, they concluded that your place next to me was up for grabs and crowded Lisa right out."

Susan smiled, seeing the whole scene. "And you let them get away with it."

"I preferred those seating arrangements myself. It had already occurred to me that I might have some explaining to do, as it was."

He had known she would be jealous and would put him through this third degree. The fact that he'd downplayed any possibility that Lisa might be a rival for his attention endeared him to Susan and made her want to keep her preferred status, at least for a limited time.

"Jim, I've been thinking tonight about what you asked me yesterday morning at the hotel. How can we live this close and see each other and not make love? Those weren't your exact words, but it's what you meant. Well, I think you're right. It's expecting too much of both of us." She waited nervously for his response.

"What are you suggesting?"

"That we can be very careful and keep people guessing as much as possible. We wouldn't be able to spend the night together, for example. There wouldn't be anything wrong in some touching in front of the children, but nothing, you know, passionate."

Again he didn't answer at once. "This is quite a turnabout. Does it have anything to do with Lisa?"

"In a way, yes. I believe you when you tell me that I have no reason to be jealous of her, but common sense tells me that there are lots of women out there who would be happy to go to bed with you, including some other blue-eyed blondes. Don't you want to have an affair with me?'' Susan broke off to ask. She was finding his response more than a little disappointing.

"I want to have an intimate relationship with you, of course, but not because you feel threatened by other women. You don't need to worry about whether I'm out womanizing any time we're not together, because I won't be."

"It sounds as if you're trying to talk me out of the whole idea," she said, more provoked than reassured.

"You're not exactly an expert at deception,'' Jim pointed out gently. "Yesterday at your parents' house you didn't relax a minute. Don't you think that I was aware of how uncomfortable you were having me there?''

"I didn't notice that you were aware of me at all."

"I was. I could repeat practically everything you said within my hearing range."

"That's more than I could do," Susan retorted. "Between trying not to look at you and pretending that I wasn't listening to your conversation, I couldn't keep a train of thought straight. It would have been some consolation if you had been having the same problem, but you seemed to be perfectly at ease and enjoying yourself thoroughly."

"I was interested in meeting your family and getting to know them, and the situation didn't cause me any guilt or shame or embarrassment, the way it did you. The only thing I could do to try to make it easier for you was to be as convincing as possible in the friendly neighbor role you'd given me, when you introduced me."

"You were convincing," Susan told him, yesterday's resentment in her voice. "Becky and Mary Ann cornered me after dinner and teased me about giving myself away every time I looked at you, but they didn't say a thing about the way you looked at me."

"I sensed on the way home that you were annoyed with me, but I didn't know why," Jim remarked, sounding pleased. "With the kids in the car, I couldn't ask you. Then when you didn't second their invitation to come in, I figured you'd had too much of my company for one day and wouldn't be in a mood to discuss what was wrong."

"I hadn't had *enough* of your company," Susan corrected him. "I was hoping for a few minutes alone with you, but you didn't seem to be on the same wavelength."

"And tonight, when Billy and Joanie came out to meet me before I could come in—they weren't following your directions?"

"I was furious at them. It's terrible to be jealous of your own children," she confessed.

His sigh came to her over the line. "I'm trying my damnedest not to think about how close you are. This might be easier if we were talking long distance and weren't just two minutes apart."

"I know exactly what you mean." Susan gave an answering sigh, full of exasperation and yearning.

"Could we have dinner tomorrow night? I would insist on paying for a sitter for the kids," Jim added.

"There's no need for that. Instead of getting a sitter, I may even arrange to have them stay overnight with friends."

"I wouldn't do that," he cautioned. "It'll be better for both of us if you have a curfew, don't you think?"

Otherwise they could stay together all night, which was against the rules she'd set. "You're right," Susan agreed reluctantly. "What time do you want me to pick you up with the car?"

"You don't have to pick me up. I can walk—"

"I'd rather pick you up, if it's all the same," she cut in, her heart beating fast and sending warmth coursing through her.

"About seven-thirty?" he asked after a slight pause.

"That will give me plenty of time. What about you?"

"I'll be ready when you get here."

"If I'm running a little early, I might surprise you again and show up before you get your shirt on."

"I'll just leave the door unlocked. Then if I'm in the shower and don't hear you knock, you can come in and make yourself at home."

"What time will you be taking your shower?" Susan asked, pressing her hand to a hot cheek. "I'm lying here blushing in the dark," she confessed. "I can't believe this is really me talking and acting this way. It was only yesterday morning that we made love, but the way I feel right now—"

"Much as I'd like to know, please don't tell me, sweetheart," Jim pleaded. "This conversation hasn't put me in a state for going to sleep."

"I can just imagine how you look," Susan mused, shocking herself further.

"Come on. Let's talk about something else. What did you do today?"

They stayed on the phone another hour, with Susan doing most of the talking at Jim's prompting. "What did you do today?" she asked, smothering a yawn as sleepiness relaxed her body. "I passed your house several times, and you weren't there."

"I had a very successful day," he replied. "I took a lease on a building that should fill my needs for a new workshop perfectly."

"You certainly aren't wasting any time," Susan lamented. "Next thing you'll be moving to another house.

Why can't things just stay the same for now? The fall festival is more than a month away. The kids will be in school in a few weeks. It would be so easy to see each other during the day. We could have lunch together. I could drop by for a cup of coffee..." Her voice drifted off as she sensed a quiet resistance at the other end.

"My new workshop won't be more than ten or fifteen minutes away," Jim replied. "We can still meet for lunch or coffee. And I won't be moving out of this house immediately. First I have to get the working end of my life running smoothly."

"I don't wish you any bad luck, but I hope that takes you a while," she said honestly. "Speaking of working, I guess we should say good-night and go to sleep. Are you more... relaxed now?"

"My body is. Good night, darling. Sleep well."

"You, too. Good night."

Susan cradled the phone with a sigh and lay, hugging her spare pillow to her breast. It gave her such a thrill for him to call her darling and sweetheart in that tender, possessive way. He spoke the endearments easily, yet not casually.

"Jim, darling," she whispered and felt a similar thrill. Her voice contained the same sentiment that she'd heard in his, but she didn't put a name to it. She didn't dare just yet.

"I love having you hold me like this after we make love," she told him happily. "It might be the nicest part. Not that I would want to take a shortcut."

Jim chuckled, squeezing her tighter to him. "You anticipated my question. I love these rest periods myself, sweetheart," he added teasingly.

Susan blushed. They'd made love twice since her early arrival to pick him up for dinner. "It's all your fault. I was never like this before. Tonight on the way here to your house, I made myself think about what I had in mind and felt more excited than guilty. It honestly worries me that my conscience isn't bothering me any more than it is. The only explanation is that somehow being here in bed with you just doesn't feel wrong. This doesn't seem in the least cheap and sordid, like I thought having an affair would be. I know that's probably some kind of rationalizing."

"Maybe affair isn't the right word for what you and I are having," Jim suggested softly.

"How can it not be?" Susan's heart beat faster as she struggled in his embrace and he held her a moment before he eased his hold and submitted to her puzzled scrutiny. "We're not married and we're going to bed together."

"By that definition, then, I guess we are having an affair." He grazed her chin gently with his knuckles. "But I still wouldn't worry too much about your moral downslide. Do you think we should get dressed and go to dinner before it gets too late?"

Susan wasn't ready to let the conversation go. "In a minute. But first tell me your definition of an affair."

He didn't answer immediately, yet he didn't seem to be searching for the right words. "To me an affair is a temporary relationship between two people whose main feeling for each other is sexual attraction. I think we have more than that, and ours is a more meaningful relationship, which would explain why you aren't feeling guilty." He smiled. "Although certainly we do have a strong physical attraction, too."

Susan tried to smile back and then gave up the attempt. "What about the temporary part of your definition?" she asked. "Jim, you aren't...*serious* about me, are you?"

Again he didn't reply right away, and yet there was no hesitant quality in his manner or in his voice when he spoke. "I'm in love with you, but I realize that I'm not in a position to ask you to marry me. You've been very honest about what you want in a husband, and you aren't at all keen on the idea of remarrying. So don't worry your pretty little head about me," he urged, kissing her tenderly on the lips. "I'm in this with my eyes open."

He hadn't exactly answered her question, but Susan could draw her own conclusion. He didn't plan to marry her, so he must consider their relationship temporary.

"What if I'm in love with you, too?" she asked, not at all happy with his rational perspective.

"It would make me very happy to hear it," Jim said softly. "Do you love me, Susan?"

"Yes."

"Then say it," he coaxed with open yearning in his face and his voice.

"I love you, Jim."

His arms enfolded her in a crushing hug. Pressed against his big, powerful body, Susan felt a euphoric swell of happiness and a sudden, blind confidence in the future. Her life with Jim would be different from the way she had planned her future, but it would be wonderful and rich. There would be more than enough compensation for what she'd be giving up.

"We'll both have to make some compromises, but we'll be happy together," she said, looking ahead into a future that seemed settled to her. "The kids are crazy about you, and you seem to like them. I would keep working, but I'd want to do that anyway. We could fix up this house and make it very nice, or another house like it, if you still want to move..." Her tone grew doubtful on the last few words because he was releasing her.

"In other words, you're willing to give up the kind of lifestyle you'd really like for yourself and marry me?" he asked with a pained note.

"Material things just aren't all that important, when you come right down to it!" she protested.

He propped himself up beside her on his elbow and picked up her left hand. "If I can't give you a diamond engagement ring, very similar to the one Joyce Crawford has, then I won't put a ring on your finger." He squeezed her hand and let it go, sitting up. "Now let's go to dinner, shall we?"

Susan sat up, too. "Don't I have any say?" she demanded, dismayed that she'd injured his pride, but also feeling hurt and rejected. "Don't I get a choice between having you without a big diamond ring and not having you at all?"

"Darling, I'm yours, with or without a ring," he said lightly. "Battered male ego and all. I would just as soon drop the whole subject of marriage, if you don't mind."

Susan did mind. She had to bite her lip to keep from telling him that her ego wasn't in the greatest of shape either. It irked her that he seemed to be in a cheerful mood as they got dressed together. At the local restaurant where he took her to eat, the same one where she'd had the original merchants' association meeting, he gave no sign that he was giving any thought to the subject that she couldn't seem to get out of her head.

All through dinner she kept noticing his hands, which were as attractive to her as the rest of him was, and imagining a gold wedding band on his left ring finger. He might say he was hers, but with that finger bare, she had no claim to him in the eyes of the world. To women like the restaurant hostess, a young woman in her late twenties who had greeted Jim like an old friend and asked him if he wanted his usual table, he was fair game. Susan was just his date.

She worked up her nerve when they were having coffee after their meal to broach the subject of marriage again.

"Just out of curiosity, I'd like to ask you something pertaining to the discussion that we were having at your house," she said casually. "If it won't upset you."

"I doubt that it will upset me," he replied pleasantly. "What would you like to know?"

"When and if you do get married, will you wear a wedding ring? Some men don't," she added defensively when he looked totally surprised by her question.

"I've always assumed that I would, but only a plain gold band. Nothing fancy and filigreed."

"I just wondered."

"I would like to have a church wedding, too, in case you're interested."

"You would? That does surprise me. I would have thought you'd want just a private ceremony."

"No, I think getting married is an occasion that should be celebrated with family and friends. I'd want a reception afterward with champagne and dancing. How about you?"

"I'd probably go for a quiet church wedding," Susan said, thinking of the expense involved.

"Why, because you're divorced? You wouldn't have to wear white. My own personal choice would be a pale blue, like the color of the dress you had on Sunday, but floor-length and lacy. And you'd want both Billy and Joanie to have a special role. Wouldn't you love to dress him up in a tuxedo and Joanie in a beautiful long dress? Admit it."

"Of course I would," she said, smiling with wistful pleasure at the picture he evoked. "It's just that a wedding like that plus a reception would be a big extravagance. You probably have no idea of the cost, but I do."

"Regardless, that's the kind of wedding you and I would have to have," he said positively, placing his napkin on the table.

"Or no wedding at all, right?"

He smiled at her glumly knowing tone. "Exactly. Now if I can just get our waitress's attention, I'll pay the check."

"I think I know now why you've managed to stay single this long," Susan said.

He was glancing around. Another smile tugged at the corners of his mouth, but he didn't answer, and the subject was dropped.

She couldn't help noticing the amount of money he left on the table to cover the bill and a tip, but tactfully refrained from voicing her thoughts. He couldn't afford to take her out to a nice restaurant every night, any more than she could afford to hire a sitter that often. But in the car when she asked him if he would like to have supper at her house the following evening, deep down she was hoping that he would reject the idea and press for less sensible plans that would allow them to be alone together.

"I was going to suggest that we do something with the kids," he replied, giving her a questioning look. "But you don't have to cook. We could all go out and eat, preferably in a real restaurant, though, not a pizza or hamburger place, if they could be talked into it."

"I don't mind cooking," Susan said, faintly annoyed as well as disappointed. Not only was he in favor of a family evening, but he was also pressing for one with no economic advantages.

"Are you sure? You don't sound very enthusiastic, and I can't blame you. After working hard all day, it's easy to understand that you might not want to go to the trouble of cooking."

"Making a meal is no problem," she assured him. "The reason I'm not enthusiastic is purely selfish. I'd rather be able to talk to you freely, which I won't be able to do with Billy and Joanie present." Or touch him, either.

"It's a temptation for me, too, sweetheart, to have you to myself. But I don't want the kids to feel excluded or resent me."

"They would probably come closer to resenting me," Susan retorted.

"They'll get used to having me around and not pay me nearly so much attention after a while," he soothed. "You'll see. The sooner that happens, the sooner we can have some private conversations and maybe even steal a kiss or two." He reached over and squeezed her hand. "Why don't we just go out and eat, though? That's the easiest for you, and the kids seem to enjoy eating out. We'll have to see if we can't educate their palates, though. I can't take a steady diet of hamburgers and pizza."

"Jim, you can't be taking us out to eat every night," she protested.

"Not every night," he agreed, smiling over at her. "One night I do want to find out if you really can cook."

Susan sighed. "For someone who doesn't care about making money, you sure are a free spender."

"I've never said that I didn't care about making money," Jim objected. "I told you that I started hustling a buck when I was younger than Billy. When I worked for Huntington, I was in a high income bracket—"

"Don't tell me. I can just imagine how high you lived then," Susan broke in. "I know you spent a fortune on clothes and shoes, just from looking in your closet. You have more invested in ties than most men have in their whole wardrobe." Her tone was a mixture of admiration and disapproval. "I'll have to say you had good taste."

"I had to dress well and project a successful image. Besides which, I like good clothes. Whatever impression I've given you, I have nothing against the affluent life. I'm a capitalist through and through—"

"Sure, you are," Susan scoffed. "That's why you refuse to sell your furniture to someone whose looks you don't like. Tomorrow night I'll cook you supper, and that's that."

"Have it your way, sweetheart," he said, sounding exasperated. "Save me from squandering my limited funds."

Chapter Thirteen

He really didn't intend to marry her.

Susan gradually came to the realization when a month had passed and Jim never once brought up the subject of marriage. Any time she tried to discuss it, he made a light evasive remark or introduced another topic. Soon her pride kept her silent, except for occasionally voicing her discontent with the limits their situation placed upon them.

With school started up again, they had the living room to themselves on weekday evenings after Billy and Joanie had gone to bed. Sitting nestled against him on the sofa within the warm, strong circle of his arms, Susan was utterly content, except for the thought that he would have to get up eventually and go to his house and leave her to sleep alone in her bed. When the time came for him to say good-night, it was almost impossible for her not to remark wistfully, "I wish you could stay and sleep with me."

He always agreed with her that that would be very nice, but didn't ever allude to the possibility that at some future time they would be together as man and wife. Usually he managed to make her smile by emphasizing the humorous obstacles. Her bed was too short, and his feet would hang over about a foot. The kids wouldn't think anything strange about his being there the next morning, since he often dropped by and was having a cup of coffee with her when they got up, but they might notice him shaving at the bathroom sink and have their suspicions aroused. His next-door neighbor, Mrs. Alexis, wouldn't get a wink of sleep since she waited up to hear when he got home. And so on.

One night when she'd given up on getting an honest answer, he surprised her and raised her hopes by revealing that he had apparently given serious thought to sleeping with her in a house with her two children and found the idea of their presence inhibiting.

"Sleeping in the same bed and not being able to make love wouldn't be any better than sleeping apart, darling. Sound carries in these old houses. Neither one of us would feel relaxed, thinking that Joanie or Billy might wake up." He smiled. "You do tend to be vocal at times. Not that I'm complaining."

"You're vocal yourself, right at the end," Susan reminded him, feeling a stir of excitement even as she considered the point that he was making and had to agree with him. She couldn't be as totally abandoned making love with him with her children in hearing distance. "But sound carries in any house, not just old ones. Married couples with children accept the fact that they can't always have privacy and take advantage of those times when they don't have to worry about being quiet."

She didn't think it was necessary to add that the two of them could certainly arrange to have a sex life if they were married. If they didn't have to be discreet, they could make love far more frequently than they did now, since they both had their own businesses and set their own schedules. Surely he must be thinking the same thing.

"The best solution is to have a large enough house that's laid out so that the master bedroom is off to itself and private," Jim observed, again as though expressing something he had thought about. "Like the Crawford house, for example."

"Jim, the Crawford house has a master *suite*, with its own fireplace and sitting room, his and hers bathrooms and two huge walk-in closets and dressing areas. A very small minority of couples can afford that kind of house!"

"The fireplace is overkill, in my opinion," he remarked calmly, ignoring her exasperated tone. "There're some other things I would do differently in that house, too, but I like the basic floor plan. Don't you?"

"It's a dream house," Susan said wearily, too frustrated and disappointed to continue the discussion now that she saw where it was headed. If he couldn't buy her that kind of house, he couldn't marry her. Another all or nothing proposition. "Now I guess we should say good-night. I have a hundred and one things to do tomorrow, with the fall festival only a week away. I'll be so glad when it's over, and I can concentrate on my decorating clients. Thanks to you, I'm swamped." He had steered two more major jobs her way in the past month.

"Can you squeeze in lunch with me?" he asked.

"I don't see how," she said. "I have an appointment in Covington at eleven-thirty and several other things to do there afterward."

"That would work out well with my schedule. I have business in Covington tomorrow, too. We could meet somewhere."

"Okay," Susan agreed, unable to hold out against what she really wanted to do. He might not want to marry her, but he seemed to want to spend every minute he could with her.

"Why don't we eat at the Back Street Café? It has about the best lunch menu in Covington, and we would get served in a reasonable time."

Susan went along with his choice, knowing that it was pointless to suggest that they could go to a hamburger place that had a salad bar and get by much cheaper. He didn't like eating in fast food restaurants, and economy was simply no concern for him. She guessed that it came from being a single man and never having had any financial worries because there was only himself to consider. He gave no sign of wishing to change his ways and save for the diamond ring he'd insisted that he would have to be able to put on her finger before he could make her his wife.

Not that he was lavish in a showy or wasteful sense. He just seemed to have a basic philosophy that money was to be used and enjoyed. He thought nothing of taking her and the kids out to eat in restaurants and to the movies. Used to penny pinching in the area of entertainment, Susan couldn't help being aware of the money he was spending. One day before the school term started, the four of them had gone to the French Quarter, an outing that had cost him a couple of hundred dollars in total, but he obviously hadn't given a second thought to the expense.

"I know what I wanted to be sure and mention to you tonight," she said as she walked with him to the door. "The month's lease on the car must be up by now. You need to turn it back in."

"I'm not planning to turn it back in," he replied. "Not for the time being. I'm going to lease it on a regular basis, unless you'd like to exchange it for another model."

"But it's completely unnecessary for you to lease a car like that," Susan protested. "It's beautiful, and I love driving it, but I have a car, and you have two automobiles yourself. Though you don't seem to drive your sports car very much." He'd taken her and Billy and Joanie for rides, but apparently used his van almost exclusively.

"I didn't buy the Corvette with the intention of driving it very much," Jim explained. "It's a classic and was in such mint condition that I couldn't pass it up at the price."

The idea of buying a car without any intention of using it was totally foreign to Susan. "How much did it cost?" she asked, her curiosity getting the best of her. The sum he mentioned was about triple her own uneducated guess. She had to fight to conceal her incredulity, but still must have looked surprised and skeptical.

"The owner was in a big hurry to sell and didn't want to go to the trouble of advertising," Jim told her. "Otherwise, he wouldn't have let it go for that."

Susan managed somehow not to comment on his belief that he had gotten a bargain. It seemed an awful lot to pay for a little sports car that he wasn't going to drive when he could be drawing interest on a savings account.

After he'd gone and she was getting ready for bed, Susan thought back to the first day that she had met Jim. Walking around to his workshop in search of him, she had spotted the Corvette and been thrown off by the sight of it. Based on the exterior of his house, his pets and his van, she was expecting Jim Mann to be a staid, conservative type. The sports car had introduced the possibility that he might have a flashier side to his personality, unless the Corvette belonged to a son.

Leaving his premises after being bowled over by him, Susan had been no closer to reconciling his ownership of his two vehicles. Nor was she any closer now, she realized, knowing him as intimately as she did and loving him. His explanation tonight of how he'd come to buy the Corvette hadn't really been that enlightening. *Why* had he bought the car? That's what she should have asked him and hadn't, so taken aback had she been by the news of what he'd paid for it.

All the bits and pieces of her impressions of Jim hadn't fit together that first day she'd met him. She was so much more knowledgeable about him now, and yet he was still something of a puzzle to her. Everything just didn't fit.

He had so much going for him. He was intelligent, hard-working, shrewd, dependable, capable, disciplined, confident, decisive. She couldn't think of a single adjective about him that didn't add up to successful. All he lacked was ambition, which he'd had once and purged from his character when it had reached what he considered an obsessive stage.

Susan loved him just the way he was, even if she couldn't help regretting that he was wasting his potential. What hurt was that loving her obviously wasn't an incentive for him to use his natural abilities to achieve more financial success, if his pride really wouldn't allow him to marry her without it.

He wasn't much inclined to talk about his work, but he gave the impression of being very pleased with his new workshop, which she hadn't seen. He hadn't invited her to visit or encouraged her to drop by, and the location, somewhere off Highway 59, wasn't familiar to her. Now that he had a couple of guys working for him, he could presumably take on more jobs, but she wouldn't be surprised if he didn't use his extra time to build more of the lovely furniture that he didn't care about selling. The only benefit of having hired the helpers he'd mentioned was that he was now relieved from doing the easy, boring rote work that held no challenge for him.

However unsatisfying Susan found her status with him, she wouldn't push for a commitment and risk losing what she had. He was a wonderful companion and lover. He made her life a thousand times more enjoyable than it had been before she met him and much easier, too, sharing the daily headaches and chores as a husband might have done.

Her children both adored him, for good reason. In truth he gave them as much undivided attention as she did, listened to their stories, helped them with their homework, in general took a genuine interest in their young lives and seemed to care about them.

Susan would just have to go along with the status quo since it didn't seem to bother him, but it was difficult not to feel threatened when he drew the attention of other women, without even trying, whenever they were out together. Several times they had run into people he admitted having dated, who were all earthier, sexier types than Susan. It made her wildly jealous to think of him with another woman and insecure to know that he had been attracted to a different kind of feminine looks in the past.

The next day when she walked into the Back Street Café and saw him sitting at a table, carrying on a conversation with the waitress, she tensed up immediately. It was obvious at a glance that they weren't strangers, and the brunette fit the general mold of the type of women he'd dated. Tall and shapely, she had long brown hair combed back loosely from her face and held in a barrette at the nape of her neck. She wore no makeup, not even lipstick, and was smiling at Jim with a frank, interested air.

Aware of the total contrast that she would present on her arrival at the table, Susan headed toward it, her high heels tapping on the planked wooden floor. Jim looked around and stood up at once, pulling out a chair for her.

"I hope I haven't kept you waiting," Susan told him crisply as she sat down.

"I've been here about five minutes," he replied, dropping back down into his chair. "This is Lisa. She met Billy and Joanie the night you couldn't go with us to the movies a couple of months ago. She was just asking about them. Lisa, this is Susan."

Susan managed a polite smile, remembering the name immediately.

"You have a couple of neat kids, Susan," Lisa told her.

"Thank you," Susan said stiffly.

"I got a big kick of their being so well-mannered."

"It's nice to hear that they were."

"So what can I get you to drink?"

"I'll have iced tea, please."

The waitress left, moving with a kind of languid efficiency. Susan looked at Jim and found him smiling at her with amused indulgence.

"If looks could kill, you would have a couple of murders on your conscience," he said in a tone that matched his expression.

"She's 'full-bodied,' all right, the way you described her," Susan remarked, not smiling back at him. "Especially at the top. I see what you meant, too, when you said that she's a liberated type. It's pretty obvious that she isn't shy with men."

"When I suggested that we eat here, Lisa didn't even come to mind," Jim said with a patient note. "If she had, I wouldn't have thought it would be any problem for you. I've never even been out with her. I met her after I had already met you, and I wasn't interested."

"Are you saying that you might have been interested in her if you hadn't met me first?"

"I might have been," he admitted. "She isn't bad looking and she seems pleasant enough. But what does it matter? Come on, let's look at the menu and decide what we're going to eat."

"I just have one more question I have to ask," she persisted.

"Okay," he said with resignation. "What is it?"

"Have you ever been this involved with another woman who's anything at all like me?"

"I've never been this involved with another woman, period."

"Well, then *not* this involved, but just involved."

"I thought you said just one more question." He sighed, conceding when she looked at him imploringly. "The answer's no. I haven't." He smiled. "You're one of a kind. Is that what you're fishing for me to tell you?"

"No," Susan denied in a troubled voice. "I'm trying to figure out why you were attracted to me in the first place, when I'm so different from the women you were attracted to before. Weren't they all liberated types, similar to Lisa?"

"The past six years they have been. Before that, I was attracted to career women, for the most part. Speaking of Lisa, she's headed this way with your iced tea. How about taking a peek at the menu, sweetheart, so that we can give her our order?"

Susan reluctantly complied. She approached the whole matter from a different tack after Lisa had come and gone.

"Would you rather I went for a more natural look?" she asked him. "I wouldn't have to polish my fingernails or highlight my hair. I could use less makeup—but I couldn't go out without any at all on without feeling naked," she admitted, making a face at the idea.

Jim was smiling, but also shaking his head with exasperation. "I wouldn't like to change a thing about you, except for your one-track mind. And I knew what a stubborn little cuss you were, going in. If you stop polishing your fingernails to match your lipstick, I won't be seen in public with you." His smile broadened into a grin. "I can see that that threat comes as a relief to you."

"I'm surprised that you noticed," she remarked, absurdly pleased.

"I notice everything about you. How cleverly you mix and match your clothes and use accessories to come up with different outfits. I look forward every day to seeing what you're going to come out in."

"Just wait until I can afford—" Susan bit off the sentence in the middle, seeing his expression become constrained.

"It would be fun taking you on shopping binges," he said lightly, his tone denying that anything was wrong. "I would enjoy turning you loose in the designer departments of good stores and watching you try on clothes and pick out what you liked, without looking at price tags."

"I probably couldn't do it," Susan declared. "Besides, shopping wouldn't be nearly the same challenge without bargain hunting. I've spent years becoming an expert, and my talent would be wasted."

He didn't reply. She changed the subject, trying to hide her deep discouragement.

After that, she was careful not to voice any wishful thinking that might make him feel inadequate. During the next week she was frantically busy with the fall festival preparations. The weekend event drew good crowds and was deemed an overall success, though some problems did crop up, as Jim had warned from the beginning. She got favorable publicity, and the participating merchants were pleased with their business.

Afterward they operated their various establishments as they had before, and she devoted herself full-time to her interior decorating work. There was no migration of prospective shop owners to Old Mandeville, as she'd originally foreseen, but it was obvious now that improving her present business location wasn't necessary. She had as many clients as she could handle without taking on an assistant. Once again Jim had been right.

On the surface everything was the same with them but as one week after another passed and he made no mention of marriage or of a future together, her hurt and puzzlement began to fester into resentment. She found herself trying to pick fights with him on smaller issues, but he wouldn't argue with her or lose his patience. His self-control only increased her frustration and built up the urge to force him into a confrontation.

Ironically Joyce Crawford presented her with the opportunity when she flew in from Atlanta to consult with Dave Myles and Susan on the house's progress. Susan had workups of several decorating plans to show her with wallpaper samples, paint chips, and carpet and tile variations. They had productive sessions and succeeded narrowing down Joyce's preferences.

"If we go with the black and white ceramic tile for the foyer, wouldn't an old-fashioned park bench look striking there?" Joyce asked, smiling. "Or perhaps an antique church pew. What do you think, Susan?"

"I think either one would be fantastic," Susan exclaimed and then snapped her fingers excitedly. "So would a Shaker-style settee. I can show you one that's exquisite. It's a reproduction of an original piece. Did you know that Jim Mann, who's building your cabinets, also makes this kind of furniture?"

COMPROMISING POSITIONS 241

"No, I didn't know," Joyce replied. "I'd love to see the settee. Maybe he has some other pieces that I can use as well."

"I think he might," Susan said. "He's a neighbor and doesn't mind my showing his furniture to clients when he isn't home. In fact, he leaves the key to his house with me," she added, feeling a guilty twinge.

Joyce wanted the settee on sight, plus the music stand, one of the secretaries and a table.

"As you can see, Jim doesn't have anything priced," Susan told her. "I'll find out and let you know."

"The man is a real craftsman," Joyce replied. "Whatever he's asking, I'll pay. I'm sure he can't be that unreasonable."

Oh, yes, he can be, Susan said grimly to herself. Feeling primed for battle, she left a note for Jim, taped to his back door, where he'd be sure to see it: *Call me when you get home. Have business matter to discuss with you. Susan.* If he took an independent attitude toward the favor she'd done him, she was going to have it out with him.

The rest of the afternoon crawled by, and her nerves tightened as it got closer to the time when Jim should be knocking off from work and coming home. She sat at her desk, going through the pretense of working while she waited for the phone to ring. When it finally did, she jumped at the sound.

"Hi, honey." His deep familiar voice, warm with affection, came to her over the line. "I hope your note is code language. You wouldn't want to come down and discuss your 'business matter' in person with me right now, would you? I'm ripe for negotiation."

"Actually it wasn't code language," Susan replied, fighting an instant softening at his intimate tone. "But I will come down and talk to you about it right now."

"I'm going to hop into the shower."

He was assuming that she would seek him out as soon as she walked into his house, whether he was in his bathroom drying off or in his bedroom, so that they could make love. Part of Susan longed to do that as she stood in the middle of his living room a couple of minutes later and heard the gush of water stop and his shower door slide open. Instead she went over and sat on the sofa, her footsteps making no noise on the carpet. He was whistling as he dried himself off, unaware that she was there.

Picking up the remote control from the coffee table, as Susan snapped on the television set and fixed her gaze on the screen, where a news anchor was reporting a local disaster.

"Hi, there." Jim spoke to her from the open door, sounding surprised as well as welcoming.

"Did you hear about this awful fire over in Slidell?" she asked, glancing over to see him standing naked with his towel around his shoulders. The sight of his body stirred her against her will. He had evidently been thinking about her in the shower since he was fully aroused. "Almost a whole subdivision burned down," she went on, looking back at the screen. "Miraculously no one was killed."

"I heard about it on the radio," he replied. "Why don't you come over and say hello to me? We can always catch the news at ten o'clock."

"I'm too tense right now to make love," Susan told him bluntly, torn between wanting very badly to go over to him and wanting to hold out and get her resentment out in the open.

"Then we won't make love," he said. "I'll just give you a massage and work out the kinks while you tell me why you're so tense. Turn off the TV and come into the bedroom with me."

Susan picked up the remote control and flicked the Off button. He tossed his towel in the direction of the bathroom and waited for her at the door, then hugged her and gave her a tender kiss before he led her into his bedroom with his arm around her shoulders. His voice was gentle with sympathy as he asked, "Did you have a bad day, darling?"

"Not really," she answered, the little hard core of opposition inside her melting. It was too difficult to be angry with him when they were this close.

In the bedroom she helped him undress her and then put her arms around his neck, pressing her body against his. "I'm feeling more relaxed already," she told him. "I'll take a rain check on the massage and take a real kiss for starters."

"You're just saying that because you know I'm turned on," Jim accused affectionately, caressing her back and shoulders with big gentle hands. When she pulled his head down, he kissed her with hunger and his arms closed tight around her as she responded. He broke his mouth apart from hers to say huskily, "I've been wanting you all day, sweetheart."

"Make love to me," Susan commanded him.

She was ready for him to be inside her as he picked her up and carried her over to the bed. She quickly became urgent with her need as he kissed and fondled her, clearly in no hurry himself. When she insisted that she couldn't wait any longer, he didn't delay, though, but entered her, going deep. Susan cried out, the shock of her pleasure too exquisite to absorb in silence, telling him what she felt. At the precise moment when the wave of sensation was subsiding, he thrust deeply again, unleashing another surge of delicious, tormenting pleasure.

Afterward Susan tried to express to him how the pace and depth and variation of his lovemaking was unbearably perfect for her, prolonging her rise to release and threatening her with total devastation when it came.

Jim chuckled and replied, "You don't leave me wondering what feels good to you, darling." He hugged her. "Much as I hate to move, I guess we'd better get dressed, hadn't we? We can pick up the kids and go out somewhere for supper. If you've had a hard day, you won't feel like bothering with cooking."

Susan was silent, feeling her lazy contentment breaking apart and her frustration forming anew in the wreckage. They'd had wonderful sex, but it changed nothing. They would spend the evening together like a married couple, and then he would come back to sleep in this bed by himself, while she slept in hers. And he, apparently, found the arrangement perfectly satisfactory. That's what maddened her. He whistled a cheerful little tune as they got up and dressed.

"I do have a business matter that I need to discuss with you," she told him in a taut voice that drew a quick questioning glance. "That's why I put the note on your door."

"What is it?" he asked.

"Joyce Crawford wants to buy several pieces of your furniture to go in her new house. I need to know your prices so that I can tell her. That is, if she passes the ownership test."

"You brought her here today?"

"Yes. The subject of furniture came up. I told her about yours, and she wanted to see it. I didn't think that you would mind."

"I don't mind, but I wish you had spoken to me about it first," he said. "At the present time I'm not interested in selling any of my furniture."

Susan stared at him. "Not *any* of it? Why, if I may ask?"

He was buckling his belt and finished before he answered. "Because I want to keep some pieces, and I haven't decided which ones yet."

"So therefore you're willing to pass up the sale of four pieces to a buyer who won't quibble at price," she said unbelievingly. "We're talking four or five thousand dollars."

"I'm sorry if it causes you a problem with her," he said apologetically, obviously not wanting to discuss it any further. "There are other furniture makers around. She could commission whatever she wants."

A fuse went off in Susan's head. "It doesn't cause me a problem with Joyce," she blurted out furiously. "It causes me a problem with *you*. I am sick and tired of your independent attitude toward money and all of your pathetic excuses about why you can't marry me. You don't *want* to marry me! So why don't you go ahead and admit it? If you did, you would either ask me to take you the way you are, or else you'd show a little ambition and become a better provider! Between the money you have sunk in your sports car and the retail value of your furniture that you won't sell, you could buy me an engagement ring and pay for a big wedding, too! I can get along without both, but I have to know something definite about what you intend, one way or the other!"

Defiantly, Susan stood facing him, her hands on her hips and her whole body trembling with emotion. His face, full of concern and regret, blurred as her tears welled up. She blinked hard to clear her vision, determined not to break down.

"So this is what you were uptight about earlier," Jim said quietly.

"Just tell me what you have to say from there," she said as he started toward her. "I want a straight answer." The quaver in Susan's voice betrayed her, and her fresh tears made him go out of focus again, but she could see well enough to know that he wasn't heeding her words. He was coming to her with his arms open, and, despite her hurt and anger, Susan couldn't make herself turn away.

"The straight answer is that I'd like nothing more in the world than for you to be my wife, darling," Jim said, hugging her tight to him. "I've had every intention all along of asking you to marry me."

"Well, why didn't you then?" Susan demanded wistfully, her stiff resistance melting at the words she'd so wanted to hear. She circled his waist with her arms and, with a sigh, nestled her face against his chest. "What were you waiting for? You must have known that I would say yes. I certainly haven't made any secret of the fact that I wanted to marry you."

"It was a matter of pride," he admitted. "I wanted to be in a stronger financial position when I asked you to be my wife. I didn't want to offer you just the promise that I planned to increase my income and become a better provider, but the accomplished fact."

Susan pushed herself back and looked up into his face, a new insight dawning. "Your reason for moving your workshop and hiring employees was to take on more jobs and make more money."

He nodded. "Remember that day we were coming home from New Orleans I told you I would be married in six months to a year? It would take me that long, I calculated, to expand my business operation and have some solid figures to back up my plan to at least double my income, which isn't as low now as you might think," he added ruefully.

"You mean you knew that day you wanted to marry me?" Susan asked wonderingly, a little thrill flushing away the last vestiges of her disappointment.

Jim smiled down at her tenderly. "I started shopping for your engagement ring the next week."

"It all makes sense now that you were content to go along with the way things were," Susan reflected, too happy to feel any sense of reproach.

"The situation wasn't fair to you, though," he said with gentle apology. "But every time I was on the verge of talking about the future I wanted us to have together, you would tell me again how you were willing to compromise and settle for less with me. That isn't easy for a man to take, darling."

"I never meant to come across as saying that!" Susan protested. "I just kept trying to make the point that all the luxuries in the world wouldn't make me happy, if I couldn't be your wife."

"You're going to be my wife and have all the luxuries you've always wanted, too," Jim stated firmly.

"If I have them someday, fine," she said, to pacify him. "In the meantime, there's no reason we can't have a very comfortable life-style. I have no doubt that you'll be successful expanding your operation, and my business is going great. We could fix up this house for now, move your furniture out of the two front rooms and use them—or just keep living in the house I'm renting," she went on quickly when he started shaking his head.

"If we decide to buy property and build our own house—which is what I think we'll probably want to do—then we can live where you are temporarily. I'll either sell or rent this house. Or you could take it over for your business."

"That would be a good idea," Susan agreed. "Then you wouldn't have to worry about moving your furniture somewhere else." Plus she'd be freeing up the two front rooms she was using now. That would give them more room during the "temporary" period that she expected would last a number of years. They were going to need another bedroom, she hoped, for a nursery.

"My furniture won't be a problem," Jim replied. "After you decide whether you'd like to keep some pieces for our home, I'll sell the rest of it."

"But won't you be making more?"

"No, I enjoyed it while I had time on my hands, but now that I'm going to be a family man, I'll have other things to do with my spare time."

There was a ring of anticipation in his voice. She saw no sign of regret in his expression to indicate that he was making a sacrifice. "I'd definitely like to have some of your furniture in our house," Susan told him eagerly, and then made a face. "I just wish I'd known what was in your mind when I brought Joyce here this afternoon. I talked her into buying some of my favorites. But I love all the pieces, so I can pick from the others. It wouldn't be practical—"

Jim cut her off with a kiss. "You pick out what you want and don't give a thought to being practical, for a change," he ordered her. "Now, aren't you a little curious to see your engagement ring?"

"I'm dying to see it and to *wear* it," she declared with a broad smile, glad to postpone any discussion that would spoil the closeness and harmony. "Tomorrow I'm going out and buying your wedding band. I can't wait to get a ring on your finger that says you're all mine. We are going to get married right away, aren't we?"

"A ring won't make me any more yours than I already am, darling," Jim assured her, underlining his words with another tender, possessive kiss. His expression was indulgent as he raised his head and continued, "You can set a date and start making plans for our wedding. One with all the frills, like we discussed, and a big reception afterward."

Susan bit her lip to keep back a protest and watched him as he went over to his bureau, opened the top drawer and took out a small jeweler's box.

"I hope you like it," he said, bringing the box to her. "You don't know how much I've wanted to give it to you. I've had to fight with myself every time we've been here together in this room."

"I'm going to love it," she told him with absolute certainty, feeling a deep thrill as she lifted the hinged velvet top to see the ring that he had picked out for her. She was more than half expecting to see a marquise-cut diamond, but nothing like the one nestled in the satin slot. The ring was a solitaire, with a stone that could only be described as spectacular. Susan caught her breath and stared, awed into speechlessness.

"It should be your size," Jim said. "I borrowed one of your rings out of your jewelry box and took it along to the jeweler's." He lifted the fabulous ring out and slid it onto her finger.

She moved her hand, letting the facets of the stone catch the light, at a total loss as to how to handle the situation without hurting his feelings. The ring was entirely out of his price range.

"Is it what you had in mind buying for yourself someday?" he asked. "You haven't said a word."

"That's because I don't know what to say," Susan answered honestly, fascinated with the sight of the ring on her finger, even though she knew it couldn't stay there. "It's too incredibly beautiful for words. But the stone must be three carats. As much as I love you for wanting to give it to me, Jim, it's far too expensive." She steeled herself to tear her gaze away from her hand and look up at him.

He was smiling, looking thoroughly pleased with himself. "It was worth every penny to see the expression on your face, before you started worrying about how much it cost," he said. "Wait until you see your Christmas present. I've already been shopping around for it."

Susan didn't have to guess that he intended to buy her a black mink coat as unaffordable as the ring. "This is so difficult," she said, sighing. "Of all the times in the world when I don't want to hurt your pride, it's now. I know you want me to have everything I've ever mentioned wanting, but we have to live within our means, Jim. We don't want to be head over heels in debt and put a lot of unnecessary financial pressure on ourselves. There are other priorities." She lowered her gaze to her hand as she started to ease the ring from her finger, hating to take it off.

Jim stopped her. "We'll have to sit down soon and have a frank discussion about my net worth. I'll give you a run-down on my investments and assets, but for now, just take my word for it, darling. I can well afford to buy you this ring. It's paid for and insured, and it's yours. You can wear it without a single worry." He squeezed her hand and released it to take her into his arms. "You're going to have your dream house, too, and a pretty wardrobe with the latest fashions and a nice car of your own to drive. Billy and Joanie won't lack for anything, either. When it comes time for them to go to college, there will be money for their tuition. We'll be financially secure. I promise you that."

Susan held his steady gaze and believed him, but she was still troubled. "What about what's best for *you*, Jim?" she asked. "You gave up a life of stress once before when you decided that the personal cost was too much. I want you to be happy, not under a constant strain. Any house we live in together will be a dream house, as long as it's big enough at least for a family of five."

She didn't have to explain her numbers. His face kindled with love and wonder, and his voice was husky with emotion as he answered her, "I am doing what's best for me and what will make me happy. Earning money was just a way of keeping score before, in a cutthroat game that didn't have any real meaning. Now I have a purpose—taking care of the woman I love and of our children." He kissed her deeply but tenderly. "We'd better see about our two oldest, hadn't we?"

"We really should," Susan agreed, taking her arms from around his neck with reluctance. "They'll be thrilled that we're getting married."

"Do you think so?" Jim asked in a pleased voice, steering her toward the door.

"I'm sure. They'll love the idea of having you live with us."

"I can't wait."

"Neither can I. It's going to be so wonderful not to have to say good-night and close the door behind you."

Susan would have been full of bruises by the time they reached the car if Jim hadn't kept his arm around her shoulders and guided her through the house and safely down the back steps. She was too busy admiring her ring and looking into a happy future to watch where she was going. She could depend on him, she knew, to keep her from walking into walls. He would catch her if she happened to stumble and never let her fall....

*   *   *   *   *

Award-winning author Carole Halston has written twenty novels for Silhouette Books. If you enjoyed COMPROMISING POSITIONS, *you won't want to miss the reissue of* KEYS TO DANIEL'S HOUSE, *an all-time Silhouette Special Edition favorite, coming next month in Silhouette Classics.*

ATTRACTIVE, SPACE SAVING BOOK RACK

Display your most prized novels on this handsome and sturdy book rack. The hand-rubbed walnut finish will blend into your library decor with quiet elegance, providing a practical organizer for your favorite hard-or soft-covered books.

Only $9.95

Approximately 16" x 8" when assembled

Assembles in seconds!

To order, rush your name, address and zip code, along with a check or money order for $10.70* ($9.95 plus 75¢ postage and handling) payable to *Silhouette Books.*

Silhouette Books
Book Rack Offer
901 Fuhrmann Blvd.
P.O. Box 1396
Buffalo, NY 14269-1396

Offer not available in Canada.

*New York and Iowa residents add appropriate sales tax.

BKR-2A

Silhouette Special Edition

COMING NEXT MONTH

#505 SUMMER'S PROMISE—Bay Matthews
Burdened with grief, Joanna felt empty, old, weary of living. But when her estranged husband, Chase, appeared on her doorstep, need and desire took hold...and a new life began.

#506 GRADY'S LADY—Bevlyn Marshall
Ladies' man Ryan Grady had tangled with Blythe Peyton's type before—blond, beautiful, deadly. He had to protect his brother from her poison, no matter how sweet it tasted....

#507 THE RECKONING—Joleen Daniels
Once, Cal Sinclair had offered her an ultimatum. Laura Wright had chosen college over marriage...and Cal had chosen Laura's sister. Could heated passion ever sear away burning regrets?

#508 CAST A TALL SHADOW—Diana Whitney
Juvenile investigator Kristin Price was gutsy, but a harrowing stint on Nathan Brodie's ranch for delinquents truly tested her courage. Even for love's sake, could she confront her most intimate terrors?

#509 NO RIGHT OR WRONG—Katherine Granger
Single mother Anne Emerson didn't need another man—or another scandal—messing up her life, and her best friend's ex-husband was a candidate for both. Somehow, though, being wrong had never felt so right.

#510 ASK NOT OF ME, LOVE—Phyllis Halldorson
Was Caleb's past too dangerous to speak of—even to his love? What terrible secret had made him dodge Nancy's questions and desert her in a time of need?

AVAILABLE THIS MONTH: